JUSTICE IS NOT BLIND

JUSTICE IS NOT BLIND

JUSTICE BEGINS™ BOOK FIVE

MICHAEL ANDERLE

LMBPN Publishing
PMB 196, 2540 South Maryland Pkwy
Las Vegas, NV 89109

Version 1.00, February 2022
ebook ISBN: 979-8-88541-102-8
Print ISBN: 979-8-88541-103-5

THE JUSTICE IS NOT BLIND TEAM

Thanks to the JIT Readers

Wendy L Bonell
Diane L. Smith
Dorothy Lloyd
Deb Mader
Rachel Beckford
Jeff Goode
Zacc Pelter
Dave Hicks

If I've missed anyone, please let me know!

Editor
The Skyhunter Editing Team

DEDICATION

*To Family, Friends and
Those Who Love
to Read.
May We All Enjoy Grace
to Live the Life We Are
Called.*

— Michael

CHAPTER ONE

"More guns, I see," observed Dr. Gaje "Gage" Gurung with a nod of his balding head. "Well, that is good. There is no such thing as too many, provided they are in sound working order."

He stood on the threshold of the garage door he'd opened. It looked out on the back lot of their headquarters, which sometimes served them as a loading bay. The present moment was one such time.

Amahle Nikoze had been leaning out the driver's side window of her armored truck. She nodded to acknowledge what Gage had said, then settled into the vehicle and backed in through the door. Gage stepped aside and waited for the truck's hood to clear the threshold before he pulled the door shut and locked it.

The driver hopped down. She was a good ten or fifteen years younger than Gage was. He didn't know her exact age and hadn't bothered to ask, but she was spry enough that climbing off the big, rather clunky vehicle was easier for her than it would've been for him.

She faced him, brushed her hands off against each other, then ran them through her short, knotted hair, tilting her face back to take a deep breath as she often did at the end of a successful mission. It was her way of calming down and congratulating herself.

Gage sipped strong coffee from a Styrofoam cup. Dante had made it. Traditionally, Gage had preferred tea, but perhaps the rigors of his duties were pushing him toward greater concentrations of caffeine.

"So, then," he asked Amahle in his residual Nepali-British accent, "shall we go down to the locker directly? Or do you wish to have breakfast first?"

It would not technically be *breakfast* since she'd likely been up all night and was approaching the end, rather than the beginning, of her day.

She lowered her hands and opened her eyes. "Let us unload my cargo first. Then I will relax. If I sit now, I won't want to get back up." She was originally from South Africa, of the Nguni people, but her way of speaking had picked up traces of accents from all over the globe.

"That is understandable," Gage conceded and finished his coffee before he helped her open the truck's back door.

The Executives had dubbed the vehicles Autocutioners, which Dante found hilarious, but Gage thought it was appropriate enough. It certainly distinguished them as what they were—the specialized fleet operated by the Executioners of Atlantica and no one else.

Amahle handed down boxes and crates of weaponry to Gage, who loaded them onto a couple of handcarts. Then the pair took them down the ramp, each pushing one, to the door that lay at the bottom below ground level. Gage punched in the security code, and the doors swung open.

He asked, "Do you know how many we'll be able to keep? It's okay if you haven't had time to look them over. I am not busy today, yet." He backed in through the door, pulling the load behind him. Once he was a good two meters in, he turned to push the cart the rest of the way.

Amahle followed him in, pushing her cart, and let the door shut and lock itself behind her. "I have no idea. Some of them were damaged and are probably useless. We will have to examine the others to be sure."

Beyond the door that led into the basement from the garage area, there was a broad storage cellar. The Executioners had piled their more mundane supplies against the walls, mostly boxed up or on cheap metal shelving. In some places, random items, cans, boxes, or machines lay loose and orphaned amid the overall jumble of stuff. Nevertheless, there was plenty of room for the pair to wheel their heavy payloads across the floor.

At the far end of the cellar lay a service elevator. It led up to each of the above-ground floors but also down into the sub-basement. That was where the locker was.

Gage wondered why they hadn't chosen to call it something more traditional, like "the armory," but the others seemed attached to the current nickname. Probably, he surmised, because the rather dingy quality of the place reminded them of a high school locker room, although mercifully without the mold or moisture. The building's foundation was strong and watertight.

As the elevator's doors *clanked* open and the two with their carts took their places within it, Amahle let out a long, deep sigh. "Once we unload all of this stuff, I think I should have a cup of coffee, after all. Will you be able to get started without me?"

"Of course. I ought to be able to inspect two or three weapons while you get a cup. There should be at least half a pot left in the break room. Dante made it."

She nodded. "Good. Thank you."

There was a slight lurching sensation as the elevator dropped a level before coming to a jerky, grinding stop. They opened the doors and wheeled the carts out into the short, broad hallway that lay before the locker proper.

Down here, there was no advanced keypad technology sealing off their cache from the rest of the world, only a traditional mechanical lock. Gage fished in his pocket for his keyring, pulled it out, and found an oddly-shaped brass one, which he used to unlock the heavy iron door. It swung open inward on its own with a whining metallic *creak*.

He went first with Amahle following. Within the locker, there was far less room to maneuver, but there was enough. They stopped next to a table, offloading the first two boxes of guns onto it and putting the others on the floor nearby.

"All right, then." Gage opened the first box. "Do please go and get yourself a coffee. I will be fine here for a short while."

The younger woman smiled in a muted, rather weary way. "Thank you. I will be back."

She turned and walked off, her footfalls light and careful. Even in environments poorly suited to it, she could move while making frighteningly little sound.

CHAPTER TWO

Gage turned his attention to the contents of the box. He pulled a chair up next to the table, reached in, and pulled out a submachine gun from World War II. At first glance, it looked like a Soviet PPSh-41. After a few seconds of studying the details, Gage determined that it was a Suomi KP/-31, a similar-looking firearm produced by the Finns a few years before the war began.

"Most interesting. I have not seen one of these in…fifteen, perhaps sixteen years. Yes, sixteen."

It had been in 1950. It was now 1966.

As he looked the gun over in a thorough visual inspection, ensured that he'd unloaded it, then worked the action and otherwise tinkered with the visible parts, his thoughts wandered. Not enough to distract him from his duties. Only enough to make the task more relaxing, putting him into a reflective, contemplative mood.

The locker had first been pressed into use about eleven months ago. That was approximately two months after Amahle had joined them and they had, at last, uncovered the disturbing connection between two particular groups of people.

The Executives were a semi-anonymous collective of Atlantica's wealthiest and most powerful citizens, major businesspeople responsible for the island's development. Increasingly, they also handled the security of the populace. They'd formed the Executioners nearly two years ago after recruiting Tyler Katakura. The other four of them had gradually joined.

Not long after the order's inception, the Executioners began running their justice missions across the island. Rumors of a shadowy organization called the Coven of Miracles reached them during one of Daria's solo ops. The Executioners knew little about them, other than they were secretive, power-hungry, and well-connected. They seemed most interested in harvesting, stealing, and experimenting with Atlanticore crystal, which they used to power devastating weapons.

The Executioners had all searched in vain for clues that might lead them closer to the Coven. Then, at last, Gage had discovered one—only to wish that he *hadn't*.

He had doctoral degrees in archaeology and engineering, with the former in particular being the passion he'd pursued after he retired from his military service as a Gurkha. Thirteen months ago, Ty, Daria, and Amahle had recovered a case full of devices that belonged to the Coven. The items combined ancient Atlantican artifacts with cutting-edge technology.

Studying those accouterments and the tiny rust deposits that clung to them, Gage had put two and two together. All of the artifacts had been dug up from excavation sites owned by, invested in, or associated with the Executives.

Gage's hands moved across the submachine gun, his thoughts snapping back to the present. It would require a more thorough inspection, including disassembly to check for any broken internals, but nothing was *obviously* wrong with it.

He placed it into the large crate they used to separate guns that were good candidates for stockpiling. The best of them would go into the Executioners' emergency supply. The rest might be resold for petty cash to various Atlantican citizens, provided they didn't seem too criminal or dangerous. Although Ty was increasingly reluctant to put too many weapons back into circulation, now that the Executioners were bringing in more money from their investigations and various side activities.

There was another crate for guns that were defective or unsafe. Those would go to the incinerator rather than taking up space or risk their getting out on the street and injuring someone or getting peddled for spare parts on the black market.

With the Suomi cleared for the next stage of the vetting process, Gage examined the rest of the hardware in the first box. A half-dozen pistols and revolvers, as well as a Bowie knife and a sawed-off shotgun. He selected one of the revolvers, found it to be suffering from poor timing and cylinder lock-up, and tossed it into the reject bin.

Amahle returned before he started on a third item.

"Ah, welcome back," he greeted her. "So far, we have one workable submachine gun and one defective handgun."

Amahle held a tall Styrofoam cup filled three-quarters of the way to the brim with steaming black coffee. "That makes sense. If even half of these guns are usable, though, will we have room for them all? The locker is nearly at capacity unless we plan to bring in more storage cabinets and stack them atop one another."

Gage chuckled. "We shall need a conference soon to address that. I would say that Executioner Katakura's plan has been a success."

Drinking deeply from her cup, Amahle climbed onto the table's surface and sat next to the box so she could remove the weapons and perform the initial visual scan before handing them to Gage for a mechanical check. He moved his chair closer to the two bins. They'd done this many times before.

"Tyler is often successful," Amahle observed. "Although he tends to overdo things." She picked out another pistol and looked it over.

Gage chuckled while he waited for her to hand over the weapon. "I have observed the same tendency. He means well."

It had been Ty's idea to gather an emergency cache of weapons and ammunition. The more, the better, he felt. He was hedging his bets against the day they all dreaded—when those among the Executives who were Coven members or sympathizers turned against them.

Such a day might never come. For a year and a month, there'd been no specific warning signs that their benefactors were planning to dispose of them. Yet such a conflict wouldn't be unprecedented. Tyler had come into conflict with one of the Executives, Lucas Montrosse, mere days after becoming the first Executioner. Gage hadn't been around for that, but he'd heard all about it.

Daria Barruk and Dante Costa had agreed with the plan. At present, they had enough firepower to equip a small army.

Amahle informed him, "This one seems fine to look at." It was a Makarov pistol, unblemished enough that its former owner had probably never fired it.

Gage accepted it, checked the magazine and chamber, worked the slide, and examined the trigger. With a nod, he deposited it into the "good" bin.

As the pair worked through the next couple of weapons, they chatted about recent changes around their headquarters and the ever-expanding size, wealth, and population of Atlantica Metro. The city, once little more than a blueprint where some people nevertheless lived, played, and did business, had become a true metropolis and would likely only grow bigger.

They also discussed the case from which Amahle had returned. For months, a ring of extortionists had been extracting money from several well-to-do citizens. They tricked their marks into compromising situations by posing as people who had the connections to destroy them if anyone discovered their indiscretions. Of course, the extortionists backed up their claims with the threat of force.

When one of their victims tried to go public, they'd dispatched a pair of their enforcers to kill the man. He'd miraculously survived being shot five times. The first people he'd insisted on speaking to once he recovered were the Executioners.

Amahle had gone off to deal with the problem. The fact that the extortionists chose to resist had made things messier, but also...simpler.

Gage sensed that the subject of the Coven was on both their minds, but neither had mentioned it aloud. Instead, he accepted the sawed-off shotgun and tested it. Despite their obvious drawbacks of limited capacity and slow reload, double-barreled shotguns had the definite advantage of simplicity and robustness. Gage put it in the bin alongside the other weapons worth keeping.

Amahle perked up as she examined the next one in the crate, raising her eyebrows and holding it gingerly between her hands —not giving it over but retaining it for some as-yet-unrevealed purpose of discussion.

Gage leaned in and squinted, examining the firearm. It was a Colt 1911 pistol, fairly standard, like the kind that Tyler and Dante favored as their sidearms. It was severely damaged.

"This," Amahle began. "I took it off one of the gangsters. You can see that whatever happened to it is not, shall we say, normal."

He had to agree with her. The metal had suffered major warping, as though from exposure to extreme heat, and it still smelled of ozone. There was no scorching, however. Plus a distinct lack of the sulfurous smell that typically accompanied gunpowder detonations.

Before he could ask what could've caused such an effect, the South African markswoman went on.

"During the gunfight that broke out, I saw the man load this gun with a magazine that appeared to be full of bullets that glowed. When he fired at me, there was a flash of blue, electric light, and a *crack* like thunder. It was as though lightning went off in his hand."

She'd seen such weapons before. Gage recalled well the stories that she and Ty had told about them from the first day they worked together before they inducted Amahle into the order.

"What happened next?"

"It took a moment for my vision to clear." She rubbed her eyes as though recalling the event caused a momentary resurgence of pain or blindness. "When it did, I saw that most of the man above the waist was...gone. He'd struck the wall and stuck to it, as though someone had thrown a jar of jam."

Gage grimaced at the mental image. "You found the pistol lying on the ground, then?"

"No. I found it embedded in the wall across from him."

After a second's contemplation, Gage shrugged. "Newton's Third Law at work, I suppose." His dual degrees had given him a background in basic physics.

Amahle set the half-melted gun down, leaving it apart from the others in case anyone else wished to examine it later. "I found no evidence of anything else like that during cleanup. Only this pistol. I think it must have something to do with the Coven of Miracles."

Gage nodded. "Every time strange weapons that use Atlanti-core turn up, they seem to be the ones behind it. It sounds like this one...malfunctioned. Most terribly."

"Yes, yes," Amahle concurred. "So much destructive power. If it's making its way out into Atlantica like this, we could be looking at serious problems."

She reached into the crate and pulled out the next gun, a small .32 caliber pistol similar to the one she wore as an emergency sidearm. She handed it to Gage. He looked it over and determined that it was probably in acceptable working order.

"The consequences of such power, properly harnessed, might be beyond our ability to deal with through normal means. I believe we should call the entire group together for a discussion about how best to handle it."

"Agreed." Amahle paused to sip her coffee. She'd risen late to deal with the all-night mission but was growing fatigued. Nonetheless, Gage had observed over the months that she possessed an incredible ability to manage her energy reserves and maintain focus for long periods. He supposed it came with the territory of being a professional sniper.

The two of them were about to resume their tasks while discussing when and how to call a meeting when the portable two-way radio sitting in the corner crackled to life. Amahle and Gage snapped to attention, turning toward it as the static resolved itself.

The voice of Eleanor Cervantes, their contact and handler with the Executives, came through loud and clear.

"Attention, all Executioners," she began in a hurried tone, her Mexican accent growing more clipped. "There is a situation in the Metro plaza at Broadway and Seventh Avenue that requires attending to as soon as possible. Please respond at once with your availability. Over."

Midway into her report, Gage had rushed over to the radio and unhooked the microphone. He raised it to his lips.

"Yes, this is Gurung, and Nikoze is with me. The other three are scattered across the island on missions. We are likely the closest to the site. Is the situation hot? Over."

The plaza in question, if he recalled, was less than a mile from them but located in a part of downtown that often saw heavy traffic. If active violence was already occurring, they might not get there in time to prevent the loss of innocent life. At which point, their only function might be to live up to their name's grim suggestion and punish the guilty after the fact.

Eleanor replied, "No, not yet, but you must go immediately.

Our Executive security forces have cordoned off the area. However, the damage has already happened. Please depart at once. Out."

The radio crackled again, and her voice faded.

Gage stood in place, allowing himself a second or two of rest and somber reflection before he acted. It was unusual for Eleanor to be in such a rush and fail to provide any detailed information. All she'd done was order them to drive to a particular location and deal with whatever mysterious contingency had arisen.

He turned and took a couple of steps toward Amahle, who was also back on her feet. The solemn look in her eyes told him that she, too, had noted the uncharacteristic concern in Eleanor's tone.

"My Autocutioner is the best positioned to leave right away," she pointed out. "I will drive."

As she fell into a brisk trot toward the stairs, Gage stepped in behind her, keeping pace. "Yes, of course. I have been spending too much time in the lab lately, doing little but examining evidence and poking around with machines. I do believe it would do me good to stretch my legs and get some fresh air."

For this particular type of outing, though, he made sure that his trusty Webley revolver lay at his hip and his pair of kukris crossed over his back. He grabbed an armored vest off the rack in the garage as well.

Amahle still had her protective uniform on, as well as her rifle in the truck. If they were lucky, they might not need it. Where luck failed, there was always preparation.

CHAPTER THREE

Amahle couldn't be certain, but she'd long suspected that when she'd joined the order, someone had given her a hand-me-down Autocutioner before claiming the fifth and newest one for themselves.

The truck's interior had a definite lived-in quality. The seats had somewhat molded to the frame of a person built differently than herself, and it had a faint smell she couldn't quite identify. Additionally, bullet dents and scorch marks scarred the armor. The tires had seen better days although she'd replaced them about four months ago.

Then again, the Executives might have simply scooped up a used, mundane truck and transformed *that* into an Autocutioner, perhaps using armor plating they'd tested against various weapons, which might explain the scarring.

Either way, the vehicle's handling was less than optimal. She could still manage to get where she needed to go. After the years she'd put in with the Ghost-Makers, the ruthless company of snipers for hire she'd run with until she'd come to Atlantica, it irked her to be the person with the least seniority and subject to the usual barrage of hazings and minor indignities.

Still, she got along well with the others on the whole. They didn't actively mistreat her, and they were a talented, sensible, and efficient bunch.

Besides, while most of them could shoot adequately well, none could shoot quite like her. Ty had once said that the single shot from a .32 she'd pulled off while hanging from the side of a ship—the bullet that had killed her former boss and mentor, She-Wolf—was the most jaw-dropping feat of marksmanship he'd ever seen.

Now, as the vehicle rolled down the freshly-paved streets of Atlantica Metro, Gage blurted, "Careful! That light nearly turned yellow." He pointed at it to make sure she saw.

They were already past the intersection, so she barely shrugged. Driving wasn't her forte. Since Atlantica didn't technically have any laws, excessive concern with traffic lights was more of a suggestion than anything. Courtesy to other drivers, when multiple cars reached the crossroads at the same time.

When Amahle had reached it, she estimated that there was a minimum of one full second before any of the vehicles on the cross street might've struck her.

Traffic thickened as they made a left turn and entered the original core of downtown. This was the epicenter of money and power in the city, the neighborhood from which everything else flowed.

As the taller surrounding buildings fell away to the sides and the plaza's more open space came into view, Amahle and Gage leaned forward, taking note of the most unusual and striking aspect of the scene before them.

Multiple different groups of people, ranging in size from mere trios and quartets of friends to entire crowds unto themselves, had massed around the plaza's edges and pressed in to gawk, point, chatter, and try to get a better look. Temporary cordons and wooden barriers kept them back, and various members of the Executive Security Force were on hand to discourage them further.

Amahle's attentiveness, her acute reaction to any potentially dangerous situation, went up a notch as she scanned the area ahead of them for more clues about what was going on. For such a large crowd to have formed in Atlantica was unusual. She couldn't recall seeing it happen more than once or twice before in the last year.

Gage squinted and voiced a similar thought. "That is odd for so many people to take an interest in things. In a city such as this, elaborate spectacles, strangeness, and even cruelty are daily occurrences. The people are too desensitized to be much impressed by such normal affairs. What would have drawn such a huge mob?"

The Autocutioner's normal rattles, creaks, and tire hum grew quieter as Amahle slowed to a crawl, gradually creeping up on the main avenue into the center of the plaza. Executive Security knew who they were and would admit them without much fuss. The jumbled press of citizen onlookers made everything far more complicated. The security personnel had yet to notice the approaching truck.

Amahle contemplated whether to stop, dismount, and shout at them to get their attention. If there were any danger—in the form of, say, a sniper waiting and watching the whole scene from a window of one of the surrounding skyscrapers—leaving the safety of the vehicle would be unwise.

Something else occurred to her as well.

"Is it me," she mused, "or has the Executive Security Force grown much larger of late? Large and more prevalent. They are everywhere now, it seems. When I first joined, I saw them only occasionally when guarding highly valuable assets or when we needed help on exceptionally dangerous missions."

Gage brooded in silence for a moment. "No, Amahle. It is not only you. I believe they've tripled the number of their personnel this last year. It has made Atlantica safer, perhaps. Yet, what are we to do with a large police force when in fact there is no *law?*"

She chose not to comment. In her home country, and in many other nations she'd visited with the Ghost-Makers outfit, she'd encountered or heard of many warlords with private armies. So far, things in Atlantica didn't seem to have grown that bad—in part thanks to the actions of the Executioners.

So far.

A couple of the security guards approached the Autocutioner. Gage rolled down the window and briefly explained to them what was going on. The men nodded and rushed off, relaying the Executives' orders and trying to clear a path. Security personnel gradually shoved the teeming locals back, forming a corridor amid the human throng. Another man moved aside one of the wooden barricades and waved them through.

Amahle pressed the gas gently, rolling forward at a crawl. There was a chance that some of the onlookers would break through and try to shout questions at them or pound on the truck's armor. She would rather maintain a slow speed and risk that minor inconvenience than chance accidentally running someone over if she were driving too fast.

Then the crowd and the line of armored men and fortifications fell away behind them. The space beyond was starkly empty and quiet compared to everything surrounding it. The rising morning sun, rather than conveying peace or beauty, seemed eerie in its contrast with the scene ahead.

The Broadway Plaza, as it was customarily named, was one of the older public square-type areas in Atlantica Metro. It had been among the first to be developed for general use and opened to the public. Some of the city's first skyscrapers and functional offices had sprung up around it, along with a small but pleasant park adjacent to and arguably part of the plaza proper.

Despite the ambitious designs of its planners, Broadway was still the product of a time when duct tape and elbow grease held together more or less everything on Atlantica, its problems solved by whatever method was available, convenient, and affordable. On an island that people had inhabited for less than a decade, that often meant *crude*.

The city had power before it had a proper underground electrical grid. As such, power in Broadway Plaza ran from building to building—or building to streetlight, or a generator to wherever else—by a network of crisscrossing wires and cables. They arced over the square and park at different angles and heights, forming an artificial canopy of steel, copper, and rubber.

Someone had added something to the latticework of power cords—three things, in fact. As the Autocutioner rolled forward, closer to the plaza's center, Amahle and Gage saw what they were.

A trio of human bodies. They hung from nooses tied to the thickest cable and now dangled limp and lifeless, turning from side to side in the slight gusts of breeze that made their way into the artificial ravines between the many tall buildings.

Each of the corpses had something on its chest. Amahle had seen such things before and had seen photographs from other parts of the world as well. Placards hung about the shoulders to identify either the victim or the motive for their slaying. She couldn't read what was written on them from here, though.

She pressed gently on the brake, and the armored truck ground to a stop. Amahle shifted into park and turned off the engine. She glanced behind the seat where she kept her rifle but decided it probably wouldn't be necessary.

As a sharpshooter herself, it was difficult to dismiss the possibility that someone had set up the whole scene specifically to lure out the Executioners and put a rifle scope on their heads. She doubted it, though. Besides, if she *did* have to shoot back, it would be easier to guess the sniper's location from within the vehicle's safety.

Gage unbuckled his seat belt. "Well, let us go have a look at this latest atrocity. I can see why Eleanor wanted us here so quickly even though there doesn't seem to be any immediate danger."

Despite his words, he left the revolver on his hip, and the kukris crossed behind his back.

Both of them opened their doors and hopped down to the pavement. A security officer was already striding up to them. He wore a black armored uniform, much like Amahle and Gage, but without the distinctive skull-and-sword shoulder patches that identified the Executioners. Instead, a normal rank insignia identified him as a lieutenant. He wore a full helmet with a visor and carried an AR-10 rifle on a sling over his shoulder.

"Good morning, Lieutenant," Gage greeted the man. "What can you tell us, so far?"

The officer began in a gravelly voice, "Glad you arrived. We found these three about an hour ago. Not sure how long they'd been hanging there, but a crowd was forming, and people were trying to find a ladder tall enough to cut them down.

"We dispersed 'em and received orders to wait. Someone says the signs around their necks are in Latin. Hope one of you can read that stuff. Also, they tell me the Execs have other people headed here too."

Amahle frowned. "I would hope they think to send a truck with a lift or a crane. There would be no way for us to get the bodies down unless we shot through the ropes. That would be terribly dangerous, and the results of the bodies falling would not be pretty."

"Yeah," the lieutenant agreed. "It would be nice if someone in charge was smart enough to think of that."

Gage peered at the placards. "Latin. I've encountered some of it. In academia, one cannot help but do so. I am not a fluent speaker or scholar of the language. Still, I am sure we can find someone who is."

As though in answer to their questions, another car rolled

into the plaza via the same path the guards had already cleared for the Autocutioner. It was a silver Aston Martin DB4, which suggested that the new arrival was someone important. Or, at least, wealthy. Amahle saw two people within, but she couldn't yet distinguish their features.

The sedan pulled up to about five meters from the Autocutioner and wheeled around so the passenger's side faced the Executioners. The door opened to reveal their handler and contact, Eleanor Cervantes.

She was in her late twenties, with an air of sultry sophistication, and most men found her extremely attractive. Her dark hair hung loose, and she wore a charcoal-colored suit dress. From what Amahle had heard, she was the scion of wealthy landowners in Jalisco, Mexico. She'd come to Atlantica to pursue a career rather than simply manage the family business back home.

Eleanor didn't climb out, though. She was finishing a conversation with someone on the other end of a radio receiver like the Executioners kept in their vehicles and at headquarters. Her voice came fast and heated, in a barking tone that switched between rapid English and Spanish. Amahle couldn't make out any meaningful phrases.

Until, at what was doubtless the end of the conversation, she snapped, "No!" and tossed the receiver to the seat in a fit of temper. Then she got out of the car and stood in place, smoothing out her clothes and facing away from the pair.

Amahle frowned and whispered to Gage, "Have you ever seen her act this way?"

"No. Which, in its way, might be more frightening than the sight of those bodies."

Behind them, the lieutenant drifted off to oversee his men and close the pathway they'd opened for the two vehicles.

Gage looked up and adjusted his glasses. He could barely make out the words inscribed on the three placards. He read them aloud, grasping some of what they meant, but not enough to pass full judgment on their intent.

"*Pythonissam Rex. Magus Regina. Veneficus Tyrannus.*"

Amahle moved a step closer to him. "It certainly sounds like Latin. Some of it seems familiar."

"Yes," Gage conceded. "The name of the game is leadership. And magic. That much I can say." He adjusted his belt, and his eyes went distant.

Amahle had no difficulty putting two and two together. She folded her arms over her waist. "What are the odds that this has nothing to do with our friends who trade gunpowder for lightning?"

With a sardonic smile, Gage riposted, "Slim to none, as Ty would say."

Eleanor moved toward them with a fast, purposeful stride, her heels clicking. Although maintaining her usual cool, the nervous movements of her fingers and the grim set of her mouth made it obvious that she was disconcerted and still ruffled by the conversation she'd finished a moment ago.

By the time she made eye contact with Amahle and Gage, she had herself back under control. Still, a definite undercurrent of agitated worry remained.

Amahle raised a hand. "Hello, Eleanor."

Gage smiled and said the same.

"Hello," she repeated and went instantly to business. "Thank you for arriving so quickly. I'm here to report that this unfortunate event has just become priority number one for the entire order of Executioners." She flicked her eyes toward the hanging corpses. "We expect that all five Executioners will convene as soon as possible to give it their full attention."

By *we*, she meant herself and the Executives.

Amahle and Gage glanced sidelong into each other's eyes, confirming what they both suspected. Whatever was happening, it was unprecedented.

They'd all agreed that one of the major reasons their order had been so successful in its relatively brief history was because, for the most part, the Executives had left them alone. They provided material support and leads, raising particular issues to deal with, but otherwise allowed the Executioners to operate as they saw fit.

Never before had their benefactors tried to dictate the priority of assignments or who would take which case. Such things had always been at the discretion and expertise of the Executioners themselves.

Gage raised a finger. "This might not be possible. The others are amid investigations that are dangerous and sensitive. Their lives, and many others, might be at stake. We might not even be able to get hold of them if they are away from their radios."

Amahle added, "The problems that could result from leaving jobs half-finished could cause far worse things to happen in the future. Why is this one so important?"

Eleanor bristled. At first, it seemed like she might be personally offended by their defiance, but as she spoke, it became clear that it was something else.

"We hired you to deal with problems identified by the Executives, and you are paid and supplied for that purpose. Now, they have told me to tell you what you are to do next. That is all."

Understanding dawned, and Amahle's eyes darkened. Eleanor might disagree with the orders, but she considered it her duty to pass them on and see that the Executioners obeyed them. She didn't consider herself responsible for what the Executives demanded.

Gage pushed back, pointing out the technical difficulties, not to mention logistical and communications impossibilities, of gathering all five of them simultaneously. Amahle backed him up. While incensed at the Execs' sudden shift of approach, she tried to keep things rational and unemotional.

Eleanor essentially repeated the "orders are orders" line and finally threw up her hands in exasperation. "Do you not understand it? Is this really that hard for you? The Executives have done a great many favors for you all. Now, it is time to return the favor. Is it too much to ask that you show a little professionalism?"

Amahle squinted. The Execs felt that they *owed* them something. "Why this case?" she inquired. "Who are these people to provoke such a reaction?"

"I am sure that once you begin your investigations, you will have plenty of information to answer those questions," Eleanor asserted coldly.

Gage shook his head. "If the Executives wish for us to make this a priority, they will need to provide us with as much information as we can get. Yes, we could probably find out everything ourselves, with some effort. That will take time. A good deal of time, depending on how deeply we must dive. You told us they are most concerned with haste."

The contradiction was obvious. He allowed it to settle in so Eleanor couldn't pretend to deny it.

As the young woman fumed in silence, Amahle chimed in as well. "If the concern is that other people of interest to the Execs might come to such a fate as this, or that similar events will occur, it's in their best interest to help us in any way they can. Yes?"

Eleanor maintained her silence, and another realization became impossible to ignore. She was *nervous* and growing more so by the minute. She glanced to the sides, moving her eyes but not her head, and tightened her posture as though suppressing an unconscious urge to tremble. That, too, was downright strange.

Eleanor took a step closer to the pair and spoke, at last, in a low voice, barely higher than a whisper.

"All right. I will reveal some of what we know for the sake of making your jobs easier. You must understand that this needs to be kept *very* quiet and dealt with *very* quickly."

Amahle grew tired of belaboring the obvious but kept her head. "Yes, that's what we are trying to do."

"That," Gage interjected, "and obtain justice for these poor souls, of course. I don't suspect that they hanged themselves."

Eleanor began pacing. She turned it into a brief stroll toward the side of the Autocutioner so the vehicle's height would offer them a little extra cover from sight and sound. She tried to make it look like a natural, random movement. The two Executioners followed her, grasping the nature of the charade.

With a surreptitious flick of her hand toward the dangling bodies, Eleanor explained, "These three individuals would appear, after a normal, surface-level investigation, to be upper management personnel for a particular real estate development firm. One currently engaged with high-value properties in the island's less-developed portions. However..."

She stopped as though debating how much to reveal. Or whether to speak at all.

"However," she resumed, "they are in fact members of the Executives' Junior Board. They were in the process of dismantling the real estate firm so it could be acquired piecemeal by the Executives."

Gage gave a slow nod as it all started to come together. Amahle looked at the ground. She had little use for the business intrigues of such people, but her role as an investigator had forced her to better familiarize herself with them.

Eleanor went on, "This morning's event appears to be an open move against the Executives by a hidden enemy, although no one seems to be taking credit for it so far. Needless to say, the Executives are more than a little concerned. Three members of their supposedly secret organization have been plucked with relative ease out from under the Security Force's noses, murdered, and put on display for the entire city to gawk at."

The crowd surrounding the plaza looked a little thinner. The novelty must have been wearing off, especially since the guards were doing an effective job of keeping them away from getting too good a look.

Gage pushed his glasses up his nose. "Ms. Cervantes. Do you speak Latin?"

"Enough," she responded. "Why?"

He nodded at the spectacle above them. "The placards hung around the necks of the dead. You do not find them to be of concern?"

Eleanor looked up at them, narrowing her eyes. It took her half a minute to read the signs due to the distance and how the bodies kept twisting while the cables *creaked* above them.

The woman's face hardened with what looked like dismissive contempt. "Melodramatic nonsense," she proclaimed. "I doubt it will be of any relevance to your investigation. If for some reason it is... That is one more mystery you must solve, is it not?"

Amahle noticed that Gage had produced a pencil stub and scrap paper and wrote the Latin phrases down for future reference. Neither he nor Amahle said anything further to their handler.

Eleanor had already turned away from them and walked back toward her waiting Aston Martin. She glanced over her shoulder. "Get to work, please."

CHAPTER FOUR

The first order of business, naturally, was getting hold of the bodies.

A service truck with a crane, the type used to repair the power cables themselves, arrived on the scene about five minutes after Eleanor departed. The workman who had to ride up and cut the corpses down, holding them in the basket beside him each time, didn't look particularly enthusiastic about the task.

When he'd finished, Amahle had placed her hand on the man's shoulder and thanked him, slipping him an extra twenty Atlantican dollars for his trouble.

After that, two paramedics who'd arrived on the scene pronounced the three individuals dead, to the surprise of no one, and provided body bags. Then Amahle and Gage loaded the corpses into the Autocutioner's back compartment, tying them down to ensure they didn't roll around.

They kept the door separating the front seating area from the rear compartment tightly closed and rolled down the windows. By the time they set off, two-thirds of the crowd had dispersed, either because they had jobs to go to or simply out of boredom.

Nothing stayed novel and exciting for long in a place like Atlantica.

When they returned to headquarters and pulled into the back lot, there was already one other Autocutioner parked there. Amahle suspected it was Dante's. It was difficult to imagine a scenario where Ty or Daria could get back before the young doctor.

She pulled the vehicle up with its rear door facing the building's back entrance, then shut off the engine and climbed out. Gage did likewise.

Amahle paused and placed a hand against the side of the truck as a sudden wave of tiredness, a dogged feeling of both physical fatigue and lack of sleep, immobilized her. She banished it within a second, used to working through such inconveniences.

Still, she wasn't getting any younger. Plus, she wouldn't be much good to the investigation if she was utterly exhausted. Once the opportunity arose, she would have to get a few hours of sleep.

Gage noticed. "Are you okay, Amahle?"

"Yes," she told him. "Tired, but I will manage for now. I can rest later once everything is taken care of."

He shrugged and pulled open the truck's back door. Before Amahle could suggest that they get a gurney, cart, or something else that might make transporting the bodies into the infirmary easier, the door to HQ opened, and Dante appeared.

"Hi there," he called, waving to them. "I heard all about it. This ought to get us started." He pushed one gurney in front of him and pulled a second one behind. Amahle also saw that he had a couple of fresh bandages across his face. He must have been wounded on his recent job and applied them himself after he returned to base.

Gage beamed. He and Dante had been friends before the latter joined the organization. "Ah, hello. It would seem you read our minds. You're short one, but we can make up for it."

He took one of the gurneys, and with Amahle's help, they loaded the first two corpses and wheeled them into the building. Amahle stood guard outside while the men took the bodies to the infirmary. A couple of minutes later, they returned for the last one.

Amahle climbed into the truck and heaved the bagged corpse down to where Gage and Dante could secure it on the rolling bed. Watching them, she mumbled, more due to thinking aloud than wanting to converse, "I hope the smell doesn't linger in my truck. I'll have to give it a good cleaning when we have time."

Dante glanced up at her. "Yeah, understandable. Sorry you were the one who had to pull hearse duties this time. I have some spray that might help mask it, at least until enough fresh air filters through to get rid of the rest. The body bags seem nice and tight, at least, so I don't imagine anything, like, leaked out and seeped in."

Gage sighed. "Yes, there should be no problems, but I imagine she does not wish to talk about it. Come, let us head in. Amahle, you can probably get some sleep now, if you want. We can handle things from here."

She waited, sitting on the edge of the truck for a moment as her two partners pushed the gurney inside. The moment became several, and soon she realized that at least thirty minutes had passed.

Oddly, she no longer felt all that tired, her consciousness having snapped back and her body finding its proverbial second wind. She hopped down, shut and locked up the truck, and went into the building, making for the infirmary. The case had inflamed her curiosity. She would watch at least some of the autopsy and see what she could learn from it.

After that, at last, there might be time to rest.

She pushed open the infirmary door as Dante sterilized his tools. Gage stood nearby, watching. The three dead people, two men and a woman, lay motionless in a line on three tables.

The two men were chatting idly, mostly about Dante's recent case. When Amahle came in, they glanced up to acknowledge her but otherwise continued conversing as they had been.

"...that it's a good thing I was almost finished with them when the call came in." Dante chortled with a nasty and combative edge to his voice. He pointed briefly at the bandages on his face. "After what happened, I was kind of hoping I'd get the chance to take all their slimeball friends out as well. Still, they won't get far. After this stuff is over with, I'll be able to settle accounts with the bastards."

Gage adjusted his glasses. "Were they indeed using Atlanticore? It shouldn't surprise me since drug dealers will do anything to increase their profits. What puzzles me is *how* they did it without simply blowing everyone up."

Dante laughed. "Yeah. They took tiny shavings of crystal and added them to the cocktails of other filth they were using. There was an 'up' version that mainly consisted of amphetamines and a 'down' version that used heroin. Both were dangerously volatile thanks to the Atlanticore.

"It seemed to stimulate high levels of electrical activity in the brain. I'm not sure if that was due to a secondary effect of metabolizing it, or if it was a direct stimulation thing via electromagnetic signals in proximity with the cerebral cortex, or what. I wasn't able to collect a sample to study."

Amahle moved closer as they continued to chat. It seemed they were taking a break after having conducted an initial inspection.

"Well, that's too bad, but at least you disrupted the operation. What happened to your face?"

Dante scowled. "That's the one thing I don't want to talk about, bud. It's the exact reason *why* I couldn't get a sample.

"One of the fucking dealers took his whole supply of burnout dust and ignited it with some rubbing alcohol and a lighter. He was trying to destroy the evidence, that type of thing. He succeeded but blew himself up while he was at it. It also sent a bunch of shrapnel out, and I got a face full of it. Goddammit. Probably no way to avoid at least slight scarring."

His friend rested a hand on his shoulder. "Now, now, don't worry. Already, women seem to find you the—what is the expression?—tall, dark, and handsome type. Yes? Now, you will simply be tall, dark, and handsome, but with *character*. Think of it that way."

Dante snorted. He turned to Amahle, bringing her into the conversation for the first time. "What do you say to that, Amahle? Do women like men's faces to have *character*? Hah."

He tensed as he thought of something—most likely, he'd suddenly recalled that Amahle's face had a certain amount of "character" of much the same sort.

She ignored the question since she wasn't in the mood for such trivia. "I'm tired," she pointed out. "But I would like to know the results of your autopsy. What happened to these victims? Determining that is more important than any concerns of someone's vanity."

Dante raised his eyebrows, rebuked by what she'd said. He cleared his throat, smoothed his hair back, and drew himself up to his full height, assuming the posture of the professional physician he was. He lowered his voice and his way of speaking turned to a somewhat more clipped and formal generic American accent rather than the colloquial New York pattern he'd slipped into.

"Right," he began. "Okay. I've examined all three of them, and while there are more things I want to look at, I can pretty safely diagnose the cause of death."

Amahle drummed the fingers of her right hand on the bicep of her left arm. "Yes?"

Dante looked down at the corpses, his face growing somber with pity. "All three were strangled from behind. I'm almost certain of it. It appears that it happened before they were hung from the lines, since they've been dead for several hours, probably longer than whenever it was exactly that the killer dangled them from the wire."

Gage interjected, "How can you be sure they were strangled and not hanged? Wouldn't the wounds be similar?"

Picking up a wooden tongue depressor, Dante pointed at the neck of the nearest stiff, a nondescript and slightly jowly man in his early forties or so.

"You would think so, wouldn't you? Here's the thing. There are small, narrow lines cut into the skin. Look closely, and you'll see them encircling the whole neck. Over that, we have a broader, less invasive marking made by the cords used to hang them.

"It looks like the narrower wound is the older of the two in both cases. How would a thick cord make a marking like that, anyway? No, the killer did this with something like a wire. Classic garroting assassination."

As the implications sank in, Dante frowned and added, "Please don't ask me how I know that."

It was unnecessary to ask, Amahle felt. By now, she'd heard most of the stories about Dante's rather shady past. He'd become involved with organized crime while in medical school, had developed a drug problem after he acquired his medical license, and finally had allowed a patient with extremely dangerous friends to die in his care.

After he'd fled to Atlantica to escape the consequences of his negligence, his addictions quickly led to him being a debtor slave to a gun-smuggling ring. When Ty Katakura had gone after the smugglers, he'd somewhat begrudgingly spared the young doctor's life and eventually, on Gage's recommendation, recruited him.

Whatever sort of person Dante might've been in the past, he was decent enough in the present. None of the Executioners were individuals whose personal histories were exactly spotless.

Instead of pressing him about his knowledge of garroting

techniques, Amahle queried, "Do you know exactly when they might have died? Did they die at different times or together?"

Dante glanced at the other two bodies. "So far, it looks like they murdered all three at about the same time. Within the last twelve hours. No more than that, but it couldn't have been less than five or six, either."

Gage nodded and pointed out, "When I spoke to the real estate firm, they confirmed that all three of them had been at work the day before. It happened overnight."

Amahle lacked any formal training in forensics but would've guessed much the same thing, simply based on the available timetable and common sense. The dead of night was the best time for assassination, and the murderers had undoubtedly planned for the public to discover the corpses during morning rush hour.

She leaned against the wall, debating whether or not to excuse herself for a nap, when Dante suddenly muttered, "Huh, that's strange."

Amahle leaned forward. Gage did likewise. The physician was bent over the middle of the three tables, occupied by the lone female among the deceased, and was prodding and examining her, paying particular attention to her head and neck area.

"What?" Amahle asked.

Dante tapped a slight bulge under the woman's chin, about where the Adam's apple would be on a man. He produced a small flashlight and clicked it on, then used the tongue depressor to hold her mouth open. He squinted. "I think there's something lodged in her throat. I didn't notice it at first because of the distension and trauma from the strangulation followed by hanging for a couple of hours. The neck is going to swell after something like that. But this... Hold on."

He fetched a pair of forceps and had Gage hold the light on the woman's mouth while he fished around for the foreign object he'd glimpsed.

Amahle watched with a mixture of curiosity and distaste. She'd killed many people throughout her life, and she knew that Dante was following standard medical protocols as part of a legitimate investigation. Still, there was something inherently gruesome about seeing people poking around in what had once been a human being.

After a moment, Dante said, "Aha! Got it. Yeah, it's something solid. Not anything that *belongs* there, I can tell you that right off the bat." He slowly retracted his arm. The tweezers emerged clamped around a small blue stone covered with what looked like a miniature net.

Gage stared at the strange object. "What on Earth? Is it Atlanticore?"

"Probably," Dante muttered. "That crap turns up everywhere, any time something weird is going on, doesn't it?" He placed the stone in a glass dish.

Amahle pointed at the other two stiffs. "Check them, too. Maybe there's one in each of them?"

Dante nodded. "Yeah, that just occurred to me. Gage, be a pal and handle the light again."

"Of course," the Nepali agreed.

They moved over to the first man and repeated the process, then to the third body, the other male. Each time, the results were the same as with the woman. An azure-hued crystal contained within a tight latticework.

When they finished the grotesque business, the trio turned to the objects they'd discovered. Each was about the diameter of a fingernail and roughly ovoid. Big enough that a person might've choked on one, yet Dante maintained that external strangulation with garrote wires was the cause of death.

Gage looked at the items through a magnifying glass. "Yes, it is certainly Atlanticore, but the crystals appear to be inert. They do not possess any signs of the unstable power capabilities of living samples. There is a wire webbing across each of them.

Which does not seem only to enclose the stones, but to extend...outward."

He lay down the glass and looked up at Dante, his face betraying a growing dread that was pushing his usual sanguine demeanor down into the depths of stoic gloom. "Dante. This looks disturbingly familiar. Can you tell me if someone shoved these crystals into their throats after death? Or something else?"

"Mm, no, I don't think so. I had to kind of rip them out by the roots. Bizarre as it might sound, it's like someone *implanted* them there. Which doesn't make a lot of sense." Rubbing his chin, he looked again at the bodies and added, "I'm probably going to have to dissect. In fact, I should've done that to begin with."

Amahle stepped forward. "I will help if I can. I don't feel like sleeping yet. The sooner we understand what we're dealing with here, the better." Her desire to know what the hell had happened to these people was eclipsing her better judgment. There was a mystery here that went far beyond the usual avaricious intrigues of Atlantica.

Dante looked her full in the face. "If you want to, sure. Just do what I say. Brace yourself. This kind of thing can get a little, you know, icky."

"So I've noticed. I've seen far worse, anyway."

Forty minutes later, Dante's scalpel had opened the throats of all three of the deceased, and he'd made similar forays into other parts of their bodies as well. The more he examined things, the more disturbed and bewildered he became.

He paused after they'd finished cutting open the second subject.

"Okay. Same pattern in both of them, and it seems safe to assume that the third guy is similar. The wire mesh we see enclosing the crystals *was* implanted throughout their bodies.

"There isn't much sign of scarring near it, though, so it's almost like it *grew* into place the way a parasite would, or how a plant grows into an area of earth. It seems connected to the nervous system since most of it runs alongside the major nerve channels. The thickest areas of it show up to reinforce various soft tissue points in the body."

Amahle clenched her jaw. The more they learned, the less sense it made. "What does all of this mean?"

Dante shrugged. "Hell if I know. Gage, you're the technological guy, and you've been studying all this Coven shit for months. What do you make of it?"

The Gurkha had fallen into a grim, contemplative silence. He spoke for the first time since they'd begun the dissections. "The crystals, with their webbing of wires... It does all look most familiar. It's like an example of what I've seen on the ancient Atlantican artifacts the Coven tinkered with. Only far more refined."

Both of his companions stared at him, waiting for him to say more. He adjusted his glasses without looking back. "As to what its *purpose* is, I cannot say. Only that whatever improvements they sought to make to their tools and weaponry, they must be attempting something similar with the human body."

Amahle had heard enough. They'd uncovered multiple new lines of inquiry while finding no actual answers to speak of. Plus, her body had reached its limit.

"I need to sleep," she stated. "Wake me up when you need me after Tyler and Daria have returned." She went over to the sink to wash her hands.

Dante and Gage both managed a smile.

"That sounds like a good idea," Gage said.

CHAPTER FIVE

Amahle stared down at the slip of paper in her hand. On it, Dante had scrawled three names.

Elijah Greenblatt, age forty-two, originally from New Jersey in the United States. Maria Reisenegger, age thirty-four, from Chile. Sirimavo Rajapaksa, age thirty-seven, from Ceylon. All of them were alive until last night or early this morning.

Dante came up beside her. She was sitting in the break room and sipping another cup of his distinctively strong coffee. The five hours she'd slept had been enough to take the edge off her fatigue, but probably not as much as she truly needed.

"Hey," he began. "Are you sure you want to be the one to handle this? We might be able to get away with pushing it back a day until Ty and Daria get back."

Slowly, Amahle shook her head. She guzzled half the coffee at once. "Yes. I want to do something about it. Such are our orders, anyway. The Executives wish for us to investigate the whole matter without delay. You and Gage are better served remaining here and conducting research. I would be of little help with such things. I'm better in the field."

Dante shrugged, as though he found her feelings on the

matter odd but wasn't about to question them. "Fair point you have there. I've probably got a full night's work ahead of me as far as continuing to cut those poor schmucks up to figure out what in God's name the Coven did to them. Same with Gage, but in his case, from the technological rather than the biological end."

"Yes." Amahle set the coffee cup down. She knew she ought to eat something, but she didn't much feel like it. "What bothers me is that we haven't yet heard from Eleanor. Usually, she's far better about responding to us when we need something."

The tall physician pulled up a chair and sat next to her. "You're right about that. Still, this whole thing has become, well, *personal* for the Execs, from the sound of it. She's their main errand girl. At least as far as we're concerned. They probably have her doing something else and hope we won't need any help until they finish with her."

It made sense. It was still galling.

Amahle quipped, "They couldn't have picked a worse time. Will Ty and Daria be back tomorrow? The day after?"

"Hell if I know," Dante grumbled. "Last I heard, they both were off half-buried in some caves or the jungle or something on the other side of the island. Even if they *aren't* captured or fighting through God knows what, there would be no way to get them back in a hurry without a private plane. Which makes me wonder why the hell the Execs don't have more of those things working in tandem with us."

Amahle wondered, too.

While she'd slept, Dante and Gage had fired up the radio and put out a bulletin of sorts, summoning Ty and Daria back ASAP. They'd also requested the personal presence of Eleanor Cervantes. She didn't visit Executioner HQ very often. They usually only saw her in person perhaps once or twice a month. Her responsibilities were manifold, and her schedule was always full.

Amahle finished her coffee and stood. "Well, there's nothing we can do about the others yet. Therefore, I will do what I can. Although, people skills are, ah, not my greatest of strengths."

Dante chuckled. "Could be worse. I mean, you're a little stiff at times, but you don't usually rub people the wrong way. Besides, everyone respects the uniform. I'd bet money that those people at the real estate place *want* to help us. Either because they cared about their three dead coworkers, or because they know we're going to show up and want to get it over with so we stay out of their hair."

Amahle threw the cup in the trash. "I will report back later. Please do the same if you find anything."

With that, she nodded her goodbyes to both Dante and Gage, then strapped on her armored vest and took up her keys alongside the slip of paper. Besides the names of the deceased, it also included basic directions to Schust & Ferne, the development company where the three murder victims had worked.

The firm occupied the bottom two floors of a mid-tier office building downtown. Perhaps unsurprisingly, it lay only about a block from Broadway Plaza. When Amahle's Autocutioner rolled up to the building's parking garage, the guard at the gate let her in without a fuss.

When she strolled into the lobby and informed the receptionist of why she was there, the squat, pink-faced woman seemed wholly unfazed.

"Of course, you may interview the staff, Executioner," the lady said. "We had expected one of you to show up and try to satisfy your suspicions. Such a high-profile tragedy demands a thorough investigation."

Amahle's face was blank of emotion. The undercurrent of caustic sarcasm in the woman's tone and choice of words didn't escape her. "Good. Because for suspicion to fall only upon the correct people, a thorough investigation is exactly what is needed."

Most of the first floor was conference rooms, comfort facilities, and the like, so Amahle took the stairs to the second floor. Most of the offices were there and where the bulk of the actual work happened. There were perhaps twelve people on the clock. She intended to interview all of them.

The first individual on her agenda was Kerensky, an older man with watery eyes who acted as supervisor of the office staff and middleman between them and the company's president and vice president.

When Amahle came into his office, he kept looking at her with his face turned partially to the side and cleared his throat more or less continuously.

"Hrrm, why yes, I know well who they are. What they got up to on their own time was never my business or the company's, provided they did nothing to embarrass us flagrantly. Do you think they might've been involved in something, er, criminal?"

Amahle gazed skeptically back at him from across his mahogany-topped desk. "I don't know yet. That's what I'm trying to find out."

Interviewing Kerensky and a handful of other workers netted her little of value. It made sense, in a fashion. Greenblatt, Reisenegger, and Rajapaksa were members of a shadowy cabal, or so Eleanor's inside information said. Such people were unlikely to reveal much about themselves or their personal lives. No one in the office seemed to know much about them besides what they'd done within the building or basic stuff relevant to their professional spheres.

There was one red thread of interest that Amahle found winding through things, however. No one stated it outright, but by reading between the lines, piecing together the clues, and applying her intuition, Amahle figured it out.

The late Mr. Rajapaksa had been sexually involved with his secretary, Iris Tilly, who was all of twenty-four and who didn't seem to mind him using her in such a fashion. There was no indication of true romance between them. It was a shallow relationship based on the usual workplace erotic tensions. It didn't hurt that Rajapaksa had bought Ms. Tilly a gift of some sort after each encounter.

The problem was that Tilly wasn't present at work today. Even if she was, Amahle didn't know how useful she would be. A callow affair didn't necessarily have anything to do with the far more serious machinations the three Junior Executives engaged in behind the scenes.

Amahle made the rounds and pressed the others for more info, hitting dead ends each time. The employees didn't try to argue with her and weren't blatantly lying about anything, as far as she could tell, but there was no great enthusiasm for helping her, either.

None of them liked her. In other places, she might've known the reason. In other areas, it might've been because she was African, but Atlantica was too much a hodgepodge of different peoples for anyone's background to matter much. In other instances, it might've been her aloof and direct way of speaking or how her scars and manner hinted at her nature as a killer. Atlantica was full of scoundrels and misfits.

No, she suspected it was something else. They disliked her because she was a cop in a land with no laws. She threatened to stir up trouble in a place where the only guarantee of protection from trouble was power.

Wandering at last to the empty office of Ms. Tilly, Amahle leaned against the wall and scowled out the window.

"This was a mistake," she mumbled. "I'm not the one for this type of work." Daria was generally their best negotiator, manipulator, and diplomat. When Gage and Dante worked together, they tended to handle such things well, too.

Amahle was more like Tyler. Pure investigation often confounded her. Like Mr. Katakura, she preferred to deal with problems by shooting them. Although as a sniper rather than a frontline berserker, she was a bit more cool and calculating about it than he was.

Her gaze went to the secretary's desk. A pile of memos lay there. Figuring it couldn't hurt to take a closer look, Amahle flipped through them.

One caught her eye. It seemed that Mr. Rajapaksa had cleared a dinner reservation because of an impromptu meeting.

"Interesting." Perhaps the threads that connected the disparate phenomenon weren't so obscure, after all.

Making the rounds again and asking to see more internal memos, Amahle found that the other victims, Greenblatt and Reisenegger, had canceled events last evening. Some of the notes were from earlier in the day and were for mere reschedules. Therefore they hadn't garnered any particular degree of attention as anything important.

She returned to Kerensky's office. "What can you tell me about the victims' schedules on their last day? Did they have a business meeting of some sort to attend? An important seminar?"

The supervisor's face was morose. He'd hoped she would go away once she'd poked around the floor enough.

He sighed. "All of them seemed to have spent the whole of yesterday making time for the evening. Before you ask, I don't know for what. It might've been a personal matter. Nothing set up by the company, in any event."

"Thank you." Amahle turned and closed the door behind her.

It took another twenty minutes to track down a note, all but lost amid the chaos of papers pinned to the bulletin board, which revealed the final puzzle piece. Potentially.

Greenblatt had made a reservation nearly a month in advance to attend a spa session last night. It, alone among his commitments, had *not* been canceled.

Amahle stood before the note, pursing her lips. Since he'd committed so long ago, he might have simply forgotten to reschedule it. Still, it was the only lead she had. She wrote down the name of the spa, tackily dubbed Crystalline Shine, as well as its address and a crude map of approximately where it ought to be in the city.

It was time to see if Eleanor was available again.

Amahle left the building directly. She wasn't sure how she felt. On the one hand was a mounting sense of frustration that her investigation was turning up more new questions than it was answering old ones.

On the other hand, at least she would be able to get out of the dull, stuffy, and faintly hostile office environment. She looked forward to hitting the street again and going somewhere else, even if a health spa was perhaps not the most exciting of locales.

If her intuition was correct and her information was good, it might be the place where she was able to tie up the frayed mass of loose ends, so many of which had emerged in less than one full day.

Once out in the parking lot, she climbed into her Autocutioner, started the engine, and gave the mirrors a swift glance or two before backing out and driving into the street. Evening rush hour hadn't yet begun, but it would be starting soon enough that she hoped she could reach the spa within half an hour or less.

As she settled into the usual rhythm of driving Atlantica Metro's busy, chaotic streets, Amahle reached out to switch on her radio and unhook the receiver. It took about two minutes for the static to clear and Eleanor to answer her. "Yes? This is Cervantes. Over."

"Good day, Eleanor," said Amahle. "I hope you received our message from earlier. I have another concern at the moment. I'm pursuing a lead at a place called the Crystalline Shine, which is a health club frequented by at least one of our murder victims. Is there anything you can tell me about this place? Over."

Something rustled on the other end of the line, and Eleanor's voice, heavy with tiredness, responded, "Yes, just a moment, please. Over."

Amahle left the radio on and glanced at her crude, hand-drawn crude map pointing out the way to the establishment in question. It was still a good mile away, so hopefully, Eleanor could provide useful information before she arrived.

Although sunset would be a couple of hours yet, the day's light seemed unusually wan. It was partially cloudy, which contributed, but there was an odd quality in the air as well. Amahle hoped it was nothing. It might only have been a distortion of her perceptions, an illusion created by the fact that she'd been up all night and slept through the early afternoon.

When she was about a block away from the club, Eleanor came back over the radio. "Nikoze? I have something for you, but it's not much. The Crystalline Shine has no particular record of significance, only a reputation as a lower-end place. It sounds like it would be beneath the usual standards of persons such as the Junior Executives. This means that, if we are to speak frankly, the place might be a front for a brothel, drug-dealing operation, or something of that nature. Then again, it could simply be a business that provides decent value for low prices. The proverbial 'best-kept secret,' you might say. Over."

Amahle exhaled through her nose. "I see. Well, I'm nearly there. I will report after I've looked around and interviewed the employees. Out."

Minutes later, she rounded a corner and almost missed the place. It was in an unobtrusive building, only one story high but with two wings branching out from the main area. The sign out front was low to the ground and not overly flashy. Amahle turned into the adjacent lot with an abrupt jerk of the steering wheel, and the car in the lane behind her honked angrily.

Her massive armored truck was probably an unusual sight at such a place. She wheeled it around toward the back of the building, parking in the most out-of-the-way corner she could find. The rear of the property included a high chain-link fence that separated it from an empty adjacent lot and the grounds of a four-story housing complex. The overall air was of seediness making a valiant effort at respectability.

Amahle shut off the engine and flipped over the map, once again studying the names of the deceased. She suspected that all three would sound familiar to at least one or two people within.

Once more, she left her rifle in its niche behind her seat. There was no specific reason to expect danger. She trusted her ability to defend herself with her little .32 revolver, if need be, despite the weapon's relative lack of punch.

Still, the plot had thickened. She felt it, and Gage, Dante, and Eleanor had sensed it as well. They might be wandering into the midst of something more serious than any of them had dealt with before.

As such, she wondered if it might be time to start carrying more firepower. Something smaller and more maneuverable than a full marksman rifle for use in close quarters, like a submachine gun. When she returned to headquarters, she would see about requisitioning one from the locker.

"I have never truly learned to live in the city, have I?" she mused as she jumped down to the asphalt.

She came from a small rural village and had spent much of her adult life in various wildernesses on the fringes of population centers. When she'd worked in cities, it was often in war zones where the normal rhythms of urban life had ceased or retreated to make room for violence.

The ways of Atlantica Metro were totally different. Violence and deception interwove with everyday activities of innumerable types. Although Atlantica was unique in many ways, in that regard, she suspected it was little different from any other large city in the world—or any other large city throughout most of human history.

Then she cleared her head of anything save the immediate feedback of her surroundings and the tasks she had to accomplish. Anyone within the spa who was paying attention would've noticed the distinctive armored truck pulling in. They might be expecting her.

She pushed through the front door and found a humble but reasonably pleasant lobby, decorated entirely in white with ferns and other potted plants in the corners in blue, faux china planters.

A woman with a beehive hairdo who looked more or less East Asian sat behind the front desk. "Hello. May I help you?" Her eyes wandered over Amahle's uniform, fixating in particular on the skull-and-sword patch on her shoulder.

"Yes," Amahle told her. "I wish to know if three people have been members here. They have had…misfortunes, and I wanted to ask if anyone had seen them recently."

The woman tried to maintain a pleasant and professional demeanor, but she was quite obviously frightened by the implications of an Executioner wanting to ask questions. "Of course, we'll be happy to cooperate. Give me their names, and I can check our records."

Amahle gave her a small yet warm smile. "That will make everyone's day much easier. Two men, last names Greenblatt and Rajapaksa; and one woman, last name Reisenegger."

The receptionist immediately began reviewing some books and folders. While she waited, Amahle drifted back into the lobby, wanting to sit but not daring to in case anything unexpected happened.

One other person was waiting, an older man, probably of Southern European or Levantine descent, balding and heavyset. He sat in a chair against the far wall and read a newspaper that obscured his face. He seemed to be paying no attention to Amahle and to have taken no heed of her brief conversation with the lady at the desk.

Amahle glanced into the spa proper, which lay beyond the lobby. It was difficult to see much, as the lobby led into a short, broad, empty hallway before branching off to either side at a T-intersection. To the left and right of the juncture point, presumably, were the two wings she'd seen attached to the building and which must have contained the main facilities.

The receptionist stood. "Madam?"

Amahle looked back at her and widened her eyes to show that she was listening.

"All three of these people have memberships here," the woman explained. "We haven't seen them in over a week. They had reservations for an all-day health session, which was to take place yesterday. Will they be rescheduling, or have their problems made that impossible?"

Amahle walked right up to the desk, ignoring the way the woman fidgeted and spoke in a voice as low as she could manage while remaining audible at all. "They are dead. I have no reason to suspect anyone in particular yet. I would like you to help me. I must find out everything I can about them, and anything you know about their time here would be a good start."

"Oh!" The receptionist gasped. "I'm sorry to hear that. Well, ah," she struggled to think of something to say as her gaze darted around.

Amahle waited, keeping her expression neutral. The woman's fear might have indicated guilt, but she doubted it. More likely she was simply the type who was easily intimidated by authorities or rough characters and hoped the whole situation would pass as soon as possible.

"Oh," she repeated, and her eyes lit up. "If I'm not mistaken, all three of them were with the same members of our staff. Bettina, a masseuse, and Ronald, a trainer."

Amahle tried to soften her approach a little to keep the woman from growing too anxious. "That is good to know. Is either of them on hand today? I would like to speak to them."

The woman winced. "Ronald is in. I can make an appointment for him to—"

"No," Amahle interrupted. "Take me to him and point him out. Now, please. I have no time to waste."

Hanging her head in misery, the woman sighed and came around the side of the desk. "Very well. Follow me. Please, though, we would appreciate it if you would not do anything to frighten the customers."

"I won't unless someone else forces me to," Amahle reassured her.

The receptionist's heels *clacked* on the tiles as she led Amahle to the T-intersection, then off to the right. They came to a large floor filled with exercise machines. Toward the far end was another hallway bending to somewhere unseen, and there was a door as well that led to a sauna or perhaps simply a public shower.

The woman stopped and scanned the floor. About half a dozen people were working out on the machines or stretching in the open areas. Amahle stayed behind the receptionist, using her for cover until the time was right to intrude.

The woman raised her right hand. "Oh, there he is. Ronald! There is someone who wants to speak to you."

Amahle followed the receptionist's gesture with her eyes and saw a short, lean, but muscular man, thirtyish and probably of mixed white and black parentage, turn toward them. He was standing near one of the far corners and overseeing the workout of a middle-aged couple who were taking turns on a treadmill.

Ronald's gaze took in the receptionist, then moved to Amahle. And her uniform. His eyes bulged.

Amahle knew what was about to happen. She stepped out from behind the other woman and was mid-stride across the exercise room floor when the trainer turned and ran.

"Stop!" she shouted as she sprinted after him. Around her, the patrons stopped exercising and gawked at her as she passed. Some of them grumbled or clucked in alarm and confusion.

It took less than a second for her to cross the whole floor. She was still in good physical condition and accustomed to moving swiftly across rough terrain. Running over a mere floor, therefore, wasn't difficult.

Ronald was no slouch either. He'd already vanished into the hallway at the rear of the exercise room, ducking to the left.

Amahle followed him. The hall led around the edge of the sauna and past some storerooms and changing rooms. It terminated at a glass door that opened onto the property's rear portion. Amahle had seen it after she'd parked her Autocutioner.

Ronald was at the door. He had a good start on her, but when he smashed into the bar on the exit, it refused to budge at first. Trembling and using the gross motor skills typical of a panicked state, he raged and fumbled before remembering to push the bar down. The door opened, and he burst out.

In the time it had taken him to get through the exit, Amahle closed most of the distance that separated them. She bolted after him, catching the door before it could swing shut, and hurled herself out into the lot.

She was gaining. Ronald's coordination had left him in his desperation to get away from her, and navigating the obstacle course of narrow halls, doors, and parked cars was enough to neutralize the speed of adrenaline. Halfway across the parking lot, she came within barely two yards of her quarry. Another second, and he would be hers.

Then, abruptly and shockingly, he stopped, spun, and yelled at her. "*Stop!*"

Amahle let out an "Oof!" as something invisible struck her like a moving wall or a powerful gust of wind. The air vibrated and echoed with a distinct metallic ring, and there was an odd smell all around her. Like ozone.

As she toppled over, her momentum killed and her balance destroyed, her brain picked up the pieces of what had happened. The man had used his *voice* as a weapon. It made no sense, but there was no other explanation. Unless he had some kind of other weapon concealed on his person and had activated it without her seeing at the same instant he'd barked his command.

She fell on her side and rolled up to her knees almost at once. The percussive blast had destabilized and disoriented her but hadn't done any serious damage.

Ronald noticed too much. His eyes bloodshot and crazed with anger, he took a heavy, stomping step closer to her, his arms spread out at his sides, and his hands balled into fists. He opened his mouth.

"Now, *you will—*"

Amahle was nothing if not a fast learner. Before he could repeat his unnatural attack with another powerful shout, she pounced from her crouching position, arm extended, and drove her knuckles into the man's throat.

He stumbled back. The beginnings of the metallic echo effect in his voice dissipated, giving way to a normal human gagging sound, but one of his flailing arms struck Amahle upside the head. She fell aside, her vision spinning as Ronald staggered across the pavement, trying to flee into the street.

Amahle tumbled to the ground, flat on her back, and through fast reflexes and sheer force of will, she propelled herself back onto her feet. She was dizzy, and her head hurt, but the pain was distant and numb, secondary to the all-important goal of running down her prey. She started after him again.

Ronald wasn't in good shape. The throat punch had hurt him more than she'd expected. He clutched his neck as he swayed and stomped around like a hapless drunk, then bumbled into the street, oblivious to an approaching car.

The sedan's driver honked, braked, and tried to swerve. They were partially successful. Instead of running Ronald over, the car broadsided him. Metal *crunched* as the impact threw the man eight feet into the air before he crashed to the pavement in front of the spa.

Amahle dashed over to him, her right hand hovering near the

holster where she kept her .32, but she doubted she would need it. Ronald was dying.

Blood covered him from his impact with the car—which *screeched* off down the street, the driver not wanting to take any responsibility for the accident—and he continued to choke. Amahle saw why. Smoke was coming from his mouth, along with bluish sparks. He coughed up blood, and his eyes bulged with desperate pain. It was awful to see.

Cursing under her breath in her native tongue, Amahle knelt beside him, trying to pry his clawing hands away from his neck. His strength was flagging. When she gripped his wrists and forced his hands aside, it looked as though the malfunctioning device had burned a hole the size of a golf ball through his throat. He gurgled one last time and died.

Amahle let his hands fall and stood. Things were still going rather less well than she would've liked. This wasn't the sort of investigation she'd be able to shoot her way out of.

There was one thing she *could* do, though. She pulled out her pocketknife and brought it to the dead trainer's throat.

CHAPTER SIX

After Amahle had announced her return, Gage and Dante must have guessed that she hadn't bothered to eat while she was out. She came back to find that they'd ordered an assortment of deli sandwiches and that Gage had made a beautiful pot of strong green tea. It made their labors to come far easier to deal with.

"All right," Dante announced, emerging from the infirmary after twenty minutes or so. Amahle sat with Gage outside, eating and drinking tea, while she filled him in on everything she'd done and discovered.

They both looked up as the physician clapped once. Dark circles had formed under his eyes, but there was manic energy in him. The case had captured his attention and piqued his intellectual curiosity and sense of adventure.

Amahle set down her teacup. "Yes?"

Dante held up the blue stone and what remained of the wire webbing. "It's damaged, yes, but I'm fairly sure it's the same type of implant we found in the other three stiffs earlier. Which is interesting because this guy was what, a personal trainer at a day spa? I mean, maybe he had all the connections in the world behind the scenes, but kind of an average-level guy. So these things, whatever they are, aren't only going to the upper echelon of the Coven's people."

Gage swallowed a bite of club sandwich. "It would seem so. When the others return, we will hear what they have to say as well."

Amahle nodded.

Dante excused himself to clean up. Once he finished, he would join them for their preliminary conference. The three of them could at least get enough important discussion out of the way to reduce the amount of talking the other three would have to do.

It was almost nine o'clock in the evening. Tyler and Daria, surprisingly, had both sent messages indicating that they would be back in the city soon. Eleanor had also promised to show up, but she'd been carefully vague about the time.

"Gage," Amahle said, "I have to confess that I've never felt I was a good detective. It doesn't come naturally to me, and I don't know what to do next."

He grinned with a mixture of sympathy and amusement that made her feel better at once. "If that is so, you're in much the same boat as nearly all of us. So, don't worry too much. You have done enough and provided us with more leads and clues. Besides, the whole purpose of calling a conference is so everyone can contribute their knowledge and opinions."

It was true. But... "I feel like someone should be out hunting down the masseuse from the club. Yet that would make it harder for us all to decide on what to do next."

Gage waved that off. "You tried your best. We might be able to pursue other avenues."

The masseuse, Bettina Karo, had yet to turn up anywhere. After the death of Ronald, Amahle had gone back into the spa and tried to calm down the terrified receptionist before asking for Bettina's contact information. After the woman's hysteria subsided, she'd given Amahle an address in exchange for a promise that she wouldn't be harmed or punished for anything Ronald had done.

There was one problem, though. It seemed to be Ms. Karo's *former* address. Amahle had gone directly from the spa to the apartment, only to find that an elderly couple who'd never heard of Bettina now inhabited it.

Seething with aggravation, Amahle had interviewed the neighbors, but most of them hadn't the slightest idea where the masseuse had moved to. Two did, but their reports conflicted wildly. One asserted that the young woman had relocated to the other side of town to stay with an ex-boyfriend. The other seemed confident that she'd taken the ferry off Atlantica altogether to live with her family in Canada.

So, Amahle had gone back out to her truck, sitting in the dark of the housing project's back lot and trying to think. Before she could make up her mind, the radio had *crackled*, and Gage and Dante had asked her to come back to base.

She had complied, melancholic and discouraged as she drove through the neon-lit city.

Given the awful scene at the spa and how the staff seemed to want her to go away and stay away, finding the masseuse could prove highly difficult. If the Executioners returned, the employees might warn Bettina to get out. A covert stakeout could work but might further damage their reputation in the neighborhood. No one liked it when the enforcers of justice used underhanded techniques against people who technically hadn't done anything wrong.

Dante emerged from the lab with clean hands and his lab coat off. "Okay, done. Hand over one of those sandwiches."

Gage was about to shove a section of salami and cheese toward the doctor when the doorbell rang. And a second or two after it faded, they could hear the door itself opening and footsteps moving into the building.

Dante pivoted toward the sound. "I'll get it." He patted his hip.

He was wearing his 1911 in a holster. It had been concealed beneath his physician's coat earlier.

Gage stood. "Allow me to come with you. Amahle, stay and finish your dinner."

She shook her head and pushed her chair back from the table. "It will still be here in a moment. I think all three of us should go."

The men didn't object. In unison, they moved through the building toward the lobby behind the front door.

Seated in a plastic chair and waiting for them was neither Tyler nor Daria nor some mysterious enemy, but Eleanor. "Hello," she opened. "I didn't know if you were available and felt it would be pointless to stand around outside, so I let myself in. I have a spare key."

Amahle bristled inwardly. It made sense that Eleanor would have access to the place. She represented the people who'd given them the use of the building to begin with. Still, something about it seemed arrogant and disrespectful.

Dante quipped, "Welcome back. We were starting to forget who you were, no offense. We have sandwiches and tea if you want them. No sign of Katakura or Barruk yet, but they're on their way."

"Excellent." Eleanor stood. "Yes, I'll have a bite to eat and a cup of tea, thank you."

Amahle noticed that the woman seemed mostly back to her usual unflappable self. There was still a dimly perceptible edge to Eleanor's demeanor, an underlying recognition that she was here because the Executives were abnormally worried. However, she'd banished most of the agitation she'd displayed earlier.

They moved themselves and their meal to the break room and tried to relax. While they waited for the last two Executioners to show up, the three present regaled Eleanor with all they had done and discovered.

Eleanor spoke little. She only nodded periodically to indicate that she was listening.

When everyone else finished with their stories, Ms. Cervantes only said, "That is interesting. I'm glad you've been hard at work."

Amahle couldn't dismiss the feeling that Eleanor was deliberately holding something back from them. She opted to probe for a reaction and see what happened.

"Eleanor. In your opinion, why would this man, Ronald, have the same type of advanced implant as the others? It's already suspicious enough that three Junior members of the Executives' Board have devices in their bodies that could come from no one except the Coven of Miracles. He was a mere trainer."

The other woman sat in tense silence, looking not at Amahle but a random point far distant. It was tough to say whether she was legitimately lost in thought as she pondered the questions or simply pretending to be to disguise her discomfort.

Dante chimed in before Eleanor could say anything. "A trainer and a masseuse aren't that different from a doctor, in a way," he observed. "They would have the excuse of being in regular close contact with the victims. Physical contact, even. They might be the go-betweens between those three and the Coven. So if that's the case, they have enough responsibility for the Coven to want to invest in them. It wouldn't really matter what they did for a living."

Eleanor remarked, "That is an excellent point. I don't believe I have anything to add to it." She ran her slender fingers through her long, dark, wavy hair.

Amahle silently cursed Dante for inadvertently giving Eleanor an easy way out. Before she could turn the pressure back on, a further complication arose. Someone else came through the front door.

Everyone's heads snapped toward the sound, but this time the intruder had no intention of waiting for them to greet him. "Hey!" Ty shouted. "It's us. We're finally back."

Presumably, he meant himself and Daria. As two pairs of footsteps moved down the hall and into the break room, the presumption was proven correct. At least, the entire order was together in the same place.

Gage smiled and waved. "Good evening to both of you. We were worried that it could be another day or more. Please, help yourselves." He gestured at the food and drink. "Let us fill you in on everything."

Amahle's mood improved at once. Having Tyler present meant that things might truly get accomplished now. He seemed to be in a jovial mood, but he was also tired and stressed from the rigors of his recent assignment. As the others talked, regaling the new arrivals with the events of the last twenty-four hours, Ty's brooding antagonism slowly swelled to the forefront of his mood.

Amahle also watched Daria. Though she lacked the "book smarts" of the two doctors, her knack for dealing with people, understanding what people were thinking, and playing people against one another exceeded all the others combined. Something cold and hard was growing in her eyes as the information piled up, leading anyone who heard it toward increasingly obvious conclusions.

Daria glanced at Eleanor as the spiel wrapped up. Then Amahle glanced at Daria. Something passed between the two women. They both looked at Ty.

Tyler Katakura had fallen silent midway into his friends' account. Gage and Dante had done the bulk of the talking, but Amahle contributed when necessary. His hands gradually tightened into fists, as they sometimes did when he ached to clutch a weapon.

Eleanor cleared her throat. "You've been sufficiently thorough that the Executives will no doubt be pleased with your progress. I cannot thank you enough. However, it sounds as though any conclusions we might try to draw will have to be—"

"*Conclusions*," Ty interrupted her in his quietly authoritative way, "are drawn from evidence. Based on everything I've heard, the evidence that there is a direct connection between the Execs and the Coven is *incontrovertible*."

Now, Amahle thought, they would start to get some real answers.

Daria kept quiet and still while Gage and Dante blinked in confusion. They knew the facts of the case. Still, they seemed behind the curve in terms of grasping the dynamic that had emerged among Tyler and the women.

Ty rose to his feet and left the lounge behind with quick, direct movements. He was gone before anyone could ask where he might be going. Amahle noted that his footsteps moved toward the infirmary...then came straight back.

Eleanor stood, smoothing out her dress. "Well, thank you again for reporting all of this. I will see to it that the Executives are aware of all that you've done."

Ty appeared again in the doorway, blocking off her escape. His face was a mask of cold intensity, and clutched in his bony, callused hand was one of the bizarre implants his comrades had dug out of the throats of human beings.

"What you will do," he proclaimed in a low voice that cut through the air and killed all other sounds, "is *fucking explain this. Now.*"

Eleanor's mouth opened and closed. "What? Why would you think that I could explain it any better than your friends did? What are you talking about, Katakura?"

"Don't try to bullshit me," he snapped. "You're holding back on us. We *know*, Eleanor. We've known for over a goddamn *year.* Since around the time Amahle was first inducted. That the same people who sign our paychecks, or at least *some* of them, are the people responsible for the lightning guns and insane Atlanticore harvesting schemes that have come within a hair's breadth of killing us all."

Eleanor blinked and swallowed.

Dante, who had a slight history of leaping to the defense of women whether he could trust them or not, stood. "Don't be *too* hard on her, Ty. She only works for them. She might not know everything."

Daria snapped, "Be quiet, Dante. Eleanor is far too attractive for your opinion on these matters to be entirely objective."

Eleanor looked around at each of them in turn, growing frantic. "What is going on here? You're all acting ridiculous. I've never done anything except help you whenever you needed it."

While she turned her attention to Amahle for half a second, Ty sprang forward. The wakizashi he always wore at his side flashed from its scabbard, and suddenly the blade's tip pressed against Eleanor's throat.

"Don't play dumb with us," he hissed. "You're going to start talking, or I'm going to take a page from Dante's book and engage in a little exploratory surgery. Do you understand?"

Now Gage, who had been trying to remain neutral, stood beside his friend. "Tyler, please. It is true. Something is going on here that demands further explanation. You must not go too far. Dante might be right—perhaps Eleanor truly *doesn't* know enough to tell us what you seem to want to hear from her. Think carefully about it."

Ty flicked his eyes briefly toward his friend, then turned them back on Eleanor. "I *have* been thinking carefully about it, Gage, which is exactly why I'm doing this. None of it adds up unless we assume they're setting us up. Or at least holding out on us, probably to cover their asses regardless of what it means for us, or the rest of Atlantica."

Eleanor was speechless. She'd gone perfectly still, staring at Ty with eyes far wider than usual but not cowering or squirming. She was afraid but in a way that had sharpened her senses and resolve rather than unraveled them.

Amahle exhorted, "Tyler—killing her will do us no good. I

will agree that she owes us some answers or explanations." She looked at Eleanor with a cool, almost icy gaze through half-lidded eyes.

Ty made one small concession to her. He took a single step back so his short sword no longer pressed against the woman's throat. It still hovered only a hand's breadth or so from her chin. Well within reach for him to slash her face or neck if he felt sufficiently motivated.

"Correct," he said. "I would rather *not* kill you, Eleanor. But you do owe us some answers. *Right now.*"

Ms. Cervantes glanced from side to side, moving her head as little as possible to avoid looking like she was about to try springing to safety or lunging at Ty in desperation. As usual, she was under a fair degree of tight control, but they all saw the blend of emotions on her face. Subdued terror, pleading for someone to come to her defense...and a defiant expectation that she was probably on her own.

No one sprang up to save her or demanded that Executioner Katakura back off.

Suddenly a pistol appeared in Eleanor's hand. A little Walther .380 or something similar. Ty blinked in shock. She'd drawn it fast enough to get through his attentive guard. If she'd chosen to fire it on the spot, the bullet would probably have struck him at the same instant he plunged his sword into her throat. She didn't. She was giving them a chance to avoid bloodshed.

Taking advantage of their surprise, Eleanor demanded, "Have you all gone insane? Do you not realize what you're doing, or how crazy it sounds? I've been your friend and ally all this time, and now you're threatening my life based on conjecture!"

She kept the pistol trained on Ty, but something in her vibe and demeanor told them that she could as easily pivot and aim it at any of them. She had no hope of taking them all out. Still, she could perhaps shoot one or two of them before she went down.

No one wanted *that.*

Daria cleared her throat. "When powerful people dabble and meddle with unnatural and dangerous technology, it makes us a little uneasy. Surely you can understand that, Ms. Cervantes?"

In a grumbling tone, Dante added, "Especially when those same people are the ones holding the purse strings. Ugh. They're worse than hospital administrators."

Eleanor shot him a half-disgusted look. "You're ready and willing to go to war with the ones holding the purse strings?" Her face turned to the others, evaluating each of them in turn. "Are you?"

Silence fell over the room. While the woman in the center stood with her gun extended, breathlessly waiting for their response, the five Executioners said nothing.

Instead, they exchanged a long chain of glances, each making eye contact with the other and passing along the unspoken understanding that bloomed between them. They didn't need to speak aloud. The bond they shared after so many months of working together—and shedding blood alongside one another—was too strong for that.

Ty inhaled through his nose and took Eleanor's attention. "I am the first Executioner. I was there for the order's formation. Back when it all started, I did as instructed. I exercised my judgment in seeing to it that I served justice. So I provided an object lesson in the case of Mr. Montrosse. You remember that well, I'm sure."

Eleanor said nothing, but there was no need to. She'd been there.

"No one is above consequences or investigation," Ty continued. Throughout his spiel, the wakizashi stayed in his hand, its point aimed at Eleanor's face. It was the same blade he'd used to execute Montrosse. "Just as no one is above taking a trip out to sea if that's what it takes."

He was referring, of course, to the new policy they'd adopted about a year ago. The guilty ones they captured alive were brought aboard a boat and sailed out on the Atlantic, along with those they'd wronged. The victims had the choice of sparing them, relinquishing their claims, or simply having the Executioners end the offenders' existence and bury them at sea.

Once more, Eleanor scanned the whole room, trying to assess each of the five in turn. The pistol remained steady in her hand, and her finger hovered by the trigger. "So, then. You will not let this go. You really are willing to take it as far as it goes?"

Her only response was a wall of cold silence, a matrix of iron resolve.

Eleanor's gun hand began to lower, and it appeared for an instant or two that she was melting or collapsing, her shoulder slumping and the tension leaking out of her body. It looked as though she might fall. Dante watched in alarm. Ty stayed alert to some trick she might try to pull.

As Eleanor's face dropped out of sight, she began to make a breathy, rhythmic motion. Amahle could hear it readily, and her first guess was that the woman had started to weep. In fear, sorrow, or horror, perhaps. It took only a second to realize that she was wrong.

Eleanor was laughing. The sound of it grew as her torso heaved more strongly, and there *were* tears in her eyes, which she squeezed out in a brief fit of nearly hysterical mirth. Then it gave way to good-natured chuckles of relief.

Amahle glanced at the others, who looked every bit as puzzled as she felt.

Eleanor stood straight and wiped her eyes with her left hand. "You have no idea how long I've been waiting for this."

CHAPTER SEVEN

Amahle stared at the other woman. After a few seconds, it occurred to her that her mouth was hanging open, so she snapped it shut. Her compatriots looked equally befuddled. That Eleanor wasn't going to try to kill them to escape was certainly encouraging. Still, her reaction wasn't what *anyone* had expected.

By now, Eleanor had composed herself again. There was still a moist sheen around the rims of her reddened eyes, and her clothes and hair looked a bit ruffled. Otherwise, she once again resembled her usual self.

"For some time," she began, inhaling deeply and speaking in her standard professional register, "I have noticed that the Executives have been...changing. They as a group, and what they stand for, are not what they once were."

Amahle hadn't been part of the order for as long as the others, and she immediately wondered if she'd missed anything important.

Cocking an eyebrow as he kept looking straight at Ms. Cervantes, Tyler prodded her, "Oh? Go on."

"Yes." Eleanor sighed. "I must confess that it has been disturbing to witness, and it grows worse when I think back on how things were even a year and a half ago. They were always people of great power, with an aloof quality, shrewd and calculating. Yet at first, their concerns were...mundane. Perhaps we might call them benevolent, to some extent. They primarily wanted only to bring stability to Atlantica. To transform it from a ragged frontier outpost in the ocean to a stable, legitimate nation-state with a respectable and thriving economy."

Amahle kept silent. Such individuals—rich elite types who felt that they were helping humankind to "progress" while also conveniently enhancing their money and power—weren't exactly her favorite people. Yet she understood the general meaning of what Eleanor was driving at.

And the implication that something worse, maybe *far* worse, was now going on.

Eleanor went on, "From being a more or less benevolent organization, they've changed much. They're more secretive—less open about what they wish to accomplish. Their priorities are different. I don't know the whole of it.

"They're no longer simply a Board of Executives who treat Atlantica as part investment, part philanthropic endeavor. They operate as a cabal whose intentions are as esoteric as they are ruthless. A shadow has fallen over everything."

Ty glowered at her. The edge of his hostility had dulled, but he remained alert and intense. "When? When did the change happen? What caused it? You're close to them. You must have seen or heard something to clue you in."

The woman's face fell, and she stared through space and time toward the past, reviewing it the way one would flip through photographs in an album.

"I believe the shift has come along with a change in the Senior Board. Some members retired or recused themselves, and other, newer members have taken up important positions. That must be it. It's the only thing I can think of. All things would be as they should, were it not for this switch to more sinister motives."

Dante asked her, "What do you mean?"

Eleanor looked at him with a slightly pinched expression of condescension. "Say what you will about the ways of the rich, about cutthroat business practices and stacking the decks. It is nevertheless far better that everyone abides by the rules, even if the rules seem unfair."

Scowling in her direction, Amahle remarked, "Yes, of course. I am sure that all the people who get exploited will see things your way."

Eleanor's eyes turned toward the South African. Her patronizing expression hadn't changed, but some of her restless energy was back. She began to move her arms a little while she spoke.

"Now is not the time to get into a philosophical tangent. You should understand—*everyone* exploits others. The worker and the foreman overestimate their labor value because it behooves them to do so. The high executive doesn't appreciate the suffering of the workaday drudge; fair enough. Yet the drudge cannot comprehend the constant pressure and the scope of responsibility that is the executive's domain."

Amahle didn't have an immediate answer for that. She remained skeptical but was willing to consider that Eleanor *might* have a point.

Ms. Cervantes concluded, "So you see, the question isn't how we might stop all exploitation. It's how do we balance out that factor in ways that aren't too terrible for everyone, and by so doing, create something stable and good?"

Ty leaned a little closer to her, and the dark blaze in his eyes grew brighter. The tension in him was palpable, like moisture or electricity in the air. "You've been using us all this time to do that? Balance exploitation?"

Eleanor tried her best to maintain her cool demeanor, and Amahle estimated that she was about halfway successful. She knew that she was at a disadvantage, surrounded by dangerous individuals who had reason to distrust her. She also appeared confident in the power of her logic.

"Do not get lost in the weeds here. I believe that is the expression. Focus on the big picture. When I first brought you in and formed this organization, we were clear on our goals and motives. We need Atlantica to be stable and productive, which is certainly far better than the alternative. Think of how things were before."

Gage ran a fingertip over his lips and rolled his eyes as he thought it over. "To be fair, there is some merit in what she says. When was the last time we had to protect a community from a clearance team?"

Clearance teams were groups of thugs hired by rich folks to forcibly remove squatter settlements from land they coveted. Their operations frequently devolved into bloodbaths. Ty, the first Executioner, had been acting as a small village's protector against such gangs when Eleanor had recruited him.

Gage added, "I do not like some of what Eleanor says either. But I see what she means. There is some value in it."

Daria leaned forward and snapped her fingers. "We're getting away from what this conversation is truly about. Eleanor! You're saying that things have changed, yes? Tell us more about that. Is it because of new people who are in charge of the Executives? Or have they altered their plans? We must know this because it does make a small difference. Or perhaps not so small."

The others fell silent as Daria spoke. Once she finished, they all stared at Eleanor, waiting for her response.

Ms. Cervantes sighed, and it was obvious to them as well as her that she'd been trying to divert them from asking too many questions about the inner workings of her benefactors by steering the discussion toward "the big picture," as she called it.

Eleanor was smart enough to know when she had no choice but to fold.

"Very well, I can tell you more. You must understand that I

cannot tell you everything because I simply don't know. I don't sit on the Boards. I am not *one of them*. I simply work for them in a closer capacity than you do. They don't tell me what happens behind closed doors. So I can explain to you only what I do know from experience."

"Well, that's a start," Ty quipped. Talk."

Eleanor inhaled deeply and did as she was told.

She extrapolated upon what she'd already said, plus the estimates and deductions the five had made on their own thus far, describing the operations of Atlantica's most powerful group from the perspective of her office.

Most things the Executives wished to accomplish, or simply needed to address, were discussed by a group called the Junior Board. Its members constituted the entirety of those individuals who called themselves "the Executives," and they were a somewhat motley band of power brokers, business leaders, and information directors, virtually all of whom knew each other personally or professionally.

Daria ran a finger through her hair. "If all of the Executives are part of the Junior Board, then who on Earth are the Senior Board?"

"I'm getting to that," Eleanor replied in a curt tone.

The Junior Board operated in various ways, using whatever resources and connections were available to its members, to pursue the directives set by the Senior Board. Everyone in the lower level of the organization had *some* say in their objectives, but ultimately it was the upper echelon who had the *final* say.

"The Senior Board is composed of select, secret members of the Junior Board. It is a smaller handful that exists within and alongside the larger group. The only ones who know who a Senior Executive is are other members of the Senior Board. You see?"

Daria nodded. "Yes. Several secret societies employ a similar structure."

Ty flexed his free hand. The knuckles *cracked*. "What about everyone else in their operation? What's your formal rank, for example?"

Amahle noted that Tyler had automatically assumed something that resembled a military hierarchy. He'd only been in the U.S. Army for a couple of years, but at heart, he was a soldier through and through. In a way, that might have blinded him to the subtler and more fluid ways in which the Executives seemed to operate.

Eleanor extended a slim hand in front of her, gesturing like a college professor concluding a major point during a lecture.

"So, you could say that the Senior Board is like the brain, which is the ruling function of the body, sending out signals which everything else must obey and which dictate the course of action. The Junior Board, then, are as the higher and more essential body functions such as respiration, perception, and fine motor coordination."

Ty muttered, "I'm not sure I like where this is going." He understood the metaphor, and for that reason, he could jump ahead to a few possibilities for where it might end.

Eleanor paid him no heed and finished with, "People like me are the hands and feet of the Executives, directly interacting with that which the Junior Board members have begun to move toward, under the ultimate direction of the Senior Board."

Folding his arms over his chest, Dante inquired, "And what does that make us, exactly?" Nods went around the room. Each of them had been about to ask the same thing.

Eleanor blinked as though it had suddenly occurred to her that such a question would be impossible to avoid once she'd used such an elaborate metaphor to get her point across. She took it in stride.

"You are a tool," she stated in a flat tone. "A tool in the hands of the Executives, used for whatever purpose you're needed."

"You mean a weapon," Ty shot back, his mouth twisting into a sardonic jeer.

Eleanor shook her head. "Not necessarily. A sharpened piece of metal can be a scalpel for performing life-saving surgery, a sickle for harvesting food crops, or a sword for striking down enemies. It depends on how you use it."

Dante grunted. "Ehh, yeah, you have a point there. I would *not* want to use a sword for surgery, though. Or a sickle. That's even worse, for Christ's sake."

Daria gave a sharp wave, once again seeming impatient to reach the end of the discussion and therefore trying to keep everyone on track. "In what ways, specifically, are the Senior Board members behaving differently, Eleanor? You haven't bothered to tell us in much detail yet."

It looked for a second as though Eleanor was about to try to dismiss the request, maybe by telling them to focus on other things, but Ty glared at her and leaned forward by an inch or two. She wouldn't get away with dodging the question.

Eleanor sighed. "Before, in the times when things were more...sane, more normal...all of the directives were, you might say, centered inward. It was all about *legitimizing* our thriving young island.

"Then, when the next great international summit or conference occurred, Atlantica could secure an invitation to attend and be treated as deserving of real respect. The world would see us as a functioning nation, not merely some overgrown trading post rife with violence and corruption."

Amahle quipped, "I see." She felt that the wellbeing of the population was more important than the island's reputation, but as a motive, legitimacy made sense. "Where are these directives pointed now?"

"Down and in," Eleanor elaborated, with the shadow of a deep frown playing about her mouth and eyes. Before she spoke again, she appeared to wallow for an instant in the cumulative strain and depression of many long and difficult months' worth of concern and dismay.

"It has, in recent times, been about getting hold of as much Atlanticore as possible. They're extracting as much ancient Atlantican technology as can be had from the dig sites and ruins. No matter the cost or the risk involved, these concerns now trump everything else. They've been reaching out to various players, people of all sorts whom they think can help move the process along and develop the spoils of Atlantica into new, experimental technology."

Amahle glanced at Gage and saw the Nepali looking back at her with a controlled expression of interest. Their conversation in the locker that morning replayed itself in both of their heads.

Gage raised a finger. "So, Ms. Cervantes, you are talking about how the Executives have begun to ally themselves with the Coven of Miracles? That is the conclusion we must reach from this, yes?"

"That or possibly *becoming* the Coven," Eleanor muttered. "Some insane marriage of the two. The motives of the Coven and the resources and influence of the Executives, maybe."

Ty's nostrils flared as they did when he was furious, but his tone was low and restrained. "You have a problem with this, despite being their loyal servant?"

Eleanor stood a little straighter. "Yes, I do. I'm a pragmatist. I might lack your zeal for righting wrongs, your idealism. But I have never been reckless, wasteful, or needlessly cruel." She paused, and her gaze turned to the floor. "The fact that I'm telling you all of this puts me in far more danger than it does you."

Brooding silence settled over the room. The truth of Eleanor's final statement was self-evident. She might've been a quick draw with her pistol, but she lacked the heavy weaponry, and more importantly, the combat and survival experience of the Executioners. Not to mention, she was more intimately involved with the people above her. They likely knew more of her secrets than she knew of theirs.

Then the security alarm went off. Everyone tensed, half-jumping out of their shoes as the abrasive, high-pitched blaring sound shattered the quiet.

"Already?" Dante groaned.

Gage, being closest to the small console in the corner that included screens for the closed-circuit TV system that monitored their property through multiple cameras, rushed over and looked at them, trying to assess the situation with all possible haste.

He reported, "Someone has breached the exterior fence. I saw a form moving just past the edge of the camera's field of vision, and part of the fence has been cut with an electric saw or bolt cutters. Two of the screens have gone black; they may have covered or destroyed some of the cameras themselves."

Ty sheathed his wakizashi, pulled out his pistol, and went over to the counter where he'd laid his rifle. "Somehow I doubt it's only one guy. The timing is awfully convenient, too, isn't it?"

The other Executioners, too, took up their weapons and readied themselves for whatever came next.

The alarm's tone was especially unpleasant, as though designed to induce panic and mental discomfort. Amahle gave silent thanks for long years of experience dealing with stressful and deadly situations. A person for whom such things were completely new might easily find their terror driven over the edge into total panic simply by the way the repetitive noise grated on and frayed the nerves.

She said, "Gage, please turn that alarm off if you can." Despite her confidence that she could fight with it wailing in the back-ground, she would *prefer* not to. Eleanor was now visibly sweating and trying not to tremble.

Gage remained glued to the console. His hands worked the controls, almost absentmindedly, and after a couple of seconds, the alarm fell silent. In the brief span of peace that followed, Gage said something even worse than the obnoxious blaring.

"I can see them. There are approximately two squads of eight people each, as far as I can determine. There might be more who have remained hidden from the cameras. It appears that about half of them are professionals and have armor, helmets, and rifles. They, ah... They might be Executive Security. It is difficult to tell, and well-financed mercenaries would likely similarly outfit themselves.

"The rest are likely to be thugs who don't seem to possess the same quality of gear. No armor, I think, and probably shotguns and war-surplus submachine guns or older rifles."

Daria cursed in Polish. Dante sighed and shook his head, a crazy half-smile on his face as he loaded 12-gauge buckshot shells into his Ithaca 37. Amahle said and did nothing.

Ty asked, "Where are they, and what are they doing right now? What's their likely plan of attack?"

Without hesitation, Gage explained, "One of the groups is trying to breach the main gymnasium doors. It looks as though they're attempting to overcome the lock by doing something to the keypad rather than simply breaking through with brute force.

"The other group is going to the garage. Presumably, they will try to force the doors open and come at us through the rear entrance at the same time as the other force comes through the front. A rather basic pincer maneuver."

"Right," Ty growled, working the charging handle on his AR-10. "Easiest thing to do would be to neutralize one group before the other can slam us from the other side. If we need to split up later to mop up the leftovers, so be it."

Eleanor's eyes bulged. "You're going to try to kill them all? If it's Executive Security, they might be content to arrest us." She glanced around.

No one seemed very interested in her suggestion. She raised

her pistol again. "Well, if you insist on acting like complete madmen, at least allow me to—"

Ty pivoted without warning, and with a sharp clapping motion, knocked the Walther from Eleanor's hand with his right. He caught it with his left and swept it away and out of her reach.

"*What?*" she snapped, her voice rising and cracking. "How dare you! Don't you—"

"Sorry, but I still don't completely trust you, Eleanor. Nothing personal. It would be best if you sit this one out until we finish and the smoke clears."

Eleanor's jaw dropped as she stared at him with a mixture of shock and seething anger. Amahle recognized it as the kind of indignation that Westerners had in mind when they had coined that saying about "Hell hath no fury."

Ms. Cervantes sprang at Ty, her hands clawing madly. He caught one of her wrists and tried to push her away, not wanting to hurt her, but her feistiness and the strength of sheer adrenaline meant that he might well get his face torn off unless he was willing to use extra force.

Amahle stepped in toward Eleanor's left flank as Daria moved toward the woman's right. Both of them dashed in and grabbed at Eleanor's arms in unison, surprising her and keeping her hands away from Ty's face.

Ty nodded. "Thanks. Let's put her in the pantry. She'll be fine for a bit. Dante, Gage, clear us a path and take point."

"Roger." Gage moved ahead. Dante followed him, and the pair stood near the doorway to the rec area, keeping watch. Their enemies would arrive soon unless they sallied forth to meet them first.

Ty opened the pantry door. The room beyond it wasn't overly spacious, but Eleanor could sit or lie down if she wanted to, and if by some chance they had to leave her there for an extended time, she certainly wouldn't lack food. Amahle somehow doubted that it would become an issue, though. Deadly combat encounters between small armed groups rarely lasted very long. Either the Executioners would free Eleanor shortly... Or the intruders would.

Amahle and Daria struggled to force the other woman inside. She was snarling and chattering in Spanish while she tried to pull away and kicked their legs and groins. Ty frowned. "Okay, fine." He moved in behind the three and grabbed the back neck area of Eleanor's jacket, helping to stabilize her and urge her forward. All three of them shoved her so she stumbled into the pantry, then they slammed the door. Ty produced a key and locked it.

"She'll be fine," he repeated. His demeanor was rife with discomfort, even embarrassment. He probably felt bad about humiliating a person who'd helped them all so many times.

Under the circumstances, though, Amahle couldn't fault him in the slightest.

As Ty, Daria, and Amahle walked toward the front of the room to join Gage and Dante, Eleanor's voice shouted through the door, "You idiots! You're going to get us all killed—trying to fight when we're outnumbered four to one!"

The five Executioners looked at one another, blank-faced. Then, at the same instant, they all burst into raucous, side-splitting laughter.

CHAPTER EIGHT

Ty made a coughing, grunting sound, bringing his sudden outpouring of mirth to an abrupt end. "Gage, kill the lights," he commanded in a low yet sharp voice. "We know the layout of this whole place by heart. They don't."

Nodding, the Gurkha headed back over to the switchboard and made a few fast flicking motions. One by one, the overhead lights went out. Room by room, the entire building plunged into darkness.

Night had fallen outside. The invaders had probably figured that the shadows would hide their approach through the city. Now, darkness would become their enemy within the building. Even with flashlights, they would be at a disadvantage versus those who spent so much of their lives in the halls and chambers around them.

Ty turned to Dante. "Stay here and guard Eleanor. Not to mention the passage."

He referred to the hidden narrow hallway that led downstairs, the one in the same pantry where they'd locked Ms. Cervantes. It lay hidden behind a shelf and required an access code punched into a keypad. For those who could activate it, the passage led to a staircase. Then another short hall opened into the same service elevator that would take them to the sub-basement and the locker.

Dante at first squinted in irritation, as though miffed that they were leaving him out of the main fight. Then he realized that later, if he survived, he could tell Eleanor that he'd been personally responsible for protecting her. "Yeah. Roger."

Ty nodded. Then, exchanging glances with the others, they opened the door and rushed out, ready for anything.

The first Executioner took point, toting his rifle. He was their de facto leader, but no one had ever bothered trying to restrain him from leading from the front. Aggressively plunging into the fray, often in the most unsubtle fashion he could get away with, was in his blood.

Behind him, Gage and Daria moved along with their weapons at low ready, prepared to fan out to the sides if necessary to cover either an advance or retreat.

Amahle brought up the rear. She could handle herself in close-quarters combat if necessary, but she did her best work at range, where there was a little more breathing space to focus on accuracy and decisiveness rather than pure offense.

The hallway was pitch black. Ty swung around the corner by the infirmary, which took him into the corridor that ran toward the entrance lobby to the left, and the garage straight ahead and to the right.

This second leg of the halls was brighter due to the yellowish-white beams of two flashlights that shone through the lobby windows, dispersing the darkness around them as they swept and jittered around the seemingly empty space.

Gage was about to catch Ty's attention in the hope of getting a hand signal, a nod, a look, anything to tell them exactly what to do next. Ty, however, chose to cut out the proverbial middleman.

Screaming at the top of his lungs, the first Executioner bolted straight down the hallway, his rifle shouldered and aimed off to the left. He opened fire on full automatic the instant the lobby windows passed in front of him. The weapon's thunderous report was painfully loud in the enclosed space, and the gun's star-shaped muzzle flash was briefly as bright as the flashlights.

Daria cursed in Polish, Gage swore in Nepalese, and Amahle cussed in Xhosa, their mutterings masked by the sounds of gunfire, cracking plaster and wood, and shattering glass.

They knew what to do next.

Men shouted, and the intruders returned fire, haphazardly blasting into the space their attacker had vacated. Ty had jumped and rolled to the far end of the hall beyond the lobby entrance, putting him out of their sight, and he stayed low. Bullets smashed through walls and windows. Dust and showers of glass flew through the air, catching the erratic beams of light and reflecting it like frost under moonglow.

Gage moved to the lobby's near edge and fired a couple of short bursts from his AR-10 around the corner, enough to provide cover and keep their enemies on edge.

Meanwhile, Daria ducked low beyond him and fired an entire magazine of nine-millimeter from her Uzi. The pistol-caliber weapon wouldn't be able to penetrate the body armor of the more elite security guys. However, it could potentially still wound their limbs, damage their gear, or simply knock them off-balance from impact. The auxiliary thugs accompanying them had no such protections.

In the darkness and chaos, there was no way to see if they'd hit anyone or anything, but screams of pain amid the general cacophony suggested that they wounded at least two men. If they were lucky, another one or two might be dead.

As some of the gunfire died down, Amahle paid close attention to the voices of their foes. She'd hung back from the others, but now she calculated position and distance, raised her Winchester, and fired two rounds of .308 through the wall. After the crack of the second died down, someone bellowed and gurgled, and it sounded like a body dropped to the floor with a heavy *thud*.

Though they could barely see anything, Gage and Amahle could somewhat make out the forms of Ty and Daria at the farther end of the lobby's edge. Ty was making a sweeping motion of his rifle toward the right-bending corner ahead of him as he reloaded, indicating that he'd probably seen or heard something from that direction—the other squad approaching from the garage.

The voice of a man, presumably the lobby squad's commander, barked, "Evac! Regroup at—"

Ty didn't let him finish. Instead, he hopped back to the corner and fired half of his magazine into the lobby, then pivoted and blasted the other half down the hall toward the garage. In the ringing echo that followed, they could barely make out the sounds of boots shuffling away.

It wasn't over yet. They all knew that. As the intruders beat a temporary tactical retreat, they made a slight error and left a gift for their adversaries. One of the flashlights had fallen to the floor, still switched on, its beam shining through the lobby doors and into the hallway.

Ty looked at Gage and Amahle, then at Daria, who was right next to him. He pointed at Daria and himself and swirled his hand at the lobby. Next, he nodded at Gage and Amahle and pointed down the hall toward the garage.

Amahle frowned in the shadows. They'd done significant damage to the first squad, neutralizing perhaps a quarter of its members, but she wondered if it was enough to justify splitting up into two groups. Then it occurred to her that the squads might be planning to combine forces and simply assault them as one team, overwhelming them with massively superior firepower.

If that were the case, it would make sense for Ty and Daria to go on the hunt after the weaker squad, finishing them off, while

Amahle and Gage picked off a few of the stronger in the larger and more tactically advantageous environs of the garage. They could regroup later.

Nonetheless, she didn't like fighting in such cramped conditions if she could help it. Even when prowling through the jungle, there tended to be more distance and greater freedom of movement than in a dark labyrinth of rooms and corridors. On the other hand, the garage would offer extra cover and more places to lay traps.

Daria reloaded and popped up over a shattered counter, the barrel of her submachine gun moving across the lobby and ready to unleash suppressing fire. It appeared that the squad had retreated out of the immediate line of fire. Satisfied, Ty ducked past her into the lobby proper, crouched behind a couch, then motioned for Daria to join him while he kept watch.

Once Ms. Barruk was clear of the hallway, Gage and Amahle trotted down it toward the next corner. They hoped Ty's burst of rifle fire had driven the second squad far enough back for the two of them to infiltrate the garage before they had to engage the enemy.

Gage leapt around, gun shouldered, and advanced with Amahle about two meters behind him. So far, there was no sign of the second squad anywhere in immediate sight.

As soon as they went through the door into the garage, a flashlight's beam swept over them, and the shooting started.

Amahle's heart jumped into her throat. She dove and rolled to the right, tucking her rifle beneath her as automatic fire crackled all around and blasted dusty holes in the wall behind her. Then she was behind a tall crate of spare parts. It wouldn't provide real cover against the powerful penetrative capabilities of the 7.62 rounds from the security men's rifles, but it would offer concealment.

For a second. Which was exactly how long she waited before

sprinting deeper into the structure's depths, where the shadows were her friends, and it was like the jungle all over again.

Gage sprinted in the opposite direction and took cover behind the front end of a half-disassembled car he'd been working on. More gunfire followed him, but the engine block stopped it. Based on the reports of the rounds and what he could see of the guiding flashlight beam, he had a fairly good idea of the men's location.

They were passing right underneath the frame of another car suspended from the ceiling. Gage aimed the cords holding it there and fired three shots in quick succession, severing the lines. The mass of steel plunged and *crunched* against the concrete floor, taking at least two men with it. Their screams echoed against the walls.

Then someone burst around the other side of the gutted car, aiming a sawed-off shotgun. Since Gage's rifle was braced on the engine block and trying to pivot without getting it stuck would be too slow, he dropped it and drew one of his kukris instead. The thick recurved blade *swished* through the air. It struck the shotgun and knocked it aside as the man fired.

"Shit!" the attacker exclaimed under the gun's *boom*. The recoil from accidentally firing sideways knocked him off-balance. It was all the opportunity Gage needed. He swung the kukri again, and this time it clove through the man's breastbone and most of his throat. He fell back, clutching his neck and choking on his blood.

Then Gage retrieved his rifle and shot five times, more or less at random, in the general direction of the enemy team. He would have to trust Amahle to do her part in the meantime.

Amahle had seized her advantage in the chaos to slip into the darkest corner and climb atop a sturdy mass of shelving. Lying prone on the dusty surface, trying not to move lest it creak beneath her, she braced her rifle and stared into the gloom.

She couldn't see much. Using the scope was relatively pointless in such conditions, especially given the shorter distances. Instead, she relied mostly on iron sights and intuition.

Her eyes were adjusting, and the wandering flashlight beam helped her orient the remaining squad members relative to the many obstacles within. They were moving through the garage's center and trying to flush her and Gage out with a skirmish line, she saw. Given how much junk lay piled everywhere, only one or two of them at a time could accomplish much of anything.

Silhouettes took form. Two of them clicked on flashlights, bringing the yellow beams up to three. Amahle focused on a pair of men slipping between the central mass of spare parts and an empty lift near the car where Gage crouched.

She could've attempted to shoot both their heads off in quick succession. It might have worked, but it would also offer the second man time to react and escape. So she did something else.

The rifle's muzzle hovered over the leg of the man in the rear. She squeezed the trigger.

The gun's thunderclap seemed to tear the building apart from within. The security goon she'd targeted collapsed on top of his mangled leg with a shriek. As Amahle had hoped, he fell laterally across the narrow space that he and his partner had been navigating.

The other man fired a couple of poorly aimed shots in Amahle's general direction and turned to retreat. He hesitated when faced with his comrade's body. There was a moment, a second or less, when he couldn't decide whether to leap over the other man and leave him there or to crouch and try to help him.

Using the first man as a living trap for the second was a cold thing to do—but it worked. Amahle took advantage of the second guy's indecision and fired again, putting a hole through his skull. He dropped like a toppled statue. Then she finished off the first man with another headshot, bringing his screams to an abrupt end.

Someone shouted, "Fall back! Regroup outside!"

Amahle couldn't see enough to take another good shot, and the sound of the squad leader's voice echoed too much to pinpoint it, but she fired one more round anyway simply to drive the men off.

Gage did similarly, blasting a short volley of full auto fire from his rifle over the top of the gutted car. Then there was silence, aside from the *crashing* and *crackling* of whatever trouble Ty and Daria had got themselves into near the lobby.

Amahle climbed down from her perch. Having an elevated spot to snipe from was of lesser value in conditions of thick darkness and without a light of her own. She rejoined Gage, and they nodded at each other.

The team had done a few drills in procedures for defending HQ from an incident like this. Someone should, if at all possible, guard the entrance into the building proper from the garage, as well as the basement entrance. Gage took the former and Amahle the latter. Then they waited.

Meanwhile, Ty and Daria advanced in tandem through the first portion of the lobby. Ty was about to swing himself around the corner into the entrance area, but Daria preempted him by picking up a clipboard from the reception desk and tossing it ahead of them both. It sailed through a lighter patch of air next to the exterior window and clattered against a chair.

At least two guns opened fire, shooting at sound and motion but not at definite targets. To some extent, the first squad's retreat had been a ruse. Ty grimaced. They might have gunned him down if Daria hadn't baited the men lying in ambush.

The clipboard had distracted them, pulling their attention about twelve feet to his left. He leaned out around the corner, exposing as little of his upper body as he could, and emptied another entire magazine into the entrance hall area. He didn't know exactly where the men were—but they were *probably* against the wall by the other side of the reception desk or behind the kiosk near the front doors. Ty sprayed lead at both locations.

Someone screamed, and a body tumbled out from behind the kiosk. Then two other things happened at once. A pair of men exploded into the lobby from right beyond the front doors, aiming their rifles at Ty, and a third figure who'd barely escaped Ty's first barrage darted past him—toward Daria.

Ty roared and plunged toward the newcomers, drawing his pistol and blasting away while they opened up at him with an AR-10 and a submachine gun. Bullets slammed against his armor. One of the men stumbled, wounded by the pistol rounds, while the other ducked.

Ty ejected the empty mag from his rifle, slammed a new one in, and opened fire again.

The man who'd darted past fired semi-randomly in bursts of two or three rounds at a time toward the other side of the reception desk. He'd guessed that Daria must be somewhere in that vicinity. Glimpsing her flitting silhouette as she tried to dive behind a couch, he fired four rounds at her before his submachine gun *clicked* empty.

Daria collapsed to the floor with a *thud*. The man cursed under his breath and advanced toward her, his shaky hands pulling the empty magazine free and fumbling for a new one. The woman wasn't moving. He must have hit her.

Then suddenly she rolled over, pistol in hand, and shot him in the face. He never knew what hit him, falling straight over backward and dying in midair.

Daria climbed to her feet. "Why do they always fall for that one?" she mused. The gunfire was receding, and Ty was limping toward her. Her heart thumped faster with sudden concern.

Ty mumbled, "I'm hit. In the side. Should've gone for cover."

"But you didn't." Daria sighed. It was almost impossible for Ty to shy away from a fight when the opportunity to crush an opponent lay within his reach. She holstered her Browning, raised the Uzi, and fired half a magazine toward the entrance to discourage any other intruders from trying to rush them. No one came in.

Ty gestured with his chin toward the main hallway. "The bad guys are probably all going to regroup in the lot. Let's check on —*shit!*"

Someone popped up from behind a chair and rushed into the hall, headed toward the lounge. The invaders had left a man hiding there when they began their false retreat, and he'd waited through all the other violence for his opportunity.

Daria shrugged. She wasn't about to abandon Ty while he was hurt. She had a certain amount of faith in Dante. Still, the man trying to infiltrate deeper into the building suggested that the brutish murder of everyone present wasn't necessarily the intruders' goal.

They were looking for someone. Someone like Eleanor, probably.

Back in the lounge, Dante crouched next to the stove, the Ithaca clutched in sweaty hands. There had been a *lot* of shooting. That was probably a good thing. If the bad guys were winning, he figured they would only have needed to shoot a little and be done with it. Large amounts of gunfire meant that his fellow Executioners were still in the game.

Footsteps were moving toward his location, though. It sounded like only a single pair. That could mean two things, both of them bad.

It might mean that their assailants had routed his friends, and whoever was fleeing back here was the only survivor. Or it might mean that an enemy had broken through—whether for purposes of general scouring or a more specific objective.

Dante held his breath and remained out of sight. In Amahle's opinion, he was nearly as aggressive and straightforward a fighter as Tyler was, but he liked to think he could be subtle when the situation called for it.

The door burst open, and a man in black armor toting a rifle sprang in. He was neither Ty nor Gage. He was bigger than either of them, although Dante couldn't see his face. He advanced cautiously but with haste, sweeping the room quickly for any obvious foes but trying to spend as little time on it as he could.

He didn't see Dante. The shadows beside the stove were too deep. Instead, he went straight to the pantry, shined a penlight through the little window, and aimed his rifle at the door. On the other side, Eleanor half-screamed something in Spanish.

Dante could've taken the man out then and there, but he had to *know*. He had to know if the hostile teams were here to kill her, arrest her, or rescue her. To find that out would clear things up substantially.

The rifle *cracked*, and the door *banged* in, its lock blown off. The man aimed his rifle at approximately the chest height of an average-sized woman.

"So, there you are," he said in a strange, undefinable accent. "Well, goodbye."

Eleanor shrieked in terror.

Dante jumped up, pointed his shotgun's muzzle at the man's face, and roared as he pulled the trigger. The intruder started to turn toward him but was about a quarter of a second too slow.

The shotgun's blast vaporized the mercenary's lower head and neck. His helmet toppled to the floor while the rest of him slumped against the wall.

Silence settled in, briefly, until Dante stepped into the compromised doorway. Eleanor was frozen in place, her hands extended in a vain gesture of self-protection.

"It's okay," Dante reassured her. "That was me. You know what? If they came here specifically to assassinate you, I guess you really *are* on our side, after all."

Eleanor just stared.

Then, to the surprise of them both, a metallic ringing sounded over their heads and someone's voice came through on the intercom. It must have been whoever was in the garage since there was a console out there that Gage often used to communicate with the rest of them while he was absorbed in mechanical stuff.

"Attention," Amahle said. "We need everyone to the locker. We've driven off the first wave, but more of them massing in the street, and they have a vehicle. An APC, I think, which they might use to drive through the walls."

Dante frowned. "Fuck," he grumbled.

Amahle went on, "I've also seen small reflections of light within human-sized silhouettes in the windows of some buildings around us. They've posted snipers. They are here not only to dig us out but to ensure we cannot escape. Everyone to the locker!"

Nodding, Dante strode into the pantry. "Eleanor, it's okay. We have a secret passage in here that, well." He kicked aside the shelf, exposed the keypad, and punched in a code. Right as the camouflaged doorway opened, the intercom rang again.

"Dante," Amahle added, "Tyler is wounded, somewhat badly."

Dante sighed and ducked back into the lounge to grab a spare first-aid kit. "Of course he is," he muttered.

CHAPTER NINE

Ty braced himself with one hand as the service elevator started its descent. The other hand he kept low at his side, clamping the rag over his wound. It was already badly stained a deep red, and his hand was developing a rusty crust over the fingers where some of the blood had begun to harden.

Dante grimaced at the initial jolt before it became a smoother ride the rest of the way down. He kept his eyes on Katakura.

"When we get down there, I'll patch you up better, pal. We're going to need proper medical facilities, though, one way or another. At least some little out-of-the-way veterinary clinic or something if you don't want to take the risk of going to Atlantica General Hospital."

Ty let out a sharp breath. "I'll be all right. Wait, no," he lamented, "I won't. You're right. We need to do something. I don't want to hear about it or talk about it now. First, we figure out what we do next and decide how to get out of here. We can worry about me later."

Dante nodded. "If you say so. Be careful. Let's not waste time. It's probably not going to be fatal anytime soon, but you could have some serious problems if we don't deal with it inside a couple of hours. Don't make any sharp movements. You've lost a lot of blood, and we don't need that wound getting ripped open again."

"Yes," Ty grunted while staring at the wall.

It was obvious to them all why he was so sullen. He knew, yet hoped they wouldn't bother to say aloud, that the *reason* he had a serious injury was because of how reckless and aggressive he'd been in battle. Even a modicum of greater self-restraint and patience might've saved him from becoming a casualty while still allowing them to fight the enemy to a draw.

Daria said in a soft voice, "Don't worry too much. They don't know all of our secrets. We will leave them in the dust soon enough."

Gage beamed with pride, and his grin lightened the mood for at least a moment or two. Eleanor nearly asked what they meant, but bit her tongue and kept silent.

The elevator reached the bottom of its course and the doors rattled open, disclosing the short hallway, the small alcoves to either side, and the door that led to the locker. Dante stepped out first.

"Hey! Amahle. You down here?" He held his shotgun at low ready. Behind him, Gage and Daria had their long guns slung over their shoulders, but their hands hovered over the grips of their pistols.

The door in front of them *clanked, hissed,* and opened. Amahle stood beyond the threshold. "Yes. Come in. We cannot stay here long, though. What happened?"

Gage put one of Ty's arms around his shoulder and helped him carefully trudge into the sealed chamber while Dante and Daria explained, as tersely as they could, all that had occurred upstairs. Eleanor stood in silence, staring through the things and people around her at some indeterminate point about a thousand yards away.

Amahle filled them in on her side of the story. When she

finished, Ty gave an aggressive, impatient nod and interjected, "Okay, we get it. We need to retreat, and now. Leave Eleanor. She'll be safe enough until they give up and go home, and we won't have to deal with the risk she poses."

Eleanor turned to stare at him, her jaw falling open, though she could not yet bring herself to speak.

Dante, not too surprisingly, was the first one to object. "Hey. No, she's coming with us. She nearly died back there, okay? She's on our side. Maybe she wasn't *always*, but she sure as hell is *now*. We can't just leave her. You know damn well that they're not going to 'give up and go home.' They're here on an important mission. It's not one she's supposed to survive, or I'm not a fuckin' doctor."

Ty glared at him, and the two young men stared into each other's eyes. The others knew they should intervene, but somehow they doubted it would help or make much difference. What was going on between them was something they needed to work out themselves.

Ty's lip curled. "They're here on a mission *because* of her, so you're right in a way. You want to vouch for her? She's your responsibility. You keep watch on her, you take care of her, and if she fucks anything up, it's on your head, Dante. And you will take her head *off* if she tries anything that's liable to screw us over or get us caught. Is that clear?"

"Yeah," Dante growled. "Perfectly clear. You hear that, Eleanor? Keep nearly getting murdered occasionally, and otherwise do nothing, and maybe Ty will get the message. Eventually."

Daria snapped her fingers. "Yes, we will take the risk. There is no reason to mistrust Eleanor, I think, yet she is no match for all of us, either. Next, we need to investigate why this has happened. Eleanor might be able to help. It would be *profoundly* useful to locate some members of this Junior Board and have a friendly talk about what is going on. Why the corruption? Why the aggression against us—their people? I would like to ask them both of those questions. I think we all would."

Everyone looked at her. Ty gave a deliberate nod. "You're right. She could be our key to unraveling this mess. We also need to find out who killed those three Execs hanging from the cable. Were they only Junior Board, or were they Senior? Eleanor said no one knows who is who. It has to tie into all this. It wouldn't make any damn sense if it didn't."

Amahle suggested, "Let us split up. We can accomplish more things that way in a shorter time. I'm accustomed to working in small independent teams. Since I was investigating the murders already, let me take one or two of you and continue with that while the rest take Eleanor to track down the Junior Board members who are still alive."

Dante's aggressive disposition had faded enough to allow his Hippocratic Oath to reassert itself. He was now reexamining Ty's wound, making sure the blood was clotting enough for him to remain conscious until they could get him to a care facility of some sort.

Ty winced under a gentle poke from the physician's long finger. "Good idea," he rasped. "Who knows. Maybe we have some friends out there, but we don't know about them yet. If the Execs are willing to do *this,* maybe our murderers are really the good guys."

Eleanor said, in an oddly distant and detached way, "I do not think we should be making friends with those who string up their enemies and leave them dangling in a public square. Such barbarity does not indicate...good intentions."

Ty squinted at her. In a cold tone, he snapped, "As far as I'm concerned, you still aren't part of this. Based on everything you told us a little earlier—you know, before all hell broke loose and your bosses' people tried to kill us—I'm not convinced that whoever hanged those bastards *doesn't* have the right idea."

Gage tried to change the subject. "I will go with Amahle and help her look for the murderers. That will allow the three of you and Eleanor to focus on finding the Junior Executives. Since it may be better to wait a day or two before attempting such a thing, you will have time to get Tyler patched up at a clinic. Now, let us take spare ammunition and weapons, and then take our leave."

"Finally, someone is talking sense," Daria quipped.

Nods went around the chamber. They snatched up spare magazines and boxes of ammo, and also grabbed a couple of extra pistols, submachine guns, and a sawed-off shotgun or two.

While they loaded up, Eleanor asked the obvious question. Amahle was surprised she hadn't heard it from her sooner.

"How will we escape?" she began in a small voice. "There is no way out of here. Is there?"

Eleanor was still badly frazzled by the whole experience. Everything about the look on her face and in her eyes, the way she moved, and the raspy edge her voice had taken on suggested that she was on the verge of shock.

From what Amahle had heard, the woman was fairly tough in her way. She'd been all over the world and dealt with a variety of people, some of them dangerous or unsavory. Still, this was clearly Eleanor's first experience with outright life-or-death combat.

She was handling it better than some, though. Amahle had seen people dissolve into complete wrecks, incapable of doing anything whatsoever, under the strain of battle and the horror of violent death. Ms. Cervantes was at least *functional* at a certain baseline level.

However, the question she asked revealed how close she was to coming apart, and as the Americans would say, *losing it*.

"How are we going to get out of here, may I ask?" she repeated and looked at each of them in turn with fast, jerky head motions. "We left all of the vehicles upstairs, in the garage. Now we're stuck down here, in this hole, with no way out. They must be moving in by now. We would have to fight our way through the garage. They might have reinforcements coming in. What do we *do?*"

Gage, who seemed surprisingly calm, held up a hand palm outward and gave the woman a faint yet reassuring smile. "Not to worry, Ms. Cervantes. You haven't been down here before. There is more to it than greets the eye at first glance."

Dante interjected, "It's supposed to be *meets* the eye, Gage, but close enough."

"Yes, thank you." The Gurkha walked over to the switchboard that controlled the lights and pressed a couple of buttons.

Eleanor half-jumped in place as the *grinding* and *clanking* of metal suddenly filled the subterranean space with an undertone of humming machinery. Ahead, around the storeroom's corner, light spilled out from some previously hidden nook or cranny.

Ty said, "You didn't think this one room was the whole sub-basement, did you? The gymnasium had a few secrets it was hiding, I'd guess, and we've done a few expansions and renovations of our own over the last year. It helps to have a Plan B. And a Plan C and D, if at all possible."

Despite his wounded state, there was a certain fierce pride in how well his team had done against a numerically superior foe. It sustained him, kept him composed and alert.

Eleanor exhaled in a slow, controlled way. "Very well. Let us see it, then, please."

Dante stepped up, holding his shotgun to his chest. "I'll lead the way." He was the youngest and tallest person present, and he'd escaped without wounds, so it made sense. Still, Amahle wondered if on some level he was simply looking for an opportunity to impress Eleanor.

It was none of her business, though. She hung back, waiting to take up the rear. Dealing with threats by shooting them from a distance, even if other people were potentially in the way, was her stock in trade.

Gage went second, then Eleanor, then Ty, Daria, and finally Amahle. They left the locker proper and walked through the narrow passage that had opened beside it, which wended a short way forward before turning sharply to the left and opening into a cavernous cell-like room. Aside from its low ceiling, it was effectively a garage unto itself.

The cheap but effective fluorescent lights overhead illuminated what lay within. Seeing it all, Eleanor stopped and gawked in surprise while the Executioners fanned out to make certain no foes were waiting for them.

Amahle highly doubted anyone could've invaded the sub-garage. It was a secret to everyone but the five members of the order, and its exit was well-hidden and never discussed in public. Still, she kept a close watch on everything with her rifle as Dante, Gage, and Daria poked around the nooks and crannies for ambushers. Ty remained by Eleanor's side. That way, he could still fulfill the important function of protecting her but without having to move around too much.

Meanwhile, Eleanor stared at the three vehicles on the bare concrete before them.

The largest of them was an armored personnel carrier. Ty had captured it from a group of wealthy degenerates—with ties to the Coven of Miracles—who had maintained a lodge up in the mountains from which they hunted human beings for sport. He'd told Eleanor they'd broken the massive vehicle down and sold off the spare parts. Ms. Cervantes might well have been realizing that she'd been lied to.

The other two were de facto Autocutioners that the five of them had modified over the last several months. They'd used cheaper vehicles as their base and powered them with a system that alternately combined a traditional gas-burning engine with one that employed the sophisticated Atlanticore crystal matrix typical of the Executioners' main rides. The crystal engines had been gifted them by the Executives about eight months ago, as

Amahle recalled, as replacements in case their main engines failed.

The two Autocutioners down here, though, had considerable visual differences from the ones they used in their standard daily work. Enough that the average person on the street probably wouldn't recognize them as official trucks driven by the island's notorious dispensers of justice.

The first was still identifiable as the same basic type of vehicle, a mid-range truck of vaguely military caliber. Several modifications served to mask its true status. They'd added a custom grille to the front, plated with brass, making it gaudy and arguably attention-grabbing. Yet it wasn't too out of place by the standards of Atlantica, a place where excess and ostentation were considered normal.

They'd also fitted it with new and different bumpers than what came with the original vehicle. They were nothing special, but noticeable enough to be significant. The headlights were of a different pattern and cast a dimmer cone of illumination than the ultra-bright ones on the main, official Autocutioners, but the secondhand ones were still sufficient for most nighttime usage.

Finally, they'd disguised the armor plating with a simple paint job. No longer was the truck a deep iron-gray but a dull off-white. It nearly passed as a construction vehicle or some oddity that someone might peddle through a consignment firm.

As for the other Autocutioner, the modifications had gone further still. This one had an entire false frame attached to it, deep blue and featureless, resembling a large unmarked service van rather than a paramilitary vehicle. Close inspection might reveal the trick. However, it would pass muster as far as driving down the street or sitting in a parking lot someplace where people would probably never give it a second look.

Beyond the three vehicles, in the same direction that their front ends pointed, was a tunnel. It was narrow enough for one truck at a time. The two disguised Autocutioners could navigate it with at least a little bit of elbow room, but the APC would be a tighter fit and would barely squeeze through.

The tunnel appeared to slope gently upward. Perhaps thirty yards beyond the staging area of the trucks, right around where the glow of the overhead lights began to fade, the passage also wound off to the side and out of sight.

Eleanor let out a dry chuckle of disbelief. "You people are truly amazing. Perhaps we underestimated you. I don't know how you hid all of this from the Executives, but with things as they are now, I'm glad you did. Where does the tunnel lead to?"

While Dante and Daria finished their sweep of the garage, Gage turned back to Eleanor. "It opens on an alley about two blocks away from here. The exit is well disguised, and one of us will check before we all drive through it. We might yet be able to escape without them knowing where we've gone."

Amahle raised her voice enough for everyone to hear. "Does that mean we're decided not to go back into headquarters? If so, let me close the secret doorway."

Ty grunted. "Yeah. It's fallen to the enemy. The whole city is our headquarters now, at least until further notice."

Nodding, Amahle stepped back, found the controls, and shut the same portal that Gage had opened from the console within the locker. There was a chance that the Executives' goon squads might figure out the combination to open it from the other end, but by the time they did, they would find nothing but an empty chamber and a tunnel that seemed to lead nowhere.

A *mostly* empty chamber.

"Leave the APC," Ty instructed the group. "I don't like the thought of it falling into their hands if they find this place, but we can't take that damn thing out on the streets without the whole city noticing. We have to lie low and avoid attention for a little while."

Daria, satisfied that her sector was free of hidden adversaries, trotted back toward the rest of them. "I agree. Who shall take which one, though?"

Ty gestured at the Autocutioner that had been repainted and re-outfitted but still resembled its original design. "Gage, Amahle, you two get in the white one. The rest of us will take the blue one with the fake van frame. Fire 'em up and check the radios. We need to get the hell out of here once we know those are in working order."

Eleanor's eyebrows rose in concern bordering on alarm. "The Executives will be monitoring the frequency we usually use, so I would not recommend using the radios at all, unless..."

Gage gently put a hand on her arm and flashed one of his patented reassuring smiles. "Unless we have other, emergency ones that use a different frequency? Yes, yes we do. I installed them not long ago, perhaps three months, if memory serves me correctly."

The woman relaxed a bit. "Well, that's good. I'm glad you were able to think ahead of such things."

Ty took her by the hand and led her toward the blue van. "Yeah. We can discuss the details later. Dante! You coming?"

The tall physician had run somewhat ahead to the tunnel's mouth to peer into it and check for any signs that enemies might have breached the exit. Encountering nothing but darkness and silence, he jogged back to the staging area. "I'm coming, bud. Hold up."

While the other four piled into the blue-framed vehicle, Amahle joined Gage in approaching the white truck from either side. Without them discussing it, she headed for the passenger's side while he took the driver's seat. As their tech specialist, he'd done most of the modifications to the vehicle and the radio and thus was more familiar with operating them.

As Amahle slammed the door, checked her rifle, and mentally prepared herself to shoot while riding if necessary, Gage took the emergency radio from its hiding place behind the seat and put it on the dashboard. It was an ungainly lump of tubes, crude speakers, and wires. Knowing Gage, it would probably get the job done.

The small man fiddled with a couple of dials until the device *buzzed, crackled,* and finally gave way to a clear signal. "This is Gage. Testing. Over."

Daria's voice replied at once. "Testing. Can you hear us? Over."

"Yes. Now, we go silent. Out." Gage switched it off and opened his door to converse with the rest of them face-to-face. Since the two disguised Autocutioners were parked next to each other, they were well within speaking distance.

Ty spoke so everyone could hear him. "Two days. No communications for forty-eight hours. If by some chance they find this frequency, at least they won't hear a damn thing on it. When the two days are up, all we do is briefly check in to make sure no one's—" he paused and swallowed his words, "To make sure everyone's safe."

Amahle shook her head. Ty had been about to revert to his accustomed blunt speech but had "softened" his way of putting it at the last second for Eleanor's benefit. That might have been unnecessary, given how quickly Eleanor was adapting to the awful situation around her.

"Yes, good idea," Amahle responded. "We'll see to our tasks and contact you at the appointed time. Between Gage and me, we can do this, and I'm sure you can as well. Good luck."

Dante leaned out the passenger's window and waved. "Good luck." Then Daria fired up the engine, and the fake van moved ahead into the tunnel, the noise of its passage seeming louder than it ought to.

Gage turned the key and started their white truck. "Best of luck to us, too. I fear we will need it."

Grimacing, Amahle confessed, "So do I."

CHAPTER TEN

The other Autocutioner's fake blue van frame was visible ahead of them in the square patch of dim light that lay at the mouth of the tunnel. Behind the vehicle, faint heat waves shimmered around the exhaust pipe. Daria was idling.

Amahle watched while Gage kept them rolling forward. Seconds ago they'd finished the gently sloping ascent and were now in the passage's last stretch. It leveled out before it opened at the end of a covered shack of sorts sandwiched between two warehouses and forgotten during an earlier period of the city's development.

"What?" Amahle murmured, mostly to herself. "Are they waiting for us to see if we are okay? Or is there something wrong?" Without her conscious awareness fully realizing it, her hand crept over and down toward her rifle.

Gage slowed but didn't stop. "I'm not sure. Nothing seems to be amiss. I cannot see any sign that they're trying to signal us or tell us to go back." He kept driving forward, steeling himself for whatever might come.

As they passed out of the tunnel altogether, the imitation van began moving again. Then an arm—Dante's, presumably—

extended from the passenger's side window and gave them a thumbs-up.

Amahle let out her breath as Gage increased his speed.

She didn't let herself get too comfortable yet, though. So far things were going well, but they weren't yet free or safe. "Go in a different direction from wherever they're going," she suggested. "We should lie low and get some rest, somewhere no one will pay attention to us. Then we can begin in the morning."

"Agreed." As the other Autocutioner turned left at a side street beyond the valley, Gage crossed the road, went on to the next one, and turned right. After a moment of disorientation, Amahle determined that they were heading east.

The dark masses of buildings passed them on the sides, partially illuminated by street lamps. Regular electric ones emitted yellowish hues. In more upscale districts, the cutting-edge lights powered by Atlanticore gave off a brilliant blue-white shine instead.

Amahle said, "There's a place I saw not long ago, an abandoned lot near the corner of 16th Avenue and Fern Street. Buildings and fences mostly surround it. We would be able to park there without anyone seeing us unless they either came into the lot itself or were in one of the nearby buildings and looked out the window at us."

It was unnecessary to add that they were in a disguised vehicle.

Gage took her advice, piloting the truck for another five or six minutes to the location in question. Amahle helped point it out to him, and they pulled in without trouble, locating a nice shadowy corner on the pavement's cracked expanse where they would be as unobtrusive as possible.

"Now, let us get some rest." Amahle sighed. "I wonder if that might be unwise. But I am so tired. .."

Gage smiled at her. "Yes, I think it would be better for us to begin our efforts tomorrow when we've refreshed ourselves. You may sleep first, and I will take first watch."

She thanked him and headed into the vehicle's back compartment. They generally used the rear of the Autocutioners to transport prisoners or equipment, but it made an acceptable makeshift bunk or infirmary when necessary. Gage had thought to outfit the compartment with sleeping bags and a few basic toiletries while modifying the radios.

Amahle lost consciousness almost as soon as her head rested upon the roll of fabric that served as a pillow. She drifted off into vague, abstract, yet disturbing dreams.

She awoke sometime later, with a kind of lazy and relaxing grogginess, when it was still dark out. Gage heard her rustling and looked back at her. "Good morning. It is about four o'clock. Once you're up, I will take my turn sleeping. You may wake me up at nine or so. I do not think I'll require a full night's rest."

Amahle sat up, stretched, and yawned. "We will see." She didn't want to delay too long but also wanted Gage operating at the peak of his abilities. Some people needed less sleep than others, though.

Gage informed her that there was a small electric hotplate up front for her to make tea if she wanted it. Then he curled up where she'd lain a moment ago and was soon snoring peacefully.

While he slept, Amahle's mind turned over the problem of what to do and how to do it. She and Gage would be resuming the investigation she'd been embroiled in yesterday before the attack on headquarters. Therefore, it made sense to pick up exactly where she'd left off.

Bettina Karo, the masseuse. Finding her might be their best bet. Amahle had already pursued a couple of leads and found virtually nothing of use.

How then, Amahle wondered, could the woman be drawn out of hiding and questioned?

There had to be another way than simply knocking on doors

and asking around. For all his intelligence, Gage was too much a scientist to come up with anything. His logical and rational mind was probably not well-suited to the kinds of deception and subterfuge they might need to employ to find a person who did not wish them to locate her.

Amahle would have to be the one to think of a plan, then.

Patience had never been something she lacked. She sat and contemplated, going through scenario after scenario, as the night ended and dawn spread its dim light over the city and the sky. She barely noticed how much time had passed, and it seemed almost too soon when nine o'clock rolled around.

She turned her face to the back compartment. "Gage. Wake up. It is time."

He grunted and stirred, but it was difficult to tell if he was truly awake yet. She would give him a minute or two and go back to prod him with her foot, if necessary.

Her mind returned to the task at hand.

During her earlier forays into the mystery of the three hanged Executives, she'd resented the task of investigation and the social skills and restraint that went with it. Plus the fact that she had to observe the normal mores and standards of civilian life and couldn't deal with problems simply by finding the right person and putting a bullet in their head.

At present, under the duress of necessity, something important unveiled itself in her mind. She'd been going about this all wrong, approaching it with an attitude all but guaranteed to fail.

Outside the truck, the sun was coming out through the dissolving rain clouds, and shafts of morning light filtered down to the earth. A few of them passed through the vehicle's windows to fall on Amahle's face. The rest of it shone on the ground, the trees, and the buildings. Soon it would warm up the air and evaporate the puddles of water left over from the last storm.

The weather here reminded her of the rainy season back home in South Africa but without much of a dry season to counterbalance it. She recalled a particular man she'd had to kill years ago, on a morning much like this one.

He'd been only her third. She was a teenager, growing more confident in her abilities and more inured to the ugliness of death, yet still the act of trying to shoot someone who would kill her if he could brought with it an absolute terror that wouldn't abate anytime soon.

Because she had been at a disadvantage—a lone girl with an old bolt-action rifle left over from the Boer War—she'd had to use trickery. She'd lured the man out into the open, keeping herself out of the picture all the while, until at last the sights on her rifle had hovered over the back of his neck. She'd emptied her body of breath and squeezed the trigger.

Locating the masseuse was really no different. Once she thought of Bettina Karo as *prey*, Amahle found that coming up with ways to lure her out—albeit simply to detain her and talk to her, rather than to blow her brains out—got far easier.

Something rustled behind her, and a minute later, the Gurkha crawled to his feet and trudged into the front seating compartment.

"Gage," Amahle began. "I believe I may have an idea or two for how we may find the woman."

He rubbed his eyes. "Oh, yes? Please tell me, then."

Amahle stood, hunched since the compartment wasn't big enough for her to stand straight, and looked out the window again. "If we can find any of her contacts, we can come up with a way to send out word that she is needed, that she is in trouble, or that someone needs her help. In that way, we can lure her into a trap."

"Hmm." Gage frowned and rubbed his slightly jowly chin. "That might work, but it could be difficult, especially since it will mean that we must... jump on her, as though we were attacking. She might flee in terror or try to fight us, and things might become most ugly."

Much to her annoyance, Amahle supposed he was right. Or partially right.

Gage added, "We will expose ourselves to scrutiny and rumors if we do that. It would make it far easier for the Executive Security forces or those who might inform against us to see or hear something."

Amahle considered it. "Very well. There is another option, one which I have just thought of." It didn't involve Ms. Karo, but it did apply a similar strategy.

"Yes?" Gage leaned forward, his curiosity piqued.

"We can go back to the health club where the masseuse worked and speak to the manager. Well, I should not go in since they would most likely recognize me and kick me out. You might be able to. Someone who works there could give us information whether they mean to or not, of course. If we can find out who the owner is, that might help to point us toward the Coven's hidden connections."

Gage raised a hand, brushing his thumb and forefinger together. He apparently had never learned to snap his fingers, so that was the next best thing. "Yes, yes, that is a good idea. Why would members of the Junior Board go someplace where they did not have an assurance of cooperation and privacy?"

"Exactly. This club must have deeper connections to the Executives. Or the Coven of Miracles. Or both at once."

Gage had the same thought. His mind was already racing ahead, however, to *how* they would infiltrate the place and gain information. "I can do it. I will pose as a customer interested in joining the club, say, to gain physical fitness. I wasn't with you when you were there earlier, and in this past year, I haven't been out on jobs in public as much as I once was. I spend most of my time in the lab these days."

Amahle agreed. Since Gage was such an unassuming-looking individual, without his uniform or other Executioner paraphernalia, it was unlikely anyone would see him as much of anything save a random, frumpy, middle-aged man. He might as well have been a mail clerk or a plumber as anything else.

Amahle elaborated, "After you've been inside and had them show you around the place, you can determine where the people and security are. I remember some of it, but there was no time to learn much. You can direct me where and when to enter without being seen. Then I can have a friendly talk with the manager."

The pair spent another twenty or thirty minutes working out a rudimentary plan, coming up with a full cover story for Gage, and briefly rehearsing it. For a man who didn't seem to lie often or to enjoy lying, he took to *acting* quite well, Amahle thought. All they had to do to complete the illusion was keep him in his workday office clothes, with nothing on his person to suggest he was a warrior in the employ of Atlantica's most feared organization.

When they were ready to go, Amahle took the wheel. Having been to the spa less than a full day ago, she easily located it again. She pulled the truck into the rear corner of the adjacent lot, parking out of the way, but not in the same place she'd put her Autocutioner the first time.

No one had seen her behind the wheel. She was almost positive. As soon as they parked, she ducked and sat on the floor near the entry to the back of the truck. "All right, Gage. Good luck. I'll wait."

He nodded. "Thank you. I might be in there for quite some time, depending on how long I must keep up the charade before we can get what we want."

She waved that off. "Take as much time as you need." The vehicle had a few U.S. and Canadian military C-Rations on board, and she opened one to eat a mediocre but acceptable brunch as Gage hopped down to the pavement and strode toward the building.

He brushed himself off, adjusted his glasses, and pushed in the front door. Amahle had told him about the timid Asian woman working the counter yesterday afternoon. With the place opening for business in the late morning, the only person doing reception was a man.

"Heyyyy." He greeted Gage with a flashy grin the instant the Nepali walked in. "Welcome. Haven't seen you before. What can I do for you?"

Gage returned the smile, but he wasn't sure he liked the man's attitude. Tall, lean, and muscular, he nonetheless came across as someone putting on a façade of confidence. He sported a greaser hairstyle, well-groomed mustache, and a shirt left unbuttoned at the neck and upper chest so his gold medallion rested against his hairy pectorals.

It looked as though he was trying to project an image of a Latin-style Lothario and sounded like he was faking an accent to match, but traces of his real voice crept through beneath it. In which case he sounded more like a Jewish or Polish shopkeeper's son from New Jersey.

The man extended his hand. "My name's Lorenzo Solomon. I'm the manager here. Ask any questions you like, or I can give you a tour of the facilities."

"Oh, the manager?" Gage piped up. "That is good. You'll be able to tell me about all the services you offer." He paused and made a show of grimacing sheepishly at the floor. "You see, I have a problem. I find that it is difficult to attract a lady friend. Since I have neglected my fitness, I thought that perhaps getting more exercise would improve my chances."

Lorenzo's eyes lit up. "I know what you mean. My friend, I think I know exactly what you *need*. Allow me to play show and tell."

From the lobby, the manager took Gage back into the gym area and showed him the mineral baths, sauna, and facilities for performing facials, manicures, and pedicures. "Men can benefit from those too, you know," he pointed out. All the while, he rambled on about the many exciting packages they offered for new members.

Midway into the tour, one of the low-level female attendants appeared and expressed her deep concern for Gage's plight, talking to him as though he were a child. "Aww, well, I think we have what you're looking for, sir. We can help you slim down around the middle *and* bulk up around here!" She patted his arms and shoulders. "Won't that be nice?"

Gage smiled at her, hiding his annoyance. He was a friendly and even-tempered man, but their condescending and smarmy behavior tested his patience. "Most definitely nice, yes."

The manager and the attendant continued to ramble, trying to sell him every service they offered. Gym access, personal coaching, vitamin supplements, protein supplements, sauna access, the full spa treatment; he nodded vacantly at all of it, implying that he was interested in paying them as much money as possible.

Lorenzo concluded with, "There's only one thing, friend. We need to get an idea of where you're at in terms of your baseline level of physical fitness. So, let's go over to these weights here and see how much you can lift. First, we'll have a demonstration of the goal you want to attain."

He rolled up his sleeves, bent his legs at the knees, and picked up a barbell loaded with iron disks, sharply exhaling as he hoisted it above his head before lowering it back to the floor.

"There," he gasped. "In a few months, I'd be willing to bet that you can do the same thing."

Gage looked at the weighted bar. "Perhaps. Allow me to try." Before Lorenzo or the woman attendant could stop him, he crouched, grabbed the bar, and deadlifted it above his head. Since he *was* somewhat out of practice, it took more time and effort for him than it had for the manager, though.

Lorenzo stared in shock as Gage lowered the barbell back to the ground. "Forgive me," Gage remarked, "but it seems that some of my weight is muscle, after all. Still, I welcome the opportunity to grow stronger. Sign me up for..." he paused. "Everything."

The manager's befuddled expression gave way to a smirk of victory. "Well, then! Sounds great, my friend. Why don't we give you a free trial of the facilities while we get the paperwork taken care of? It's the least we can do. Heh, heh."

Gage stalled for another hour or so, going through the motions of trying out some of the exercise equipment and taking a nice hot mineral bath. He didn't like the thought of keeping Amahle waiting, but the charade would be more convincing if he lingered. Furthermore, once they completed the paperwork, the manager would likely be more... pliable.

At eleven-thirty, after signing the forms, Lorenzo declared that lunch hour was beginning for the staff.

"You can lounge around in the, ha, lounge, if you want," he informed his new customer, "but we won't have our spotters in the gym or anyone else on duty until twelve-thirty. Most customers leave during that time and get lunch or something. I'm going into my office, and I'll be busy with important business stuff. Not to mention celebrating you making the right choice by letting us provide so many valuable services to you." He grinned like a cat about to pounce on a bird.

Beaming, Gage said, "Of course. I will think it over for a minute or two. I am *certain* that I will be back soon."

Things quieted down while Gage waited in the lounge, sipping a protein shake. Once the manager sequestered himself in his office and the rest of the employees and customers left, he crept to the rear of the building, where there was a T-intersection. One path led to a door that opened on the parking lot, but it seemed to be an emergency exit and likely had an alarm.

He went the other way instead, ignoring an "Employees Only" sign and finding a back storeroom that had been left unlocked. From there, it was easy to locate a service exit that opened upon the alley-like area behind the building, including a loading bay and a dumpster. He braced the door and crept out into fresh air, sneaking around the side of the building toward the white-painted truck with the brass grille.

Gage knocked on the window, and Amahle appeared at once, her eyes wide.

"Let's go," he told her. "There is no one else around. We can have the manager to ourselves. He is a most unpleasant man, but I doubt he poses any threat."

Amahle nodded but still checked to ensure she had her .32 revolver in her waistband. They snuck back into the building through the propped-open back door, then moved slowly toward the manager's office.

The door was closed. It had no window, and there was no way to tell if it was locked merely by looking at it. Gage pantomimed a kicking motion, then looked at Amahle, who nodded her approval.

Sucking in his breath, the Gurkha slammed his foot into the door near the knob, cracking the wood and making it swing in with a groaning *creak*, followed by a *slam* as it crashed into the wall. Amahle pounced into the office, and Gage fell in behind her.

"*Jesus Christ!*" Lorenzo exclaimed, turning to stare at them bug-eyed.

He wasn't wearing any pants, and his hands were slick and shiny. Spread out on the desk in front of him were various photos of himself in various stages of undress.

Amahle's jaw dropped. "You think highly of yourself, I see. The Coven—excuse me, the Executives—must pay you well for your services."

Before the stunned man could speak or react, Amahle struck him in the face with the edge of her hand. Not with enough force to seriously injure him, but enough of a blow to snap his head aside and send him tumbling into his chair. His jaw turned red and he squinted in pain.

Gage moved in and shut the door behind him. "Perhaps, after paying you the ridiculous amount of money you wanted in exchange for so many redundant and unnecessary products and services, I too can look good enough to lust after my own 'before' and 'after' photographs."

He kicked the side of the chair so it spun halfway around and wheeled back against the wall. Lorenzo fell to his knees on the floor, pants still tangled around his ankles. When he tried to scramble to his feet, Amahle struck him again, driving the heel of her palm against his chest so he fell back into the chair.

He looked up at them, eyes flashing with anger as his cheeks reddened with embarrassment. "What the hell is this?" he sputtered. "What do you people want?"

"Information," Gage said. "If you'll kindly cooperate with us, this ordeal will end soon, and you will suffer no further harm or humiliation." He flashed his warmest, most sanguine smile again. "If, however, you do not cooperate..."

Amahle drew her pistol and aimed at his face. She finished Gage's sentence for him.

"Then I will kill you here and now, and everyone will find you *like this*. Naked, beaten up by a woman and a short, overweight middle-aged man, and..." She gestured vaguely. "Everything else we see here now."

Lorenzo blanched with horror at the very thought. Probably more at the prospect of being found in his current state than at the prospect of death, Gage suspected.

"I-I—there's only so much I can—fuck! What do you want to know?"

Gage nodded. "You are a wise man. We wish to know about your masseuse, Bettina Karo, as well as the trainer who died yesterday. When were they hired, and what do you know about them? Do not pretend that you have no idea what we are talking about. We know that this place is *connected* to certain very powerful people."

There was an obvious flash of fear on the man's handsome face, a moment of hesitation; then he saw Amahle aim at his eyeball with her gun, and he sighed in resignation.

"Those two were 'instructed hires' from the owner," Lorenzo explained. "They only ever worked with three clients. Those were the rules, okay? I don't know why. I'm not important enough to know why. I thought it was strange, but they gave me a bonus to do it anyway and keep quiet about it. Not to mention, those three paid premium rates."

Amahle pressed him further. "Who is the owner? We want a name and where to find them. Do not think of telling them that we're coming, or we will come *back* here and find you."

The man winced, then declared, "Jori Singh. He owns multiple properties and a bunch of other business investments. This place is a drop in the pan. He's with a company called, uhh, Khalsa Development Investments. Talk to them if you want to talk to him."

While Amahle stood still and silent, Gage gave a short bow. "Ah, thank you, sir. I am terribly sorry to say that I've changed my mind about my membership and all of the premium services I signed up for. Nevertheless, we will keep our end of the bargain and leave you in peace to finish up here as you see fit."

He turned and opened the door, stepping through it. While the manager sat there and stared after them, Amahle followed Gage out into the hall and quipped, "Have a nice day."

CHAPTER ELEVEN

Amahle and Gage went straight from the health club to a venture capital firm that Eleanor had them investigate several months ago. Daria had been the one to handle that particular case, but Gage at least knew where the place was and roughly what they did. They would be the best culprits to point the pair toward Khalsa. And by extension, Singh.

It took about an hour to reach the firm. Traffic thickened as lunch hour ended and Atlantica Metro's many office workers and other white-collar types rushed back to work. They competed for road space with the blue-collar laborers who built the offices and maintained the gas, water, electricity, food, and nonedible supplies that allowed everything to function.

Amahle mused, "We likely won't have time to stake out this Khalsa place and interview their people on the same day. We do not dare barge into a place connected with the Coven unless we observe them beforehand. Business hours will end before that."

Gage was driving this time. "Yes, that had occurred to me. This way, we'll be able to check in with the others before we move in on this man Singh."

He meant Ty, Daria, Dante, and their self-imposed two-day

moratorium on radio communications. Amahle didn't complain, but she wondered if it might be better for them to prioritize haste over covertness. Things had become *political*. People with money, influence, and position were now involved, making things more complicated than she could readily comprehend.

There was something else, too, that was strange and disquieting. Since escaping their besieged headquarters, they'd heard *nothing* about the event itself. News on the regular radio didn't mention that a gun battle had taken place in the middle of the city at a building widely rumored to be associated with the Executioners.

They hadn't heard any random member of the public discussing the incident, either. Nor were the Executive Security personnel roving around in force or establishing checkpoints or anything of the sort. It was as though the Execs had gone to great lengths to keep the whole thing quiet and were now pretending that it hadn't happened at all.

A couple of the black vans that Security used had driven by, from time to time, and in each case, Amahle's gut clenched in anxiety.

The capital firm was in the far northeastern outskirts of the city. "This is good news," Amahle observed. "It means that there will be fewer people who can see us than if we were in downtown near our HQ." Then she frowned out the window, watching buildings streak by. "The Execs might control such a place."

Gage shook his head. "The Execs have some control over nearly everything that is regarded as respectable or important here. It will be impossible to avoid all scrutiny. Nonetheless, I will be the one who goes in to speak to them for much the same reasons as at the spa."

The office lay in the corner of a half-completed industrial park, surrounded on two sides by undeveloped land and on another two by mixed residential and commercial structures.

There was a rather nice marble fountain out front, but the building itself was a banal cube of glass and steel, nothing special.

Amahle waited, reclining low in the passenger's seat while Gage walked into the lobby. About a minute after he'd departed the truck, a black van drove by behind them. Amahle sat up straight, staring into the rearview mirror.

For a second or two, it looked like the vehicle had slowed its pace. It might have been an illusion created by the different angles from which she viewed the small mirror between adjusting her posture. Then the van was gone.

"I am jumpier now than I have been at times when my life was in far more danger," she scolded herself. "It makes no sense."

Again, it was the political intrigue going on behind the scenes that so disturbed her. She didn't understand it, and she feared none of her friends truly did, either. Herself against another rifleman in the wilderness was something she *did* understand.

Gage returned around ten minutes later.

"I have what we need." He climbed into the truck, his face showing an odd mixture of amusement and sour distaste. "They seemed to resent that I was only looking for another company instead of wishing to do business with them. I slipped them the money I was hoping to save for lunch to keep them satisfied."

Amahle gestured at the rear compartment. "There are still several C-Rations left. I ate only one of them."

Gage chuckled. "Let's go. The bad part is that Khalsa is located right in the center of town. Not far from our headquarters, or the central financial district where the Executives seem to be most active."

It was another forty-five minutes back to their destination. Gage circled the block a couple of times to get a feel for the area and scope it out without attracting the same level of attention that would come from parking across the street and staying there.

Predictably, Khalsa was in a tall, modern office building. It wasn't quite a skyscraper, but it was an expensive and impressive structure all the same. A buffer zone of fenced-off alleys separated it from the neighboring buildings, and across the street was a line of high-end shops—jewelry stores, boutiques, and the like. Most of the people who strode along the sidewalks were wealthy-looking sorts.

Midway into his third circumnavigation of the building, Gage pulled off onto a side street and parked in a patch of deep shade that lay a safe distance from the Khalsa front windows.

"Now we watch and wait. It is growing later in the afternoon, so many of the staff will probably leave through those doors out front as they close down for the day."

Amahle nodded. "Unless Singh is the type who stays late in his office working all night. How will we know him, anyway? Should we go straight in and ask?"

Gage shook his head. "The man I spoke to earlier described Singh and said he is only there about half of the time. Today, our main concern is seeing if anyone takes too much interest in *us*. And how good their security is."

It made sense, and Amahle had no objections. However, it drew her mind back to the things that had been bothering her all day. She decided, at last, to share them.

"Gage. I'm worried about how quiet everything has been. There has been no news about what happened at HQ, no sweeping of the streets to find us. I would've thought that they would be trying to manipulate public opinion against us, but it is as though no one cares at all. It reminds me of the type of trap I would set for someone I wanted to be...complacent. Making them feel safe, so they drop their guard before I deliver the killing shot."

The Gurkha made a low sound in his throat and pursed his lips, staring through the windshield. "I see what you mean. Some of it, we can chalk up to the people of Atlantica and how quickly they forget and grow bored with things. Still, what you say is valid. There might be things going on here that we yet know nothing about."

"There must be," Amahle insisted. "Why would they try to kill us all simply because Eleanor told us a few things? It would be far more advantageous for the Executives to keep us on their side and try to convince us that their cause is just. They invested far too much time and money in equipping us and providing us with intel and support. Why would they cast us aside so quickly?"

"I must admit, I don't know, Amahle." Gage tapped his hands on the steering wheel as though he were suddenly impatient for something to happen. "I do not know."

Amahle looked through the windows, watching the afternoon's light fade. A few people filtered out of the Khalsa office, but Gage didn't identify any as the man they sought.

He added, "The one thing I can think of is that the Executives might still think they can keep the situation under control and bring us to heel. Perhaps they meant to capture us last night and only to kill Eleanor."

Amahle shook her head. "They might have tried to negotiate, or used nonlethal weapons, then. You might be correct about the rest."

Brooding over the questions, they watched as business hours ended and the office's staff left in small groups. When it became apparent that their quarry wasn't among them, they drove away and found an inconspicuous place to spend the night.

The next day saw them back in their spot on the side street, watching the workers come and go in the rhythms of their daily routines. By quitting time, the truck's confined quarters were wearing on Amahle's patience, and Gage shifted in his seat more often as well. Both felt the pressure of waiting for something to break but hadn't thought of any other avenues of investigation to pursue.

Gage said, "I don't see anyone who resembles Jori Singh. He must not be here today, or perhaps he is staying overnight. We should consider breaking for the evening and getting in touch with the others. It's close to time now."

Trying not to squirm with uncertainty and impatience, Amahle suggested, "Another half an hour. Then we can leave and try again tomorrow."

"Very well." They sat, observed, and found nothing.

Fatigued and frustrated, they drove around at random until they found a suitably obscure and discreet alley about a mile from the Khalsa building. Then Amahle took a couple more C-Rations out of storage while Gage tried to raise the other Executioners on the emergency radio—the one that the Executives didn't know about. Or so they could hope.

Amahle scowled as she unpacked the meals and brought them up to the front seat. "If we have any money, we should eat out properly or visit a drive-up restaurant," she muttered. "Besides, after these are only two more left. We shouldn't deplete our emergency stores."

Gage nodded his agreement but remained mostly focused on fiddling with the radio's dial. "Come in," he said. "It's me. Both of us are fine. Please respond. Over."

Silence and a faint *crackling* of static were his only response.

Looking at Amahle, he quipped, "Not to worry. They might be busy. We're also a little early. We might have to try several times before we catch them while they're in the vehicle."

The thought had occurred to her as well, but she gathered that it made Gage feel better to say it aloud. To some extent, it made her feel better, too.

They ate, and Gage retried every four or five minutes. When they still hadn't received a response after the fourth try, it grew harder to suppress the feeling of disquiet.

Then, after they finished their meals and as darkness fell over the city, the light crackle of Gage's fifth try gave way to Daria's voice.

"Hello, it is me. It's good to hear that you are well. We are making do, and Number One will be all right. Is there anything you need to know right away? Over."

Amahle sighed in relief. When they wanted to communicate without being too obvious about their identities, the Executioners referred to themselves by numbers, in the order they'd joined. Thus, Number One was Tyler, and Amahle was Number Five.

Gage closed his eyes for a second and smiled. "Ah, excellent. We don't have anything urgent to report or request, but if you think the risk is acceptable, we would like to update you on what we've found so far and to hear the same from you. Over."

"Go ahead, but keep it short," Daria said.

Gage summarized all that had happened, and Daria acknowledged it in a neutral tone. She probably hoped for more progress, but so did they all. Then she listed what her party had accomplished.

With Eleanor's help—she was more or less back to normal after being shaken by the battle and determined to cooperate with her friends—the team in the fake blue van had begun to assemble a "hit list" of Junior Execs. It included places they frequented, their contacts to tap if need be, and so forth.

Daria pointed out, "There's one problem. This man you mention, Jori Singh, isn't on the list. Eleanor, have you heard of him?" She paused.

"No. She feels she might have encountered the name on a list of businesspeople, but he isn't a known member of the Junior Board. This precludes him from being on the Senior Board as well, as I understand it. Therefore he's one of two things. Either a second-order associate who might not know the full extent of the Execs' activities, or an active member of the Coven of Miracles who operates outside the Executive Boards altogether."

Gage and Amahle fell silent. The alley around them was as close to pitch black as any place within a major metropolitan area could be. Only a small amount of light from the nearby street lamps filtered in.

"I see." Gage's voice was soft. "In either case, it's important that we speak to him and find out all we can. We will try the office building again first thing in the morning, and if that doesn't work, we'll seek other options."

He turned and caught Amahle's eye as he spoke. She nodded her approval. There was nothing else she could recommend or add.

Gage and Daria agreed that the two teams would speak again in another thirty-six hours, if possible, or sooner, but only in the utmost extreme of dire need. At last, they signed off and switched off.

After looking around to ensure they were still alone in the alley, Amahle opened the door and hopped down to the damp pavement to stretch her arms and legs. She breathed deep and looked up at the dim sky, where the stars were made invisible by the city's lights.

The prospect of spending another day sitting in a truck and doing nothing physical whatsoever did not appeal to her. She would suffer what she must. In the past, she'd lain still for nine or ten hours at a time while waiting for targets to cross open spaces below whatever eagle's nest she'd occupied if that was what the job required.

Gage softly called, "Please do not wander far. We should get some sleep soon since we must begin early tomorrow."

"I know. I sleep better with fresh air. Might we crack the windows tonight?"

"Oh," Gage mused, "I suppose."

CHAPTER TWELVE

Amahle and Gage were awake before dawn. They had a good two hours before Khalsa opened its doors to employees, so they went out for breakfast at a twenty-four-hour diner that served impressive platters of eggs, sausages, and pancakes along with good strong coffee.

Amahle was nervous, particularly since the waitress kept squinting at her as though trying to remember who she was. She couldn't recall having been in the establishment before, but the woman might've seen her on an assignment somewhere else in public.

Nothing happened. Again, it was as though the recent violence at Executioner headquarters had never happened at all. Atlantica had a way of swallowing up its momentous events.

The pair drove back to the same side street they'd used before, reasoning that if someone recognized them from yesterday, it would be *less* suspicious to be seen in the same location. They could always claim it was the best spot they'd found so they snapped it up as part of whatever their benign, mundane, non-investigative job was. Such a story *might* work.

"Now, let us see if our man will at last show his face," Amahle murmured.

It only took about twenty minutes.

Gage sat up in his seat, abruptly alert, and pointed. "That's him. It must be, based on what the investment firm told me."

A tall, lanky, middle-aged man with deep brown skin and a salt-and-pepper beard had strode out of the building's front door, dressed in a fine white suit. Two big bruisers accompanied him on either side. Both men dressed in black, wore sunglasses, and kept adjusting their jackets. Given how things operated on Atlantica, Amahle wondered why the deception was necessary. Openly wearing their guns would've made as much sense.

The three headed toward a pair of cars parked at the curb beside the office. Both were luxury sedans, but Amahle couldn't identify the make and model offhand. The one in the rear had an opened trunk, and two other men, attendants or servants of some kind, were loading bags and suitcases into it. One of them also added a folded-up towel in bright colors.

"Hmm." Gage scratched his nose. "He's going on vacation, perhaps?"

Amahle shrugged. "Taking a trip, I'm sure. Can you follow them without being seen? Both cars are probably going together. A man of his importance will have a security escort with him."

Gage nodded. "I believe so, yes." He glanced around, then asked, "Could you get out and scout what lies at the other end of this street? So I know which roads to follow, depending on which direction they go."

Amahle had been about to request that she do something along those lines, anyway. She climbed down from the truck, slipped away behind it, and soon stood on the sidewalk opposite the block where Khalsa's office lay. There were no surprises. This part of the city was largely a grid of streets laid out with maximum efficiency in mind. However, there was a rather busy intersection to the east.

She returned to the truck and reported her findings about a minute before Singh climbed into the second car. Then it and the escort vehicle roared off to the west, the same direction they'd been pointing.

"Go," Amahle said.

Gage nodded, fired up the engine, and stepped on the gas.

They gave Singh's motorcade a short head start. The glossy black cars were relatively easy to spot. They were more conservative than the flashy sports cars favored by many of the town's wealthy player types, yet finer than the jalopies driven by the working class.

Still, traffic was heavy enough that it was difficult to remain at the ideal distance, where they could keep their quarry in sight without being close enough to look suspicious.

Gage grimaced in concentration, staring ahead except to check his mirrors, while Amahle did most of the broader visual scanning and pointed out tips. "They're doubling back east. Why? Have we been spotted?"

"Who knows," Gage grunted, too focused on the task to be his usual friendly self.

The two black sedans zigged and zagged through the city, seemingly taking a more circuitous route than was necessary. Amahle wondered if Singh's men had spotted them and were testing them or trying to throw them off. At one point, though, they went down a one-way street that Gage recognized.

He grinned. "Aha. I know where that one goes and how to intercept it. This way, under the overpass..." He pulled onto a side street, through a tunnel, and a few minutes later they suddenly emerged on a major thoroughfare with Singh's cars about a hundred yards ahead. A semi-truck allowed them to ride behind visual cover as they pursued the sedans.

Then the city proper fell behind them, the land rising and growing irregular as they came into the foothills. The labyrinth of tall buildings, deep alleys, and fenced-off lots gave way to prosperous gated suburbs, less-prosperous shantytowns, and unfinished development sites in between the stretches of uninhabited trees, rocks, and moss.

Amahle pointed ahead. "This road has only two branches from here on. The main one, which circles the city to the north, and another that goes into the hills to the northwest where some rich people live."

Gage nodded. "The latter is probably our objective."

It was. Falling back more than half a mile, they nonetheless saw the two black cars taking the northwest exit and vanishing into the increasingly rugged wilderness. Amahle only hoped that wherever Singh was heading, one or both of the sedans would be visible from the road. The wealthy liked their privacy, so there was no guarantee of any such blessing.

She mentioned her concern, and Gage increased his speed. They'd fallen far enough behind during the crucial drive through the less populated, semi-rural outskirts that they could afford to close the distance again.

The northwest road wound through densely forested areas, crested ridges, and ascended rocky slopes mostly barren of trees. As it descended on the other side of the line of hills, Amahle sensed that they were nearing the all-but-untouched jungle that filled much of the island's center.

Here and there, they caught glimpses of the black sedans.

At last, the two cars pulled off into a drive near the utmost end of the road. Gage slowed but continued his approach. The property lay on the other side of a high stone wall, but they saw the peaked roof of a mansion beyond it. At a taller point in the road, they also glimpsed what looked like two separate pools filled with sparkling blue water. Beyond the estate, a cliff overlooked a scenic green valley.

"Such a nice place," Amahle observed, trying not to grind her teeth. She'd never entirely left behind the dislike and distrust of the rich. The antipathy had been with her since her earliest childhood memories.

Gage stopped at a curve in the road where they would be mostly out of sight but fairly close to the gate the sedans had driven through. "We must decide whether to sneak in or to try something else. If we move and act decisively, it might be our best chance to get Singh alone."

The South African looked at the mansion and the sky beyond. It would probably be a sunny day. The weather lately had been comparatively dry and pleasant. Atlantica was often rainy, but it lacked much seasonal variation in temperature—a true oddity of climate, given its location near lands with short steamy summers and long icy winters. Scientists found it perplexing.

Amahle pointed out, "We're also in the middle of nowhere. If we fail, this would be a good place for them to dump our bodies in the jungle, where others might never find them. I've been in such situations before. But... I worry about the others. What they might think, and what could happen if we fail them."

Gage gave a slow nod. "Yes. There is much risk. But you've been through worse."

Sighing, she picked up her rifle. "Yes, it's worth the chance. Get us a little closer, then follow my lead." She strapped her survival knife to her thigh as well. It was practically a machete and might come in handy for hacking through especially dense undergrowth if all else failed, in addition to being a fearsome backup weapon.

Gage smirked weirdly and pulled the truck forward another hundred yards. He stopped in a patch of ferns a short way off the road where dense trees would hide them from anything other than the most direct scrutiny. Then both climbed down to the earth, left the truck locked, and plunged into the bush, toting their rifles and secretly thrilled at being back on the hunt.

Amahle was the expert at navigating rough country on foot, but she was impressed by how well Gage kept up with her despite his advancing age, stocky build, and the simple fact that he'd done most of his work indoors for months.

He'd fought in the Second World War, she recalled, and some of his time had been spent in the tropical forests of Southeast Asia, doing his part to expel the Imperial Japanese Army from the region. Some of what he'd learned must have been coming back to him.

It took them around thirty to forty minutes to navigate the hilly jungle that separated their erstwhile parking space from Singh's luxurious vacation home. As they drew closer to it, they moved slower and with far greater caution, performing exhaustive sweeps of the territory and stopping to watch for patrols.

When the woods began to thin, and the estate proper came into view, they wondered if they'd been wasting their time. Singh didn't seem to place much of a premium on tight security.

The wall wrapped around the property on the two sides closest to the road. The terrain was rough enough on the west and north ends that they must have assumed no one would dare approach that way. Amahle and Gage bore north and passed a broad window, which they saw through the foliage. It opened onto a sitting room within.

Singh's bodyguards—the two who'd accompanied him out of the Khalsa office and another two who'd occupied the escort car —were all gathered there, drinks in hand and watching a film on a projector. One of those comedies that involved attractive women acting foolish while scantily dressed, from the look of it. One of the men glanced briefly through the glass at the forest but then turned back to the screen and laughed alongside the others.

Amahle signaled that she was moving around to the west side of the house. Gage nodded and followed.

West of the house, the land had been landscaped flat, and one of the swimming pools, shaped like a teardrop, glimmered in the late morning sun. There were a couple of tables with umbrellas and chairs around the pool proper. A lit brazier burned nearby despite the brightness of the day. Sitting on the colorful towel that his staff had loaded into the trunk was Jori Singh.

Amahle guessed that he was performing yoga since he seemed to be in a state of deep yet relaxed concentration. He was completely naked. Despite being in his mid-fifties if not older, he was in impeccable condition with lean sinews rolling beneath his chestnut-colored skin.

The pair remained nestled within the foliage on the western slope. He didn't indicate that he'd seen them.

Amahle looked at Gage and waited for a bird to sing as cover before she whispered, as quietly as she could while being audible, "We abduct him and run. Yes?"

"Yes," Gage agreed in an equally soft voice. "Although the guards might drive ahead. If they find our truck..."

Amahle waved that off. "No other choice. Let's go."

She moved to the right, allowing Gage to take the left. Each would be able to creep up nearly to the very edge of the lawn beside the pool while retaining concealment. Then a hasty rush, flanking the man and holding their guns on him to keep him silent, and they could spirit him off into the jungle. If they were lucky, they might be halfway back to their vehicle before his bodyguards noticed he was gone.

Amahle reached the end of the foliage. The muzzle of her rifle was protruding over the edge of the landscaping. She counted to three in her head.

On two, Jori Singh opened his eyes, stared straight at her, and rose to his feet with a fluid yet steady motion.

The South African and the Nepali burst out onto the lawn, making no noise but a faint rustling as they passed beyond the ferns of the woods and moved in toward the man's sides.

He stayed where he was. "Welcome," he greeted them as though they were expected guests. "Would you like some tea?"

CHAPTER THIRTEEN

Since both Gage and Amahle had their weapons free and ready to use, Singh had undoubtedly seen the rifles at the same time he saw their bearers. He was unperturbed. The fact that his new guests had loaded guns leveled at him and could kill him five times over before his security team could help him didn't seem to cause the man any particular stress or fear.

Amahle said, "Do not try anything foolish. You're at a disadvantage. I would bet money if I had the chance that you know who we are—and what we're capable of."

Singh offered an unhurried nod, and reached out for a velvet robe hanging on the pole that supported an umbrella over his poolside table. To his credit, he appeared to understand that slow, deliberate motions were his best bet and that any sudden moves might get him shot.

Amahle wondered if he might have a weapon under the robe, but she doubted it. Singh took up the robe and swung it around his shoulders. Once his arms were through the sleeves, he tied it around his waist with a sash.

"Tea?" he asked again.

Gage and Amahle kept silent, watching his movements and face for any sign of sudden aggression or disobedience.

They saw none. Singh wore an easy and genuine smile. Combined with his grandfatherly beard and bright eyes, it made him look downright pleasant. He walked about four steps to another small table nearby, where a pole and hook held a dangling copper pot near the burning brazier.

Amahle watched, almost disbelieving what she saw, as the man casually adjusted the pot so it hung over the flames. Then he set out three cups with strainers for each before taking up a small ceramic jar and measuring out equal portions of dried black tea leaves. It was fragrant enough that Amahle smelled it from ten paces away. The aroma was enticing, with hints of rose and blackberry.

Gage was about fifteen feet to her left. He flicked his eyes toward her, and she returned the gesture. They were probably thinking the same thing—that Singh was stalling until his security team had the chance to wander out to the pool patio.

Everything seemed wrong. The man was truly unafraid. Amahle couldn't detect so much as a single indication that he was bluffing them. Granted, a yoga practitioner might be more skilled than the average person at controlling his emotions. Yet she somehow intuited that if she and Gage were to rush him and drag him into the trees, they would make things worse rather than better. Doing so might *cost* them an opportunity rather than gain them one.

It appeared that Singh wanted to talk, which was what they'd intended him to do all along.

He gestured at the table and a couple of nearby chairs. "Please, sit down."

Amahle responded in a voice that was low but edged with menace. Whatever the strange man's game was, he had to understand that his visitors were immensely dangerous people.

"We're not here for tea." She advanced a single step.

Gage did likewise without looking at her. He kept his eyes fixed on their target.

Singh remained unworried. His expression was too neutral and nondescript to qualify as a proper smile, but it was close. "Oh, I'm sure that wasn't why you came here. All the same, I think we have time to be civil about things. What's the rush?"

His accent wasn't too dissimilar from Gage's. Both had learned the British Raj style of English in their youth, but Singh was undoubtedly from a different part of the Indian subcontinent. Thus, the undertones of this speech weren't the same.

Amahle flashed him a nasty smile. "Civil, yes. So we can drop our guard, and you can have your hired thugs come up behind us and put bullets in our heads."

Singh chuckled. "Miss Nikoze," he intoned, "if you're so terribly worried about such things, then by all means, put that rifle of yours to its intended use. I know you're an exceptional shot. So I am certain that my death will, at least, be quick. You were always the consummate professional, preferring the clean kill."

Amahle's right index finger wandered down over the trigger guard, brushing lightly against the side of the trigger itself. If the man was going to play games, then go back to hosting Coven members at his businesses and be involved with whatever other shady endeavors funneled him so much wealth, getting rid of him right then and there might have been the wisest option.

Gage spoke up for the first time. "Why are you doing this, Mr. Singh?"

"To distract us," Amahle snapped.

Singh shook his head with a slow, tired motion, but the look on his face was one of patience bordering on amusement. His eyes continued to twinkle. "To *educate* you. You had a rather poor series of interactions with our members, did you not? The noise was audible through half the city, and the aftermath was quite the mess."

Then the Execs *were* entirely aware of what had happened two nights ago. All the gunfire must have given rise to *some* rumors, even if they proved inaccurate.

"So," Singh went on, "I would hope that you will at least be willing to listen. I realize that my life might be forfeit, but it's worth it for the chance to keep you from committing a great and terrible error."

Amahle gave two sharp shakes of her head. She was growing tired of this charade. "If you really want to *educate* us, Mr. Singh, you can come along quietly, and we'll have this conversation on a turf of our choosing." She raised her rifle a little higher. It now pointed at the man's feet instead of the pavement an arm's length in front of him.

Singh raised his right hand, palm facing outwards, but she couldn't tell if it was a self-protective gesture or one of conciliation. Given that he remained calm, it almost seemed more like *he* was reassuring *her*, even though she was the one pointing a gun at him.

"I'm afraid that won't be possible, but you must understand it's not for *my* sake."

Amahle snorted in derision. She suspected the man might cease his little stunts if she made it clear that she had zero interest in them.

Before she could say anything, Gage leaned forward. "For whose sake, then?" He glanced around and behind him, checking for any sign of the security team noticing them. There was nothing.

Singh tilted his upraised hand and moved it to the side as though making a halfhearted flourishing motion. "The people of Atlantica, of course. If you take me prisoner, the more, shall we say, *impetuous* members of my organization will become seized with the fear that you'll try to extract information from me. The secrets we've kept so well, or some of the incredible things we've discovered. In their zeal, they're willing to do many terrible things—things which I would rather not allow."

Amahle wondered if by his organization he meant the Coven or something else. The former option made more sense.

He continued, "Talk to me now on this pleasant day with excellent tea sitting before us waiting to be drunk, or kill me and leave my body if you insist, and you will be allowed to leave here unscathed. It is true. If you try to *remove* me from these premises, whether dead or alive, you will meet with violence."

His words made little sense, and it took Amahle a couple of seconds of blinking contemplation to parse them in her mind. "You're saying that if I put a bullet in your head, your goons will *not* do anything about it?"

The lanky Indian nodded. "The only crime here, Miss Nikoze and Dr. Gurung is that of abduction."

Now Amahle was even more irritated. She leaned forward, only by a hand's breadth, but enough for him to notice, and she patted the knife strapped to her thigh. "And if I start taking pieces off you, Mr. Singh?"

His expression darkened slightly, but he was still, bizarrely enough, a long way from anything resembling panic.

"You mean torturing me for information, right here and now?" He kept still. No tension was visible in his body, nothing to indicate he might try to flee.

Amahle gave a single slow nod, while her wide and staring eyes stayed locked on his. She disliked torture. It was profoundly ugly and usually not justified or useful. Still, recent events had made her desperate enough to consider it if all else failed.

Gage shot her a look of concern and perhaps disapproval.

Singh passed a moment in thought as his eyes went distant. "Hmm. I don't think you possess the skills or the tools to get anything useful from me. Even if you did, I have to be honest— I'm entirely convinced that you don't have the stomach for it." He held up his palm again. "To be clear, that is not a criticism but praise. We always desired that the Executioners rule by force, but not by fear. Which, sadly, is a distinction that most fail to grasp."

Off to his side, the tea kettle had been steaming through its spout and the gap between its lid and body. At last, it began to sing. First in a feeble moan, then a high, clear whistle. Singh adjusted the sleeve of his robe—not bunching it up around his hand to act as a makeshift potholder, but folding it back so his lean brown forearm lay wholly exposed.

Gage was becoming noticeably antsy with growing excitement. His foot tapped gently on the stone. "*We*, you say? I was under the impression that the Executives established the Executioners, while the Coven of Miracles was a separate group that had only recently become entangled with them."

He was about to say something else—probably mentioning that's what Eleanor had told them—but bit down on his lip to stop himself from blurting out more than was strictly necessary.

Singh reached out his bare and unprotected hand for the kettle, the handle of which, like the rest of it, was made of copper.

"That seems like a discussion to be had over tea." His tone was nearly jovial,

His hand clamped around the metal ring that suspended the teapot above the flames. Amahle and Gage watched in growing amazement as the man casually lifted the kettle over the table and took his time to pour boiling water through each strainer in turn.

Singh smiled as he looked up at them. The handle, which should've been scalding hot, was still clenched in his fingers as he filled the third cup. "I will admit that I'm showing off a little here. I hope that a...less monstrous display of what we've invested in might help illustrate the nature of our objectives."

Gage turned his head fully toward Amahle, and there was no mistaking his expression. The widened eyes, pouty mouth, and faint twitch of something almost like hunger broadcast his intentions. He was *beseeching* her to hear Singh out.

Her gut tightened under a brief wave of stubborn resistance.

It aggravated her that this rather smarmy man was immune to every tool she'd ever used to force compliance from people who might otherwise harm her.

Yet, Gage might be right. Something was going on here that lay far beyond the threshold of her understanding. As a scientist, it must've downright maddened Gage with sheer curiosity as to what the hell Singh was talking about.

Amahle gave her partner a flick of her eyes while keeping Singh within her field of vision and nodded. She sighed in resignation and adjusted her posture to something more relaxed. Still, the rifle stayed at low ready. She could bring it up and fire in an eye blink if she had to.

"Fine," she said. "You may speak, Mr. Singh. But we are not drinking your tea just yet. One sudden move on your part will see the back of your head fouling up the waters of that beautiful pool."

Singh appeared borderline amused. He gave a deep bow, sweeping his arm to one side to hang the kettle back on the pole where he'd first grabbed it.

"I thank you for the gift of your time. It is a shame about the tea. It really is quite good."

Trying not to roll her eyes, Amahle stated, "I am sure it is. Now, talk."

Singh's nostrils expanded as he drew in air and slowly let it out, as though filling himself with knowledge and power in preparation for relaying it all to others. He spread his hands.

"In the beginning, Atlantica was purely a mystery. It lay undiscovered beneath its shroud of fog for centuries and millennia, until the German and American navies fought over it during the war, after stumbling upon it purely by accident. Then knowledge of the island's existence was buried once more, but this time, for not nearly so long."

Amahle and Gage followed as Singh prefaced himself with a summary of Atlantica's recent history. They knew much of it already, but the man's voice was as mesmerizing as his serene manner was perplexing. He described how the various nations and powers had agreed to place no claim on the island and enforce other countries to do the same. At the same time, they officially denied that it even existed—a policy sarcastically dubbed TINA, "There Is No Atlantica."

Soon, investors, entrepreneurs, adventurers, pirates, thugs, refugees, fugitives, and the desperately optimistic arrived in droves. Wretched squatter settlements sprang up alongside gleaming skyscrapers as the wealth of the land was exploited. In particular, the discovery of Atlanticore was rapidly changing a lot of things.

It didn't take long for an aristocratic caste to develop that presided over the island's affairs—the Executives. Despite the absence of formal laws, their will collectively steered the direction of the whole fledgling nation's evolution.

"Contrary to what it seems others have led you to believe," Singh intoned, "the individuals you know as the Executives and the organization you know as the Coven of Miracles have *always* had close connections. In any event, ever since the world took an interest in this curious clump of damp, overgrown rocks we now call our home."

Amahle squinted in puzzlement as the man's words drew her deeper and deeper into thought. Everyone knew, more or less, that Atlantica had been inhabited by a surprisingly advanced civilization eons ago. Gage had participated in one of the archaeological digs the Execs commissioned to uncover the island's ancient secrets.

Yet Atlantica as it existed today—the chaotic blueprint on which a civilization was painstakingly trying to build itself—was only a few years old. The city on the south-central coastal plain, the epicenter of Atlantican society, had been little more than a crazy idea a decade ago.

Why, then, Amahle wondered, did Singh speak as though he

were describing events that stretched back through multiple generations of history?

Although it had been late morning when they'd arrived, the time elapsed with astonishing speed. Noon passed and left the afternoon lingering behind it, and the sun began to sink through the opposite half of the sky, its light slowly gaining a bronze or orangish hue as it moved toward the western horizon.

There had been tension and opposition in the early days, Singh explained. The economic development consortium known as the Executives, who also harbored political aspirations, had goals that differed from the relatively esoteric priorities of the Coven. Things had become more complicated still when right from the start of the alliance, some members shared a dual allegiance to both groups.

"In such cases," he elaborated, "the other members of each organization remained in a state of complete ignorance about the individual's divided loyalties. Thus the line that separated Executive Board members from Coven members was often thin and hazy to the point of virtual nonexistence. *Even though* the two had an undeniable rivalry, with some of their more hidebound representatives refusing to compromise on the issues that separated them."

By this point, Amahle and Gage were both sitting in the chairs that Singh had first offered them, although they sat several paces back from the table to give themselves more maneuverability in case hostile forces should appear.

She was trying to digest the wealth of information that Singh was giving her fast enough to be ready for the next bombshell, but Amahle was growing mentally tired despite her fascination. The circumstances the man described both contradicted and confirmed Eleanor's suspicions, depending on the details.

"However," Singh declared, "the Execs and the Coven finally managed to establish a truce by the time that Atlantica's existence was formally announced to the world. The twelfth of September,

1962, about four years ago. Following that, the two groups had established a full entente by the eighth of January, 1963."

Gage raised a finger. "The First Atlantican Conference. I remember the day well."

"Yes," Singh confirmed. His demeanor grew more distant, more pensive. His gaze drifted to some point above and beyond the heads of his two guests. "Symbiosis would eventually lead to synthesis, but it would take a great deal of time for everything to work properly; for the whole plan to come to fruition. In the meantime, we needed to make sure there would be a strong hand to foster growth and protect the island against malign interests. Thus would we be able to see Atlantica thrive according to our designs."

Amahle fumed at the implications of being used as a tool by a group of wealthy individuals who thought they were playing God. She kept her mouth shut. Blurting out her immediate emotional reaction wouldn't solve anything.

Gage seemed more curious than outraged. "So," he surmised, "you created the order of Executioners as some sort of, ah, interim police force? A temporary measure to deal with the... What is the expression...'growing pains' of Atlantica?"

Once again, Singh gave a deep bow, but it was less theatrical this time. "Good, Doctor Gurung. You're beginning to apply *perspective* to this matter. I'm sure that if you could step outside your feelings toward your position and your partners, you would recognize a most important and illuminating fact. Every organization, every regime, and every social assembly is temporary."

Amahle had been relaxed, lulled into a near-trance by Singh's magnetic and yet soothing voice. Now she tensed as the killer within her reawakened.

"Some are more temporary than others," she stated.

Annoyingly but predictably, Singh took her veiled threat in stride, rolling his shoulders and giving her a placid smile. "Yes, but they're no less important for that fact. Instead, it depends upon the role they serve. The function they accomplish, and the fruits they bear."

The aging man regaled them with a description of how the Executives and the Coven had evolved during their mutual advancement and their ever-increasing dependence on one another. Over time, the goals of the two began to merge and blur. The Coven became more accustomed to working through the Execs' pragmatic outlets and using their substantial resources while the Execs became increasingly enamored with the Coven's grandiose machinations.

"As the synthesis has proceeded, there have been several, er, points of tension. Times when things didn't go as smoothly as they should have. You undoubtedly recall some of them. The archaeological dig at the buried temple that introduced you, Dr. Gurung, to Miss Barruk, for one. Dr. Limbu was not properly vetted for the position, and certain factors slipped out of control. We would've preferred for it to go differently."

Gage's face was solemn. He'd lost friends in that incident, had broken his ankle, and had wound up pulled away from his chosen vocation of archaeology toward the far tougher life of the Executioner.

Singh went on, "There was that unfortunate fracas about a year or so ago, when those fools at the lodge began hunting local villagers for sport, and you, Miss Nikoze, were among those who got to clean up the resulting mess. That, sadly, was another excellent example of certain Coven members letting pure exuberance function as a poor stand-in for wisdom."

Amahle thought back to the Ashcroft twins, Hugh and Tilda, and how they'd abducted Daria. The pair led herself and Tyler on a wild chase through the jungle before flattening entire stretches of forest with a bizarre, unstable, and dangerous weapon gifted them by the Coven. Furthermore, Amahle had been captured, beaten, and tortured by her former boss and mentor, the merciless Irish sniper known as She-Wolf.

In her view, describing the events as a "failure of wisdom" was an understatement. The one good thing that had come out of it was meeting Ty...and joining the Executioners.

As though he sensed them brooding over their memories, Singh insisted, "The goals we pursue are noble. This is something I must emphasize. If there have been problems with certain of the specifics, they do not impugn the broader whole. An organization of fallible people—mere humans!—will occasionally stumble. This is no reason to dismiss what we're ultimately trying to achieve."

Amahle had about enough of the man's pomposity. She understood that the Coven might've had some good intentions, but Singh behaved as though the lives lost during those "stumbles" were of minimal consequence.

"What is it you're trying to achieve?" she snapped, no longer trying to disguise her anger or impatience. "Global prosperity? A world united under wise and generous lords? A paradisiacal religion, brought about on a tide of pilfered miracles?"

Singh stared at her for a split second, then he threw his head back and laughed heartily, as though she'd told a good-natured joke with an especially amusing punchline. "Oh, Miss Nikoze, you truly are a warrior poet!" he guffawed.

When he noticed her icy stare, his laughter faded and he settled himself. However, he was still at ease, too much for her liking. "In all seriousness... Our goals are nothing quite so apocalyptic as that. That sort of thinking is something we senior members have tried to discourage. Such romantic and glamorous ideas remain, tragically, a common foundation for the more problematic actions of our wayward members."

Echoing Amahle's thoughts, Gage pointed out, "You still haven't said what the goal *is*, Mr. Singh."

The lanky man had picked up the third teacup—with Amahle and Gage declining his offer, he'd gradually been draining it all himself—and he nodded at the Gurkha before draining the last of the tea in a long, gulping draught.

"You are correct. I felt it was necessary to explain what we are *not* doing before revealing what we *are* aiming for because, again, it might seem...overly grandiose if someone were to misunderstand it."

Amahle cleared her throat. "I am waiting."

Singh set the teacup down. "We intend to direct the next step of human evolution."

The late afternoon was waning into the evening, with the light around them turning red. The crickets and night-birds would be out before long.

With a sharp, mocking laugh, Amahle inquired, "Is that all? That's it?"

Singh raised a palm once more. "Allow me to explain. All creatures on this planet are continuously evolving, even if only in the smallest of ways. Because changes to other organisms and the environments in which they dwell is part of this process, you could argue that we all affect the evolution of our species."

Although she lacked much formal education, Amahle understood the basic concept of evolution. Gage, who had not one but two doctorates, simply nodded.

"Our goal," Singh concluded, "is simply to use what we've found here to help guide the human species back onto the path it was heading down before the Calamity. The event that nearly consumed whatever ill-fated branch of humanity once lived upon this very island on which we now stand."

Amahle both did and did not understand. She grasped the essence of it. The Coven of Miracles felt that the ancient Atlanticans had been doing good work for humanity before whatever incident had wiped them out. Now the Coven wished to resume that work. Of course, Singh hadn't bothered to describe any of the specifics. So far.

This information had stimulated Gage's intellectual curiosity to its highest degree of agitation. He leaned forward and twitched in place, ready to explode with questions. Amahle wanted to know because it was relevant to why Executive Security had tried to kill them earlier that week. Gage wanted to know for the sake of knowing.

Then, behind them from somewhere in the house, men shouted in shock and anger for about a second before the thunder of gunfire drowned out their voices.

Amahle sprang to her feet. She would never have admitted it, but the attack caught her by surprise. Despite her well-cultivated instincts and finely honed perceptual senses, she'd noticed nothing at all suggesting that shooters were about to storm the mansion.

It had to be a setup. Her lips drew back from her teeth, and her right index finger curled around the trigger of her Winchester. Everything seemed to happen in slow motion as she pointed the muzzle at Jori Singh.

Singh had stood as well. His brow creased in concern, but even with death closing in, he showed no sign of real fear.

Amahle never got the chance to shoot him, nor did he have an opportunity to plead for her to do otherwise. The glass windows beyond the pool patio shattered as a flurry of bullets crashed through them. At least five, maybe six of them ripped into Singh's chest, drawing spurts of blood from his lean frame, which trickled down his fine robe.

His eyes bulged in alarm for the first time. He staggered sideways from the table, knocking over the brazier and scattering the burning coals within it across the pavement. Something fell out of his sleeve. His right sleeve, near the hand he'd used to grasp the boiling tea kettle. Then he keeled over, landing in the clear water of the pool with a loud *splash*.

"No!" Amahle cried. She spun and opened fire on the house. She could see only vague dark shapes moving within it. The electric lighting was off, and the sun had dwindled to insignificance.

She fired three shots, her hand working the bolt with the speed of a lifetime's practice but lamenting her choice of a weapon that only held five rounds. For sniper duties, it was sufficient, but in close combat against enemies armed with submachine guns or assault rifles...

More gunshots were coming from the jungle across the water. Their assailants had caught them in a crossfire.

Gage had dropped to his knees beside the pool. For the first time in decades, he was in total shock, consumed with abject horror as though his mind refused to accept what had happened. The bullets streaking around him hadn't yet registered in his consciousness. He stared at Jori Singh.

The man was dead. There was no doubt about it; floating in a cloud of red water, his torso had been thoroughly perforated by a good half a dozen rounds, and his eyes stared vacant and glassy at the darkening sky. Then he began to sink.

Six bullets had destroyed a vast store of vital information. Singh knew things that might have benefited them all, but now, no one else would ever learn. Gage wondered, amid his hollow nausea, if this was how the scholars of Alexandria must have felt when the Great Library was burned.

Gage's head snapped to the side, toward the small object that had fallen from Singh's sleeve. It looked like a thin bracelet that might fit snugly over the forearm of an average adult man. He reached toward it.

A bullet struck the paving stone mere inches away from the object, skipping off and scarcely missing Gage's arm. He felt the air whistle over it.

His stupor cracked apart and fell away from him. He was back in the moment, fully aware of what was going on—a battle that he and Amahle might lose at any second. He raised his rifle, steeled himself for combat and death, and fired.

CHAPTER FOURTEEN

"Get down!" Gage barked. Now that his mind was truly in the fight, he quickly grasped what had happened. Attackers had fired on them from the house with automatic weapons. Amahle was trying to shoot back but with a weapon poorly suited to the task.

She fell into a prone position as he raised his AR-10 toward the approximate point where most of the bullets had come from, switching to full auto. Opening his mouth to bellow as he fired, he squeezed the trigger and swept the rising muzzle all over the hole in the glass before him. The rifle *cracked*, spitting flames along with 7.62 rounds and shattering more of the glass. It was too dark to see much of anything inside, but it looked like his volley tore up some of the furniture as well.

He wasn't sure if he'd hit anyone. People deeper within the house, and perhaps around it outdoors on the other side, were still shooting at each other.

Amahle looked up at him and waved behind them. "More are in the trees!" she cried. She aimed and fired a single shot. Someone within the building cursed and ducked out of sight, but she didn't know if she'd hit him or simply scared him off.

More gunfire, mostly single shots, was coming through the foliage toward the house—and them.

Gage had fired about half of his magazine through the broken window. He pivoted one hundred and eighty degrees and blasted the rest into the jungle, waving the rifle around to hose the tree line with bullets.

Right now, killing their adversaries would be little more than a bonus. The true priority was simply putting the intruders on the defensive so the two of them could get to safety. They were in a compromised position.

Gage called, "We must get out of here." The gunfire from the woods had ceased for the moment, so he ejected the empty magazine from his rifle, squatted, then began crawling toward the house as he reloaded. It was an awkward posture to take, but it allowed him to make himself a smaller target without compromising his speed too much.

Amahle did likewise. She fired the last round in her rifle into the jungle and dashed behind Gage, making for the mansion's southwestern corner. It was the only object nearby that might offer them acceptable cover. Otherwise, there was only the patio furniture that Singh had arranged around the pool, which wouldn't stand up to any bullet larger than mouse-caliber. Their armor could stop intermediate rifle rounds, but only a few of them. It wasn't wholly invincible.

Worse, the whole hillside was nearly dark. The brazier had been the sole source of reliable illumination, but Singh had knocked it over when he died, and the coals had nearly burned out.

Bullets streaked past them and blasted up chunks of stone, earth, and metal as they sprayed around the patio, seeming to come from all directions. Gage estimated that at least some of Singh's bodyguards had survived the initial strike and were now grouping to fight back since shots rang out in tandem from different parts of the house.

Gage and Amahle reached the corner and jumped to their feet, swinging themselves around it and hoping that the stone, wood, and plaster of two walls would be enough to protect them.

Amahle fished in her pouch for cartridges, loading the rifle back to capacity. She also had her pocket revolver, but it wasn't ideal against armored foes unless she had a nice clear shot at an unprotected body zone.

"Get to the window," she said through gritted teeth. "We need to find out who is fighting who. Whether to join them or flee."

Gage nodded. He kept his rifle aimed at the sky and side-stepped along the wall toward the long glass portal nearest to them, but there wasn't much hope of being able to see well. They'd been on the west side of the house previously, where the sunset's afterglow offered at least a modicum of light, and yet even from that way the interior had been nothing but an indistinct blur of dark shapes.

The gunshots kept coming from within.

Gage hopped in front of the window, his rifle at chest level. Surprisingly, a candle burned on a table not far from the glass, offering a bit of illumination. Muzzle flares sporadically lit things up enough to make out the generalities of what lay before him. Amahle came up at his side right as his brain finished processing the information.

A cluster of men had taken up positions near the room's southwest corner, close to where Gage and Amahle stood. By the candle's light, they appeared to be wearing dark suits, which meant they were probably Singh's security detail. More figures were gradually advancing from the house's eastern main entrance area, blasting their way through, moving under continuous barrages of covering fire.

Further complicating the situation, it looked like the shooters out in the jungle were on the same side as Singh's men since some of the attacking force were turning to fire at *them*.

"I wonder," Gage grunted, "if these people are on our side or if the enemy of our enemy is *not* our friend."

Amahle was about to offer her two cents when one of the suits collapsed, groaning, and some of his blood spattered on the window. He knocked over the candle, which instantly caught one of the curtains alight. Then another stray bullet destroyed the window itself. Gage and Amahle jumped back from the shattering glass and ducked beneath the line of fire.

When they peeked up again, the rising flames near the window frame had cast enough light on the proceedings that the attacking group was visible for the first time.

Amahle and Gage both froze, gawking in stupefaction. Both had been all over the world, fought in many conflicts, and had been to isolated villages in war zones as well as the most decadent parts of massive cities. They'd interacted with all sorts of people.

Neither had ever seen anything quite like *this*. The bizarreness of the spectacle stunned them into momentary inaction.

The men duking it out with Singh's remaining bodyguards mostly carried weapons they'd probably stolen from Executive Security—AR-10 rifles and one or two prototype submachine guns from Germany. Some also toted the shotguns or World War II surplus firearms that acted as the standard armaments for less-well-funded combatants across the island.

What was truly strange, though, was the way they'd *decorated* their weapons. Christian iconography was everywhere. They'd wrapped rosaries or crucifixes around nonessential parts where they couldn't get in the way and painted crosses and angel wings onto stocks or the sides of magazines. Tear pendants and images of saints, or the Ichthys—the well-known fish symbol—adorned receivers and foregrips.

Contrasting with this show of deadly piety was the armor the men wore. Again, they'd apparently looted bulletproof vests and helmets from the Execs' personnel, combining them with other protective gear they'd either acquired from the black market or custom-made in someone's garage.

Their armor was adorned with traditional symbols of evil, the diametric opposite of what they'd put on their weapons. Demonic regalia splashed with red paint, horns, and fangs added to headgear, flaming weapons, skulls, bones, and all the usual morbid imagery of monstrousness, death, and the netherworld of the damned.

Amahle wasn't sure whether to burst out laughing or reel back in horror. Gage was mostly dumbstruck by the sheer weirdness of it.

"They must be the ones who hanged the Junior Executives!" Gage blurted, the insight exploding in his mind in a burst of brilliant clarity. "Remember the signs? Condemnations in Latin of magic and tyranny?"

Amahle remembered. She highly doubted that Gage was wrong.

Faintly, between the rising flames and the flashes of gunfire, they saw dark shapes emerging from the jungle through the window on the other side of the room, trying to flank the strangely garbed attackers and box them in. If they succeeded, it might well turn the tide of battle in their favor.

Amahle thought fast. "We know for sure that the Executives tried to have us killed. I say we help these people. We can find out who they are and what they want later." She had to speak fast and often pause since the gunshots kept flaring up again and drowning out human voices.

Gage squinted for a second. "Yes, very well. I will move into the house from here. You go after the ones in the forest. We will meet back at the truck."

"Roger." Amahle dashed off along the wall, ducking beneath the windows. She intended to ambush the men coming from the jungle, as well as any others who might have lingered amid the shadowy foliage.

Meanwhile, Gage stared at the window next to him. It was relatively low to the ground, but he was a short man and not as young as he used to be. Frowning and grumbling, he twirled his rifle around in his hands and used the butt to smash down and brush away the rest of the jagged shards of glass clinging to the edge.

Then he sucked in his breath and vaulted over, letting out a shrill Gurkha war cry. He knew full well that he would be in danger of death the instant his feet touched the floor.

He landed about two feet from the blazing curtain, which was hotter than he would've expected. The flames must have spread to the wall itself and perhaps parts of the floor and adjacent furniture. Ahead of him was the Executive Security team. They wore suits and dark glasses instead of full armor, but Gage suspected they still had soft armor vests under their shirts. That type of protection was only proof against pistol rounds and perhaps buckshot or birdshot. It couldn't stand up to heavy rifle fire.

"Hey!" one of the men exclaimed, pivoting toward the Nepali. He had a Browning Hi-Power in hand, and he fired it three times at Gage before it *clicked*.

Gage ducked his head and took the shots against his chest. They *thunked* against his armor. Then he opened fire, now on semiauto, squeezing off four shots.

At least two of the bullets found their mark in the man who'd shot at him, and he collapsed, howling and gurgling. His body fell against one of his comrades right next to him, a tall, heavyset, balding man who jumped in the air in shock. The others didn't seem to grasp that Gage had entered the fight. They remained focused on the bizarrely adorned group moving toward them from the hall.

Gage noted with dismay that there were three men still standing. Singh had brought a total of four guys with him. There must have been at least one or two others waiting at the house before

Singh's motorcade arrived. The invaders had certainly killed one or two already.

One of the strange men, near the front of the attacking cluster, pointed an AR-10 at the Nepali but hesitated, sensing that he wasn't one of the Executives' goons. Gage glanced at him in the half-second he had before combat resumed.

The hesitant man had a flaming skull painted across his helmet, faintly terrifying in the flickering firelight that ate away at the gloom, and a burning pitchfork stenciled onto his chest plate. His rifle had crosses carved into the butt and rosary beads dangling from the sling mount. Something in his bearing made Gage think he was either their overall commanding officer or at least a sergeant.

Then the security thug who'd had the dead man fall into him tackled Gage, knocking his rifle up and back and driving his knee against the small man's gut. Gage's armor prevented him from having the wind knocked out of him, but the force of the blow still drove him back two steps and threatened to throw him off-balance.

The tall bodyguard twisted the rifle, and Gage could barely keep hold of it. Rather than try to wrestle such a large man for control of the gun, Gage did something different. He swept his left hand behind his back, drew one of his kukris, and hacked it down at the man's knee.

The big guy yelped in alarm as his leg folded beneath him, blood gushing down his shin and calf, and his forward momentum destroyed. By the time he realized what had happened, Gage was already lifting the blade again and sweeping it into the side of the man's head. It split open his temple, and he fell over to the side, never to move again.

Right behind him was another of the goons. The last of them was engaged in returning fire with a submachine gun on the demon-garbed intruders. They, in turn, focused less on the men in the house and more on the other group of foes outside.

Gunshots crackled everywhere. No place in sight was quiet or peaceful.

Gage snatched up his rifle from the dying guard in front of him, but the next man already had a bead on him. He was wielding what looked like a long-barreled revolver, possibly a .44 Magnum, which might hit hard enough to knock Gage on his back or break his ribs even if it failed to penetrate his plated vest.

He pivoted, swirling in a circle directly toward the patch of flames. The goon fired, and the shot was deafening enough that it *had* to be a Magnum round of some sort. Gage felt no impact, only heat. He'd trodden directly into the blaze, and his right pant leg was on fire.

He sprang out to the side, aiming his rifle and blasting away. Five shots rang out. The guy with the Magnum took one in the hip and one in the face. He made a gasping, spitting sound and fell straight back as though Gage had clotheslined him instead.

That left one. The last of the Executives' henchmen within the house froze in brief panic, caught between adversaries on two sides. Then one of the weirdly dressed intruders emptied an entire magazine of a nine-millimeter submachine gun into him. He reeled and shook under the barrage. His vest caught some of the bullets, but others cut into his head and neck. He toppled over, bleeding and twitching.

Gage stood and looked at the victorious band, still puzzled by all the religious iconography. He had his rifle in one hand and his kukri in the other.

The men aimed their guns at him, seeming ready to fire but not in a hurry to do so. Before Gage could try to negotiate with them, the figure with the pitchfork on his chest pointed at the blade in the Gurkha's grasp. Then everyone lowered their weapons.

"Huh," Gage said.

CHAPTER FIFTEEN

Outside, Amahle had reached the mansion's southeast corner. Judging by the sounds, she estimated two men, maybe three, had emerged from the jungle to flank the invaders and assault them through the front door. She was dimly aware that other sharp-shooters remained hidden in the forest beyond, but there was no way to determine how many there were.

She grimaced fiercely, her teeth bared. This type of combat wasn't her forte. She'd survived such engagements before, but she preferred to avoid them—everything, in her usual view, revolved around getting the drop on the enemy from a distance and confronting them through the business end of a scope. It was usually harder for them to shoot back that way, just as she liked it.

Right now, she didn't have much choice.

Mumbling a few colorful curses she'd picked up from an old drunk in her village back in South Africa long ago, she drew her small revolver. She held it loosely in her left hand, using her left wrist to brace the rifle's barrel while her right hand would work the trigger and hold the stock against her shoulder. Then she swiveled around the corner.

She was right. Two of the Execs' thugs were there, dressed in black combat fatigues and full plate armor. It was difficult to make out the details in the twilight gloom, but she could be sure of that much.

She fired once. The .308 projectile sailed from the Winchester's barrel and found its mark in the man's side, penetrating neatly between the front and back plates of his vest. He was facing the door and hadn't seen her. He let out a ragged gasp as the bullet slammed into and through him, stumbled sideways, and rolled down a gentle slope toward the road.

As soon as she fired, Amahle dropped her rifle and raised the pistol in her left hand. The other security officer seemed to be a woman and was spinning toward her with an AR-10. She was fast, but not fast enough.

Amahle squeezed off two shots at the dark blob that represented her head. Aside from a vague shudder, and the fact that the woman didn't fire her gun, there was no immediate visual feedback. Then the head appeared to tilt back, squirting a jetty of blood into a patch of air faintly illuminated by the stars, and the woman slumped over.

No one else rushed to investigate. Amahle exhaled sharply and stooped to pick up her rifle. She worked the bolt to eject the spent casing and chamber the next round, and slipped the revolver back into its holster. Then she charged toward the final corner, intent on looping back toward the west side of the house where she could clear the jungle of its newest inhabitants.

She stopped at the edge of the wall, peeking around it briefly and retracting her head. The shooters in the bush might have turned their scopes toward her position after hearing the gunfire. However, there was enough shooting still going on within the house that they might not have been able to discern the location of individual engagements.

Seconds passed, and no one shot at her. She lowered herself to a prone position and crawled away from the building, sticking to low-lying areas and keeping behind patio furniture or anything else that might give her the slightest cover. She also kept to darker places. Her silhouette would stand out too much against the pale stone of the pool patio.

When she was about ten yards from the forest's edge, two rifles within it fired.

She froze. The snipers might have been using suppressors since she saw no muzzle flare and the reports seemed quieter than they would otherwise. It was possible they were using .22LR rifles, but given the low power of that round, it seemed unlikely.

Despite the absence of visual feedback, she focused on the sounds, the vibrations, the angles at which the leaves rustled...all the things she could *feel*, based on pure experience and instinct, without being able to explain to the average person how it was possible.

Unless she was mistaken, the first of the two was crouching behind a tree whose trunk she could barely make out, perhaps seven meters ahead. The second was about three meters to his side and another three meters back.

Now that her eyes were adjusting to the darkness and the glow from the fire at the southwest corner cast a faint orange illumination over the hill, she could just barely see the outlines of the first shooter's head.

Amahle drew in a deep breath, raised her rifle, and breathed out, emptying her lungs and leaving them empty as she aimed down the sights. Even with her advanced skill, keeping the gun perfectly steady was impossible, but she could get close. Otherwise, it was a matter of selecting the perfect moment—the perfect *instant*.

Both snipers fired again. When the closer of the two worked the bolt on his rifle, he made the last mistake of his life. He leaned his head forward by an inch or two.

Amahle squeezed the trigger. The top part of the silhouette's head simply ceased to exist, leaving a crater behind. Then the shape sank into the general mass of shadows.

As she'd expected, something rustled as the other sniper swung his gun toward her position. She was already rolling aside, putting another fat tree between herself and her adversary's approximate location.

He fired two shots at her in fairly quick succession. One struck the ground half an arm's length from her foot. The other smashed into the tree, but the dense wood stopped the bullet. Amahle didn't react in any way.

If this were a traditional, isolated marksman's duel that took place outside any other context, both she and her foe might have dragged it out for an hour, three hours, or an entire day. Each would gradually seek to outmaneuver the other as they crept through the wilderness. With the battle still raging in the house, they lacked the luxury of time.

Amahle climbed around the far side of the trunk and slipped between two saplings in a creeping squat before standing to step over a patch of ferns without making a sound. Then she narrowly avoided some vines that dangled from tree limbs above her. She knew roughly where the shooter was, but he was probably too professional to fall for an easy trick like jumping into sight after she fired a probing shot.

She would have to wait for the opportunity to finish the whole game with only one more bullet.

Unfortunately, it seemed that he didn't extend the same respect to her. His gun barked once, kicking up dirt and moss a few feet to her right.

Then foliage shuddered, and dead leaves *crunched* as the man ran away, in the opposite direction from her, leaving her alone in the night-swathed jungle. He must have intuited that the battle wasn't going well for his side. She wondered how his superiors would feel about his decision to cut his losses.

Amahle stopped, unmoving and making no sounds. Part of

her wanted to chase the bastard down, but it would be extremely dangerous. She didn't know if he had other comrades waiting in ambush deeper in the bush. Plus, she wanted to know what was happening back at the house, despite Gage's suggestion that they meet back at the disguised Autocutioner.

She crept forward, sliding under a low branch and through some weeds to emerge onto the front lawn area of Singh's estate. Part of the mansion was still burning. The red glow was rising into the sky, but it would take a little while before it consumed the whole building.

Otherwise, though, everything was quiet. The fighting within the house had ended.

Amahle crouched in place, holding her rifle at low ready, and waiting. Figures emerged out the front door and fanned out into a loose semicircle—the men with the demonic armor and angelic weapons. They'd been the victors.

Another shape joined them, squatter than they, but no less fearsome. A broad, distinctively curved blade hung from the last man's hand.

One of the taller men took off his helmet, signaling the others to do likewise. Then the first of them asked, "Is that authentic? You're the real deal?" The voice was youthful and earnest, not at all what Amahle had expected.

Gage's voice responded, "Yes."

Puzzled, Amahle crept forward, crawling closer on her belly until she could get a better look and ensured she could hear the whole conversation.

The mysterious posse were all young men, with the oldest perhaps thirty at most. The one who'd taken off his helmet first and posed the question to Gage was dark-skinned and had an almost boyish look and demeanor. Amahle guessed from the accent that he was American and most likely southern. If he was older than twenty-four, she would eat her shoe.

The conversation proceeded in friendly tones. The young

leader of the strange men was excited and impressed as Gage regaled him with tales of his training as a Gurkha and how his teachers required him to pass rigorous tests and drills with a wooden kukri before he received a real blade.

Amahle shook her head as she crawled through the grass. Even next to a burning building filled with corpses, boys would rarely miss an opportunity to talk about their toys.

Once she was around the front corner near the pool and out of sight—and therefore less likely to startle them—Amahle called, "Gage, are you there? There are no more shooters in the woods."

The chatter among the men stopped and there came the distinctive rustling of soldiers readying their weapons. Gage told them to please relax.

"Yes," he shouted. "All is well, for now."

Sighing, she stepped around the corner and saw the group close-up for the first time. Their youthful, almost cheery faces were out of place next to the human and material wreckage and made their melodramatic outfits seem all the weirder.

Gage smiled at her, then gestured at the tall young black man. "Amahle. This is Augustine Freeman, but he tells me that we may call him 'Gus.' He's the commander of the Hellbreakers. They are most happy to make our acquaintance."

CHAPTER SIXTEEN

Gage laughed. It allowed him to run his hands over his waist and belly area so he could quickly pat himself down and be sure the bracelet was still there. He'd snatched it up from beside the pool after Singh had been blown away and stuffed it under the waistband of his pants.

In all the excitement since then, he'd all but forgotten about it. The Hellbreakers, as if they weren't odd enough to begin with, seemed friendly. Yet Gage still had only the vaguest idea of who they were or what they wanted.

There was no reason for them to know he had a piece of Coven technology on his person. Particularly since it was all but certain that their guns had been the ones that sent Singh shuffling off the mortal coil.

"Ha." Gus chuckled, beaming in his gregarious way. "You were looking for us, weren't you? We figured you would be. You're the ones who do the 'investigations' here, after all, when *they* tell you to. Of course, they'd tell you to look into the deaths of three of their own..."

A slim white man with short blond hair next to him chimed in. "Well, you found us. We're guilty as charged. We're the ones who've been bleedin' the beast." His accent was blatantly Australian.

Gage nodded as though the statement made perfect sense. He could roughly guess what they meant.

Beside him, Amahle was also attempting to adopt a neutral and pleasant expression while she followed the conversation. Her nervous tension was obvious to him, though. Few people on the planet were better sharpshooters, but Amahle's people skills were somewhat behind the curve.

Gage responded to the blond man with, "Well, things have changed. For the time being, it would seem there's no reason for us to be enemies. I'm glad that we were able to work together this evening. What comes next?"

Gus blinked. His grin dampened a tad, as though the question annoyed him, but he was doing his best to hide it. "We can figure that out soon. Is it true about the kukri needing to shed blood before you can sheathe it? Lucky we found you after you'd already taken care of that part. Ha, ha."

"Indeed," Gage responded, as though they were discussing a football or cricket broadcast that both had tuned in to.

Augustus Freeman thumped his chest. "We pride ourselves on knowing about things like that. And a lot of other things. You might say we're experts."

Cutting off further talk along those lines, the blond Australian said, "More Exec Security teams will be closin' in soon. They almost always have some of their mates on backup. So we need to get goin'."

Amahle spoke for the first time since the end of the battle. "One of their snipers got away. He was too deep in the jungle for me to see him in this darkness, and I thought it would be better to come back than to chase him. He will certainly tell the others what happened."

With a ragged sigh, Gus agreed to cut short his friendly chat with the Gurkha. "Fine, yeah. Nic here is all business, isn't he?

He's right, though." His face took on a hard-set look, and the muscles of his jaw rippled. "First, I want to make sure that Jori Singh is dead."

Gage held up a hand. "He is. I saw him shot many times, and his body sank into the pool."

"Okay," Gus conceded. "Let's have a look-see, anyway."

The group rounded the corner, ignoring the growing blaze in the house. It was spreading slowly enough that Gage wondered if the builders had used fire-retardant materials. Furthermore, the landscaping immediately surrounding the structure included very little that was flammable, so it was unlikely that they would have a forest fire on their hands.

Gage noted the way the men moved, their swift, self-assured motions, as well as how they fell into a rough skirmish line without having to be asked or ordered. They had military or paramilitary training. And they'd worked, trained, and fought together before.

Then he looked at the pool. Blood still stained the paving stones and clouded the water. The pool itself was empty.

"What?" Gus exclaimed. "Dammit." He clenched his right fist.

Gage was as shocked as he was, and a glance at Amahle confirmed the same. She'd been right next to him when the shooting had started and had seen the older man topple into the water after taking about half a dozen slugs through the torso.

Nic, the Australian, lamented, "Aye, that's a shame. We were all hopin' to confirm the kill."

"Yes." Gus shook his head. He puffed himself up and turned to Gage and Amahle, his face softening once again as his smile returned. "At least we can confirm something else. The whispered rumors are true. The Executioners have turned against the beast."

Amahle gave a slow, vague nod. She probably wondered how much the Hellbreakers knew about the raid on their headquarters.

Gage gestured at the pool. "Do you think some of the Coven's people took the body away when we weren't looking? We went around to the southern and eastern sides of the house when the fighting began. One of them could've dragged Singh out while we weren't present."

There was no immediate response from the young commander. He looked distant and troubled, as though unsure what to say. "It could be that." His tone suggested that he doubted it.

Gage wanted to press him for an explanation, but he didn't get the chance. Gus raised a hand and made a few military hand signals combined with tersely barked orders. Without further words, he and his men turned and jogged away from the pool and toward the road, still moving in a loose infantry recon formation.

Amahle and Gage hung toward the back of the group, and Gus himself stayed rear and center. As the two Executioners trotted behind him, he turned his head their way.

"You should come with us. Safety in numbers and all that jazz. We'd be honored to have you as guests."

Amahle looked at Gage immediately, and he met her gaze before turning his gaze back to Freeman.

"We appreciate your offer, Commander, but we have a vehicle stashed in the bush nearby. We do not wish to leave it. It would be better if we retrieve it and perhaps follow you?"

Amahle nodded vigorously, making sure that Gus saw her.

He looked ahead again while his feet moved across the gravel. They were almost to the bottom of the hill near the privacy wall. Beyond it lay the juncture of road and driveway. "If it's okay with you, let me come with you, instead. That way I can fill you in on what's going on. I bet there's a lot of stuff you'd both like to know, isn't there?"

Amahle gave a soft but half-snorting laugh. "You would win money on your bet, Mr. Freeman. Will your men be all right with this?"

They reached the base of the hill. The gate in the wall had been cut from its hinges, presumably by the Hellbreakers. Everyone stopped there, with half of the men ducking through the gateway to secure the other side while the remaining half waited.

Gus called a halt. "I'll go with the Executioners to brief them and negotiate the next phase of the operation. You're all under the command of Sergeant London until further notice."

He turned to the Australian. "Nic, proceed with the plan. I'll catch up later. Don't worry about me."

Nic saluted him. "If you say so. Boys, off we go." He and the rest of them inside the gate filtered through and vanished into the night.

Gage pointed off to their left. "Our vehicle is hidden this way. It's not far off the road but would be difficult to see from there. Now that we don't need to sneak up on the house, we can perhaps move more quickly and take a more direct route than the one we used first."

Gus had no objections. "Sounds good. We'll need to keep an eye out for any auxiliaries the beast might have sent."

"Of course," Amahle retorted. She allowed herself a small smirk. "Try to keep up." Then she plunged into the jungle with Gage close on her heels.

To the surprise of both, Gus *did* keep up, for the most part. Despite his full armor, the battle rifle slung on his shoulder, and various pouches filled with other gear, he moved through the dense undergrowth and between tightly-grown trees as smoothly as if he wore nothing but a leotard.

Since he didn't know where they were going, exactly, he was always a couple of paces behind. Both Amahle and Gage sensed that this was because he was letting them set the pace and take the lead. Not because he *couldn't* have pulled ahead of them if he'd wanted to.

As such, they had to conclude that he was in excellent physical condition, for one. He looked trim and muscular, and he was in the prime years of youth anyway. Still, there was more.

Augustus Freeman possessed a well-developed instinct for trekking across this type of terrain on foot at speed. He anticipated changes in the lay of the land based on the angle of the shadows or the way the foliage and weed cover grew and adjusted his movements accordingly. The constant presence of branches, leaves, vines, and roots didn't perturb him or slow him down.

He'd trained for land like this. Or, perhaps, he'd already fought in it.

The young man also kept talking whenever he felt he could get away with it. The boyish enthusiasm they'd glimpsed in front of the burning estate never seemed to dull or abate. Amahle wanted to snap at him to shut up. He spoke in a low voice, but all their stealth would be pointless if any of their enemies were close enough to follow the sounds of his endless chatter.

"That's a good knife you got," he commented, directing his words at Amahle. "I had one like that a couple of years ago. Good balance between slashing and thrusting, but you have to find the right level of sharpness for the edge yourself. Depending on if you're only using it for killing, or if you're gonna use it for regular old work."

The way he spoke suggested an over-earnest teenage boy for whom weapons, like model trains or bicycles, were a beloved hobby. Yet, there was an edge to his words. Combined with his evident combat background, Amahle got the impression that he had used his knife for killing before.

"Also," Gus went on, "I bet you're wondering who we are, where we came from, and how we all ended up fighting together. Am I right?"

Amahle replied, "Once again, Mr. Freeman, you would not lose money on your wager. I fear that we *will* lose the element of stealth, however, if you keep talking so much before we're back at the truck."

Gus only laughed. "Fine, fine. As soon as we get there, I'll tell you the rest."

Perhaps another minute passed before the terrain dipped and they spotted a clearing up ahead. Beyond the trees and other plant life, they also saw what looked like a two-lane road, roughly paved. Squatting amid the clearing was a big, dark, blocky mass.

"Hey," Gus quipped, "we did notice that thing coming up, but we saw it was abandoned and left it. Had other things to focus on; couldn't do a thorough search of every random wreck we came across."

Gage chortled. "We shall have to do a better job of hiding it next time. We were also in a hurry and had our priorities."

"Shh," Amahle urged them. If the Coven's minions were planning an ambush, then somewhere near the Autocutioner would be an excellent place to do it. The men fell silent, with Gus sensing her thoughts and adjusting his demeanor—suddenly he was all business.

They worked in tandem to secure the truck's perimeter. Amahle crept around to the left, seeking the highest ground to mount her rifle and wait on overwatch. So far she saw nothing of concern.

At the same time, Gage and Gus descended through the brush toward the clearing, positioned so they could cut off any foes who popped up but still close enough to aid one another and out of Amahle's immediate line of fire. It all happened smoothly, as though Gus had executed similar maneuvers many times before.

Nothing. If indeed more armed men were coming after them, they hadn't yet arrived. Or they were somewhere else. Despite barely knowing them, Amahle hoped the other Hellbreakers would get away safely.

She climbed down the slope and rejoined the men, exhaling

with faint relief. "All right. Once we're safely in the truck, Mr. Freeman, you may tell us your story."

A minute later, the disguised Autocutioner was rattling down the mountain road, with Gage behind the wheel and Amahle in the passenger's seat, her rifle leaning against her side in case she needed it. Gus crouched between them, obviously elated to speak freely and at length again.

"So, as you might've guessed, we're soldiers. A fresh batch from Indochina. Or Vietnam, which is what they're calling the part we served in these days."

Gage squinted. "The American military is sending troops to Atlantica? That is most disturbing, given the treaties and international agreements that—"

"No, no," Gus interrupted. "Nothing like that. We went AWOL. We're not technically *supposed* to be here." He laughed as though desertion wasn't a big deal. "We didn't much like the work they gave us in Southeast Asia. Us Americans felt the same as the Australians. We saw a better offer, and we jumped at it. At least, it *seemed* better at the time."

Amahle listened without speaking, focusing intently on the man's words as well as some of his unspoken implications. She could guess some of what he was about to say.

Adjusting his somewhat uncomfortable position, Gus continued, "The people who run this island needed more security forces. The Executives, or the group that calls itself the Coven of Miracles... It's getting harder and harder to tell the two apart. Barely even matters.

"They've been doing a massive, drastic expansion of their hired guns because of 'growing need,' as they put it. Love when the bureaucrat types word things like that, never saying exactly what they mean. Anyway, the pay looked good, and the work didn't sound *too* bad—not compared to Vietnam, anyway—so we caught a boat and joined up."

Amahle's nostrils flared. "I take it you didn't work for them as long as you planned to."

Gus chuckled again. "Yeah, this time *you'd* be the one who wouldn't lose money on a bet." Then his mood darkened abruptly, the way it had back at the mansion when he'd demanded to see Singh's body.

"Well, things got dark and ugly pretty quick. I started having, uh, reservations. It didn't take long to notice that some of my other recruits, mostly guys I served with in Asia, weren't okay with it either. I'm talking about the *unnatural* shit, which we were supposed to protect like it was no big deal. Or the...excesses they wanted us to take part in, or look the other way from."

Amahle was morbidly curious about the details of what he meant by that, but another part of her was perfectly confident that she was better off not knowing.

Gus concluded, "We didn't come to this island to sign up for more of the same. We wanted to get away from doing nasty stuff. Evil stuff that shouldn't happen even in a war. So we quit. We turned against the beast. The way we see it, anyone who supports them and their ways is the enemy."

Clearly, *the beast* was the Hellbreakers' collective term or nickname for the Coven, the Executives, or both.

"I see," was all Amahle could think of to say. She had dozens of questions but wasn't yet sure how to go about asking them.

Gage changed the subject. "Well, Commander Freeman—forgive me, but you haven't told me your official rank—I'm impressed that you are the leader of this band of fighters, despite being so young."

Once more, Gus instantly switched back to being jovial. "Yeah. I have some experience with this stuff. Discouraging enemy activity. Making sure people know not to join the bad guys. You ever heard of something called the Phoenix Program? Probably not, since it's *supposed* to be secret and you've been busy here on Atlantica the last couple of years."

Amahle said, "I have heard of it. Something the American CIA was doing to pacify the country." She knew full well what *pacification* usually meant in such situations.

Gus waved that away, not wanting to talk about it. "Could you stop the vehicle here, please? I'll need to rejoin my men in a minute or two."

Although mildly puzzled, Gage braked and stopped. They were on a stretch of the ridge that had an open view of the ravines on both sides, but the slope was gentler to the south, rolling away into a forested valley.

Once they were at a halt, Gus stood, placing one hand on each of the two seats, and looked back and forth between the pair as he spoke to them. "I'm going to make you guys an offer. We should work together—the Hellbreakers and the Executioners, together against the beast. We have no agenda beyond stopping it. Them. We're doing this for the *right* reasons. Because of that, we're going to succeed by any means necessary."

Gage raised an eyebrow. "Oh?"

Gus smiled and added, "Once the beast is dead, I might just retire from fighting and become a farmer. Or maybe a butcher, ha, ha. Yeah, that seems my speed."

The Executioners shot glances at one another before Gage spoke for them both. "We will take it under consideration. Your proposal is most intriguing. I am sure you can appreciate that we wish to discuss it with our other partners first."

"No problem," Gus conceded. "There's a special radio frequency we use. It's open, and someone will be listening, every day at sunrise and sunset." He borrowed a pen from one of the compartments in the truck, wrote it down on a piece of scrap paper, and handed it to Amahle. "If you're ready to start working together toward the common cause... Call us."

Then he opened the door and jumped out, hit the ground running, and slipped into the jungle like a vanishing ghost.

CHAPTER SEVENTEEN

Gus had been gone for a couple of minutes, and Amahle and Gage had been riding in silence when they heard something in the distance, growing louder and closer until its deepening roar pushed even the truck's rattling into the background of consciousness.

Amahle was first to suggest the obvious. "I think that's a helicopter. It's moving too slowly to be a plane."

Gage bobbed his head. "Someone must have noticed the fire at Mr. Singh's house. Or the reinforcements must have arrived by now. Here, let us take a look."

He deviated from the straightforward course he'd been driving to take a side path, little more than a rutted dirt track, but which led up a hill toward a ridged peak. The Autocutioner rattled as it climbed the steep incline, but it got the job done. When they reached the top, Gage shifted into park.

"There are binoculars in the glove compartment," he pointed out. "Your eyesight is better than mine. Let us look."

Amahle retrieved the binoculars and hopped out of the vehicle. The ridge was narrow but flat, and only a handful of trees encircled its edges. The rest all grew down at lower elevations.

She had a clear view of an entire region of the lower hill country, with crags, rolling inclines, and valleys spreading out around her for miles in every direction. Since it was nighttime, she couldn't make out many details or fully appreciate the vista's scale.

One particular area stood out, though—the hill where Singh had built his vacation home. Bright orange flared from the peak like the flame atop a candle, and it spread a reddish glow into the surrounding sky along with plumes of gray-black smoke.

There were two helicopters not far apart and both flying right toward the burning estate.

Gage pointed at them. "Even I can see those." He adjusted his glasses. "What else can you see?"

Amahle raised the binoculars and aimed them at the mansion. She adjusted the dials for a few seconds until the picture gained clarity and the distance seemed right. The magnification of the lenses wasn't overly powerful. Still, it turned something little more than a vague impression of past disaster into a true *scene*, one swarming with activity.

Three black vans had pulled up to the estate grounds, and men in the distinctive uniforms of Executive Security were piling out of them, toting rifles as though they meant to use them at the slightest provocation. Someone was speaking on a walkie-talkie. Like Singh's bodyguards, the man wore a black suit and black glasses.

There was a fire truck as well. It hadn't bothered to put on its lights or sirens, perhaps because there was so little traffic on the roads in the hills anyway and because the security officers had insisted they be discreet. The firefighting crew was unspooling a hose and running it toward the building.

As for the house itself, it was at least three-quarters consumed by now. The fire continued to burn in an abnormally lazy way, but it had nonetheless done its grim work of destruction.

She lowered the binoculars. "At least fifteen Exec Security and a fire truck. It's safe to say that everyone on the Board, and everyone in the Coven, will know about this soon if they don't already."

Gage sighed. "That's what I would've guessed. Let us leave at once."

They climbed back into the Autocutioner. After he started the engine, Gage drove faster than he had before. An element of reckless desperation crept into his usually conservative way of operating motor vehicles.

Amahle rubbed her eyes. It had been another long, long day. "Where are you going? The city?"

"Yes." He stared straight ahead, gripping the wheel tightly with tense hands. "I am taking a different route, which will send us into a part of the city we haven't been in lately. We don't want to retrace our steps, and it would be best to go somewhere we won't stand out too much. We must be careful until we have a better idea of what is going on."

They were going downhill again and would likely intersect the road that looped around the northern edge of Atlantica Metro. From there, they would have multiple points of reentry into the city and various options for districts or neighborhoods where they could disappear.

Amahle opined, "We should contact Daria and the others soon."

"I agree." Gage glanced at her sidelong. "Before we do, let us discuss everything that happened. It all ended so suddenly that it robbed us of the chance to put our heads together. It seems Singh will never be able to tell us the rest of what he knew."

Amahle met his eyes and saw the grieving look in them again. He'd admired Jori Singh, in a way. If nothing else, he'd envied the man's vast knowledge and was consumed with regret that he'd died in the middle of sharing it.

"Well," she began, thinking of how best to convey her feelings. They were somewhat different from her partner's. "Singh might have known things, but I cannot think so highly of him. His pompous demeanor didn't impress me. Look at who he worked for, who his friends were. The same people who tried to have us killed, despite his talk of wanting to restrain the more 'exuberant' members of his organization."

"True," Gage conceded, looking back at the road. He turned south, guiding them into one of the older and quainter of the city's northern suburbs.

Amahle continued, "It might be that he was insane. Madmen sometimes sound knowledgeable, logical, and sensible if given enough time to talk about their madness and make it sound like sanity. In truth, I think he was simply a liar. Half or more of what he told us was nonsense. He was trying to deceive us while also arrogantly amusing himself with his talent at lying. You've met people who do such things, have you not?"

"I have, but I'm not so sure that Singh was one of them. Yes, he was most pleased with himself and wrapped much of what he said in grandiosity. I don't think it was all lies. It would make no sense to spend so many hours telling us nothing but tall tales. Much of it is consistent with what we already knew or suspected."

Amahle chewed her lower lip. The subject wasn't one she much wanted to discuss. All she'd been through was leaving her sullen and cynical. "Let us talk about Augustus Freeman and the Hellbreakers instead. He talks too much, too, but I like him and his group far better, I think."

Gage widened his eyes in an expression of honest surprise. "Oh? You seemed nervous at first. Then I thought he annoyed you."

"Yes, yes." She ran her hands over her hair, wishing for a hot bath. "I didn't know if we could trust them. But think about what they *did*. They stood up against the Executives and the Coven. Once they knew the true nature of the people they worked under, they stayed true to themselves and acted without delay. I admire that. Such...spiritedness."

Gage made a low thrumming sound in his throat. "I can see why you would feel that way. It's easy to admire those who have strong convictions and are willing to act upon them. I have my doubts.

"Commander Augustus behaves with great casualness and as though he controls everything. Yet, he seems like a most angry young man. I fear he is simply looking for something to expend his anger upon. A justification for his rage and violence. If it wasn't 'the beast,' as he calls it, then it would be something else. Do you see?"

Leaning back in her seat and glowering at the window, Amahle snapped, "I see, but why is that a bad thing? Some people *deserve* to be targets of anger."

"Perhaps." Gage paused. "And perhaps I see some of myself in the young man. I see mistakes that I made or *worse* mistakes that I came close to making but spared myself in the end. I would not wish to encourage another angry young man, like the one I once was, to make those same foolish errors."

Cocking an eyebrow in a quizzical expression, Amahle looked hard at her coworker. "You were an 'angry young man,' Gage? I'm sure you were *young*, difficult as that might be to believe. You've always been the relaxed and friendly type. I thought you went to war out of a sense of duty. Was I wrong?"

Gage didn't react to the more nettling aspects of her question. He stared ahead, going through the motions of driving as his mind continued its cycle, trying to shift into a higher gear.

"In part, I suppose you were. It involved duty. My people have a longstanding sense of commitment. Everyone knows the reputations of the Gurkhas. When I was younger, I was often frustrated, and I didn't always know the reason. Sometimes I simply wished to destroy things for the sake of destroying them. Any war or conflict would've been good enough to let me do this."

Amahle's sarcasm melted away in an instant. She knew what he meant. For her, it was somewhat different. It was more the sense that fighting was what she was good at, combined with a doubt that she could be successful at much else. Therefore, on the cusp of adulthood, she'd decided that at least she ought to put her talents to good use.

Gage continued, "I sense that something similar might be going on in the mind of Commander Freeman. He and his comrades left behind one war, only to get themselves involved in another. Maybe the same is true of me, in a way. Still, I have learned something. Violence is not to be *sought after.* It is sometimes necessary. But..."

"Oh?" Amahle interjected. "If a young person is angry and wishes to fight, and if fighting is necessary, what is wrong with that person going where they're needed? It might be wrong to use a hammer to open a glass window, but that's not the hammer's fault. Do we chastise the hammer for being able to break a window when we use it to pound nails?"

Another moment passed during which the only sounds were those of the wheels rustling against the road beneath them and the bulk of the truck rattling atop its frame.

"You have a point," Gage said. "Although a hammer wielded in anger might as easily smash the fingers of the one trying to pound the nails. But yes, I understand what you're trying to say. I'm growing old. Perhaps my age makes me too quick to pour cold water upon hot passions."

Amahle laughed, but not in a malicious way. "You have self-awareness. That is good. Speaking of passions, you seemed excited by what Singh was talking about. I have my doubts. You're a scientist. You were studying the very things that man was describing to us before you became an Executioner, were you not?"

"Indeed." There was a flash of regret on the Nepali's face. Likely, he was thinking of the path not taken. The life he might've had if he'd stuck with archaeology. It vanished almost as quickly as it had appeared.

"It's impossible for me not to take a professional interest in such things. What Singh told us was disturbing, yes, because of how the Coven seemingly intended to use their discoveries. Yet the more we learn about them, the more incredible are the possibilities. Even if the Coven intends to do evil, it might be that they've uncovered things we could use for good."

Amahle looked out the side window, her eyes lidded and her demeanor growing frosty. The world had used many "discoveries" for good over the years, but she suspected there were men who said much the same thing about nuclear fission. Which they'd immediately used to create the most horrifying weapon in history.

Gage twitched his shoulders. There was something he wanted to say, but he was unsure if he *should* say it. After twenty or thirty seconds of contemplation, he made his decision. "I have something. Singh dropped it when they shot him, and I picked it up before the fighting began."

As Amahle looked at him, he used his free hand to pull from his waist the curious bracelet. "It is Coven technology, to be sure," he declared. "It might contain the secrets of how he was able to touch that kettle without burning himself."

Amahle's face fell in distaste. "Do we not have enough of their accursed artifacts sitting in our basement already?"

"We have many," Gage conceded, "but this is unlike any I have seen before. It will require further study. Most of what we gathered came from that case the Ashcrofts were trying to escape with over a year ago. This might be something newer. It will help us discover what direction the Coven means to move in."

They were now within the outer suburbs of Atlantica Metro. People lounged around outside on corners or in their yards, and others walked beside the road, to and from their errands and amusements. Traffic was relatively light. It would grow heavier once they got into the city proper.

Amahle sighed. "Well, it wouldn't be a bad idea to find out

what the enemy is capable of. You've always been prudent about such things. Remember what happened to that man with the Atlanticore pistol? I told you about it the morning right before Eleanor called us to the square for those hanged Junior Execs."

"Ah, yes." Gage turned east, then south again, subconsciously heading toward the docks district since Daria's house was sometimes their meeting place when they didn't wish to gather at HQ. "You said there wasn't much left of him."

The South African nodded. "I am eager to be somewhere else when that device is tested. I also wonder if the risk to you is worth the possible knowledge we might gain. In the end, the Coven and their servants are only men. The best way to deal with bad men is with bullets. Many, many bullets."

As she spoke, it occurred to her that she ought to consider rearming herself with a rifle she could still use for sniping purposes but with a higher ammo capacity and full auto, or at least semiauto capabilities.

Her Winchester was excellent in its intended role. However, the fight at Singh's mansion made it all too clear that she might have to engage in more combat situations where the enemy was no more than a stone's throw away. Their weapons stash in the locker was now in enemy hands. Still, in a place like Atlantica, finding a gun from a street dealer wasn't overly difficult.

Gage's usual placid demeanor was cracking around the edges. He shifted in his seat as though restless.

"To advance human understanding isn't an inherently bad thing. The more we learn about the past, the better we understand the present and the future. If the Coven has strange technology, components of it might be beneficial even if they are misusing it. To expand the limits of human understanding is to help the world."

Amahle blurted, "Then why does everyone who does it seem to be fucking crazy?"

Not only did Gage neglect to respond, but his shoulders

slumped, and he slowed the disguised Autocutioner a bit. The air felt charged with the kind of tension that didn't agitate people so much as drain them of energy.

Putting a hand to her face and frowning, Amahle mumbled, "I am sorry. I shouldn't have said that." Gage had come to this island for the very purpose she'd criticized. "It's difficult for me to comprehend why so many people on Atlantica get drawn to things that only seem to drive them mad or kill them. I realize that you don't see it that way. You're a good man, even if I wonder whether or not you're always right."

In a low, flat voice, Gage retorted, "We come from different backgrounds."

He didn't mean their relationship to violence since both had plenty of experience with *that.* He was talking about *education.* Amahle's irritation rose again, and she bit her tongue to keep from speaking.

If there was one thing Gage was good at besides tinkering with gadgets and wielding his kukri, it was knowing when to change the subject. "We should radio the others. We must decide where to meet. I had thought to drive to Daria's house, but now that I think about it, the Executives must know about the place and might be watching it."

"Agreed." Amahle pushed the thoughts of their argument from her head. Deciding what to do next was far more important than clashing pointlessly over the impasse in worldviews between them.

Gage selected a mostly empty parking lot adjacent to an obnoxious modern shopping center. It was about three-quarters constructed but looked like it might be open for tentative business anyway. He pulled over, parked away from obvious sight, and tried the radio.

Amahle waited as her partner made three attempts. Toward the end of the third, Daria responded.

"Hello," her voice greeted them. "It seems there was some excitement in the hills, wasn't there? Over."

Gage chuckled drily. "Yes, but not enough to put us out of commission. We should meet and talk, and the sooner, the better. As far as I know, this frequency isn't compromised, but I will leave it up to you to decide how openly we should speak. Over."

Amahle could nearly picture Daria doing one of her patented dismissive hand-waves. "As openly as we must. Number One has insisted that we meet in his hometown. I will assume you know of where we speak. He has friends there who would help and shelter us if needed. Over."

Gage nodded. "Yes, that's a good idea. We will be there soon. Out."

Daria said goodbye and killed the radio from her end. Gage switched theirs off and hung up the microphone.

Amahle was puzzled. "I was under the impression that Tyler's hometown was in California. Unless she means..."

"She does," Gage assured her. "The shantytown that Ty protected and lived in before he became the first Executioner. Which, if I'm not mistaken, has since become a proper *town*."

CHAPTER EIGHTEEN

Northvale had existed for close to a year before it had a name. Amahle had never been to the place before. Her only mental conception of it came to her via the stories that Tyler and Daria told about it from their time there nearly two years ago.

From the way they'd described it, the place had originally resembled something like a cross between a particularly hard-scrabble settlement cobbled together during the days of the American frontier, combined with one of the slums that prolifer-ated on the edges of cities in places like Brazil. They'd built everything from scratch, in a hurry. Amenities were minimal. They had a couple of generators for minimal electric power but remained largely relegated to using pit toilets and gas stoves or open fires for cooking. The streets were mud. They hadn't constructed anything according to a plan or program.

At present, the place bore no meaningful resemblance to the wretched prototype community it had once been. It truly had become a town—one where any but the most pampered of modern-day persons could spend time without feeling that they were grossly deprived. Any country on the planet would've recognized its legitimacy.

Amahle scanned the place through the side window and the windshield as Gage drove the camouflaged truck down the main street. Northvale's central road began as a modest track through the low foothills northwest of Atlantica Metro. It took a bumpy and winding course through a shallow ravine before opening into the valley where the town proper lay.

Originally, the vale from which it took its name contained the entire settlement, and a couple of miles of largely undeveloped wilderness separated it from the city. In the years since its founding, both had expanded.

Atlantica Metro had spread its suburbs and exurbs northwest, engulfing most of the empty countryside other than the more rugged hills. Northvale had grown out into the ravines and on top of the hills, nearly doubling in size. It also grew in comfort, cleanliness, and organization.

"Yes, yes," Gage mused as they clanked along. "I was here once when they were still trying to become a nice place to live. They had already improved many things since the early days, or so Ty told me. This is another thing altogether. I'm proud of them."

Amahle gave a single nod. Northvale was now a respectable and established working-class township. It had different neighborhoods whose locations and boundaries were more or less logical. The public spaces were well-kept. It even had an ever-increasing number of small shops and homegrown businesses, including entertainment amenities.

Daria had told them to meet her and the others at the drive-in movie theater. She was vague as to exactly where it was, but Gage and Amahle figured that an open area in front of a giant screen couldn't be too difficult to find.

They went through most of the town proper before Amahle glimpsed what looked like a flickering, moving image in the distance beyond a rise in the land. "There." She pointed.

"Ah." Gage made a turn and found the back road that led up the incline. "There is a small plateau up here. Ty told me that he used to encamp there and patrol when he expected trouble. It's strangely fitting that it would now be a recreational area."

The theater didn't have any fencing to speak of. Ridges, cliffs, and gullies served to demarcate the viewing zone from the surrounding landscape. They paid for a ticket at the booth, but when they told the girl working there that they were here to meet Tyler Katakura, she blinked and mentioned, in a half-embarrassed tone, that she would've let them in for free if she'd known they were his friends.

Gage waved. "It's quite all right. I'm sure a small business such as yourselves could use the money."

As it was growing late, the theater was playing the kind of movie that appealed to the late-night crowd—some sort of horror film set during the years of the witch trials or perhaps the Inquisition in Europe, by the look of it. The film seemed to feature a great many buxom young women being dragged off to torture chambers by grim-faced, black-garbed clergymen.

Locating the faux van with its blue exterior was easy. Daria had parked far off to one side, near a cliff that would afford them a certain amount of privacy, but also was close to a narrow but gentle slope leading back toward the town proper. It would be a good escape avenue if anything went wrong.

Gage drove over and parked next to them. The other four spilled out of the vehicle before Gage and Amahle could do like-wise. They must have been eager to see them. Ty was the last one out of the van. Heavy bandages wrapped his midsection, and he looked pale and sweaty.

Amahle had to wonder about the quality of the medical care he'd received. And whether they had waited too long to get him to it. Still, he could stand and walk and seemed aware of his surroundings. She suspected he was on at least a small number of painkillers, though.

Amahle waved. "Hello. It's good to see you're all in one piece."

"Well, what we've been up to probably isn't as exciting as what you've been doing, or so I hear," Dante quipped. "So you should talk."

Daria summed up the activities that had occupied the four of them. Reconnaissance and stalking. Gathering information from known contacts, including issuing threats or slipping bribes when necessary. It had its hazards and tribulations, but it had paid off.

They knew who to go after. They had a good half-dozen likely prospects.

When it was over, Ty looked at Gage and Amahle in turn. "Now, tell us what happened on your end."

Gage raised a hand and looked at all of them. "Before we describe it all, I have something to show you, which may be of importance to us." He reached into the waistband of his pants and pulled out the curious bracelet he'd picked up from a blood-spattered, bullet-cracked paving stone beside a pool.

Dante prodded him with, "What the hell is that thing? Looks like a bracelet. Another old Atlantican artifact?"

"Perhaps. Or it might be a more modern invention, or a combination of the two—as with many treasures of the Coven. I took it from Jori Singh, the club owner and Coven member whom we were pursuing when another faction shot him."

They all nodded and waited to hear more.

Looking a tad sheepish, Gage rolled his shoulders and admitted, "I'm afraid I don't know how it works or what it does. I haven't had time to examine it in detail or run tests on it."

Amahle interjected, "As I said before, you should *not* run tests on it when anyone else is around. The Coven seems to make a great many things that work better as accidental bombs than they do as whatever they were supposed to be."

Despite his grim demeanor, Ty managed a short, dry chuckle at that. "True. Gage, look it over when you get time, but *be careful*, for God's sake, and don't poke around with it until we can get you back to a proper lab somewhere. Now, you say Jori Singh is dead, right? Someone else shot him, not you? That's about what we figured based on listening in to Security's radio calls and observing some of the local gossip. Still, tell us all about it."

Gage and Amahle went back and forth as they skimmed over their visit to the investment firm, the finer points of their stakeout of the Khalsa office, and the way they'd tailed Singh and his security detail to the resort in the hills. They explained their mutual surprise at how Singh had reacted to their presence with near-total calm, even when they threatened him.

Then they relayed the high points of the man's long speech, their thoughts on what he'd said, and their guesses about what lay between the lines, unspoken. Eleanor paid particularly close attention to this part. Her brow stayed furrowed, and her eyes were dark and haunted.

Finally, they described the sudden outburst of violence and their escape from the burning mansion following their victory over the Execs' men. Then their ambivalent impression of the Hellbreakers—who freely admitted to being the group that had hanged the three Junior Execs a few days prior.

When they finished, Amahle and Gage looked sideways at one another, sharing the solidarity that came from surviving such a bizarre ordeal together. Then they turned back to their friends.

"That's it," Gage concluded. "We called Daria and set up the present meeting."

Ty looked unusually thoughtful and reflective. Whatever medications he was on might have mellowed him out slightly if not totally. Although his usual smoldering rage and willful, domineering side weren't far beneath the surface.

"What a damn mess," he murmured. "This might be the most crookedly bizarre case we've handled. It ties into everything else, though." He scowled in a way that almost looked like a thinly-disguised smile. "When you get right down to it, it's still only a matter of finding the right people and shooting them."

Amahle smirked. "I agree. Finding them first is the hard part."

Gage meanwhile studied Eleanor, and he noticed that Dante was doing the same. It appeared to him that she *wanted* to say something but was forcing herself to keep her mouth shut until everyone else had said their piece. She knew well that she wasn't a fully accepted group member. Doubts lingered.

Dante spoke up. "What this Singh guy said sounds fairly similar to what Eleanor told us, but there are some major differences. Granted, Eleanor only worked for them. She wouldn't have known everything. Whereas Singh was a legitimate Coven member and kind of a major player, right?"

Gage nodded. "I have every reason to believe he was, yes."

"So," Daria surmised, essentially speaking for them all. "We know where we're at, what we're dealing with, and who are the parties involved. Our task is to decide what to do next, a far harder thing to discover than any of the others.

"We have our list of names of the Junior Execs who are likely to be Coven members or at least Coven assets, and we must move against them. The problem is these new people, the Hellbreakers. What do we do about them? Can we trust them?"

Eleanor tried to speak up again. "I would advise against it. We know they are bloodthirsty, and otherwise, they represent an unknown factor that—"

"That saved our lives," Amahle interrupted her, "and fought against our common enemies. Maybe they aren't the best of friends we could hope for, but there can be a place for them. When we cannot divide ourselves to fight on two fronts, they can fight on the second in our stead, perhaps."

Ty pointed his index finger at the South African while nodding at the others. "Good point. If nothing else, we can probably use them to create diversions, cover our retreat, stuff like that. But since we don't *know* them, I don't think we should trust them with the most sensitive or important operations, either. They don't need to know all our secrets. It's enough to confirm that, for the time being, we have certain goals in common."

Gage cleared his throat. "It seems that they regard all of the so-called 'magic' of the Coven as an abomination, perhaps for religious reasons. So it would be most unwise to tell them about our research of such things until we grow to understand their intentions and motivations better."

"Oh?" Amahle objected. "How will they feel when they discover that we've been lying to them? They might think we were working for the enemy all along."

Dante scratched his chin. "She's onto something there. If they're as gung-ho as you two say, they'll take that particular revelation without a lot of grace, I think."

Eleanor added, "There might be no good option with them. I would advise keeping them at arm's length until—"

With a sharp chopping motion, Ty snapped, "We know what you would advise. Executioners, I say we work with them as far as we can without causing any problems. Until we resolve the current situation."

Nods went around the group, but Eleanor's lips were trembling while she stared bug-eyed at all of them, especially Ty.

"God *dammit!*" she exploded. She stamped, sending a minor tremor through the ground. Everyone fell silent.

Someone sitting in a car about thirty yards away turned his head to look at her, blinked, and looked back at the screen.

Getting ahead of anyone who might try to cut her off and still speaking in an unnecessarily loud shout, Eleanor added, "I will not be talked down to like this and pushed to the side of every discussion. I'm as much a part of this as any of you. I've had more dealings with the Executives and can predict how many of them will react to things. They want *me* dead as much as they want *you* dead."

Amahle bit her tongue while she chewed on her thoughts. She understood why Eleanor was angry, but the woman had been wrong about a couple of things. Singh had contradicted her.

There was still no way to be one hundred percent *certain* that her loyalties weren't divided.

Ty glowered. "Fine, we'll try to be more polite. But if you want us to *trust* you, well, you haven't earned it yet."

"How could I not?" Eleanor demanded. "I've helped you every step of the way, and the Security team who came into your headquarters was there to *stop* me from helping you."

Dante smoothed his hair. "It's true. The guy who broke into the rec room blasted the door open and was about to shoot her when I took him out. I forget what he said, but it sure as hell wasn't, 'Oh, hi, Ms. Cervantes, nice to see you. Come along now, and you'll get your bonus when we get back.' She legitimately risked her life by speaking to us about what's been going on."

An awkward but contemplative silence settled over the group.

Eleanor, her voice back to a normal register, pointed out, "By now, I have as much to lose as the rest of you. I'm already part of this team by necessity. I *must* help you succeed, or I'm dead."

Ty let out a gruff sigh. "There's a certain logic to that, yeah."

Daria observed, flourishing her hand at their former handler, "There were many times when Eleanor could've compromised the operation by telling someone what we were doing. Or she could've escaped with ease. The information she gave us has been extremely helpful. It might have taken us a month of dirty and dangerous recon work to get where we are now, after only two or three days."

Gage, Dante, and Daria all glanced at one another and nodded.

Ty looked up at Amahle, who shared his slightly sour and skeptical expression. "So be it," he stated. "I've heard of some pretty elaborate traps, some true deep-cover agents...but I don't think that's the case here. Eleanor, it's true—with the intel you've helped us gather, we have a real crack at the Execs. Those interests of theirs that are tied up with the Coven of Miracles, anyway."

Eleanor closed her eyes as though needing a few seconds to deal with a potential outpouring of emotion. When she opened them again, all that came out of her mouth was, "Thank you."

Gage asked her, "What do you think we should do? Not only immediately regarding the Hellbreakers and so forth, but what do you feel should be our overall plan, our strategy over the next days and weeks?"

He'd posed the question in a gentle and friendly tone and clearly in good faith. Amahle took note of what he'd done. By asking Eleanor for her input, he gave her the chance to display what else she could bring to the table, including her level of commitment. It was an informal way of confirming her newfound equality relative to the others.

Eleanor's mouth turned down a tad, and her eyes lowered to the ground and went distant as she strove to process her thoughts. Normally she was quick-witted and easy to launch into diplomacy.

Perhaps in this instance, the true weight of her words was bearing down upon her. She might be intimidated by the responsibility of helping to make decisions for others. As their handler with Execs, her role had traditionally consisted of passing orders and requests back and forth and simply relaying information. Positing independent choices wasn't something she'd done professionally in years.

She admitted as much before she said the rest of what was on her mind. "This is all very daunting. But there are some things you—we—must know and understand."

"Yes?" Daria inquired.

Eleanor shook her head and was back to her usual crisp self-assurance. "The issue is that you cannot employ, ah, scorched earth tactics against the Executives. Not the way you would with the usual sorts of criminals and miscreants."

Muscles along Ty's jaw rippled. That wasn't what he'd wanted to hear. "Why the hell not?"

"Hush," Daria chastised him. "Let her have her say."

Eleanor flapped a hand. "Thank you, but I'll answer his question anyway. The simple fact is that the Executives are too much, how do you say, baked into the fabric of Atlantica at this point. To burn down their whole structure to kill them, so to speak, would hurt too many other people."

Amahle gave a long, slow nod at that. There were times when she could've completed a job more easily if she'd simply killed everyone in a given building. Still, the aftermath of a total massacre was far more difficult to recover from and to justify than a clean assassination that took down only one or two important targets.

Eleanor went on, "Not only in the obvious, physical sense. Many people would also have their livelihoods destroyed. Their dreams, you might even say. The economy would be devastated. The Executives knew how to spread their money around well. They have always understood that a strong community that built a solid infrastructure was what this island needed, more than anything else."

Daria chuckled. "Yes, I remember when there was a thriving dock town, but no paved roads or plumbing."

"Exactly." Eleanor glanced to the sides and behind her, waving with each motion of her head. "You can see the evidence all around you. Look. A couple of years ago, this place was no better than a slum in any of the world's poorest cities. With investment and economic growth, it's comparable to anything you could find in Western Europe or even the United States. If we do too much damage, we risk it all."

Ty had put his life in danger to protect the community and was still beloved of them for that very reason. He was rapidly softening as Eleanor explained her motives. "Yeah, I get it. What do we do instead, then?"

Eleanor fixed her gaze to his, then glanced at each of the

others in turn. "If we're to go after the Executives and the Coven, we need to be, ah, *surgical* about it, as Dante would perhaps say."

"Eh, perhaps," Dante chimed in. "Seems like it's mostly people who *aren't* doctors who throw that word around, though. No offense."

Untroubled by his remarks, Eleanor continued, "We must take out the key points of corruption, moving decisively against them, but without doing too much damage to the rest. That way, the entire structure that supports Atlantica will not come tumbling down. I am convinced that some of those who are directly involved with the Coven will abandon the ship once they see that things are going badly for their ringleaders."

Amahle almost sneered, but not at Eleanor herself. "No honor among thieves..."

Ms. Cervantes looked at her with an expression of borderline amusement. She must have realized that Amahle was referring to the Coven lackeys themselves. "No profit in selling your soul," she added, "if you cannot get a good enough offer."

The demonic masks and armor sigils of the Hellbreakers flashed again in Amahle's mind. It took a considerable force of will to suppress a shudder.

"Yes," Amahle said, louder. "Now, what is your plan, Eleanor? Which target do you propose we hit first, and how do we go about it?" She suspected that Eleanor hadn't thought of that part yet and relied upon the Executioners to figure out the details.

It wasn't so. Eleanor immediately launched into her answer.

"I've been thinking about it, and I believe I have a good idea. There is a particular coastal facility that the Executives funneled a great deal of money into. Their stated reason, at first, was to desalinate seawater and so provide irrigation for nearby farms. They might also use the water to run a hydroelectric station in the vicinity, which can provide power to the local community."

Gage ran a hand over the smooth crown of his head. "That is

most interesting. I always wanted to know more about hydroelectric engineering. But, go on."

Eleanor did. "Despite all the money sent into that place, neither electricity nor clean water has come back out to the locals. Something strange is going on there. I believe that the interests of the Executives and the Coven are enmeshed there, which would make it a good place to hit. Furthermore, a pair of Junior Board members have been on site for three months."

Ty ran his thumb absentmindedly over the hilt of his wakizashi. "Any Junior Board member might *also* be on the Senior Board, right?"

"Correct," Eleanor confirmed. "Although it is never certain. Also, near this facility, the population of local villagers is small enough that it should be easy to avoid them. Or, at worst, to evacuate them so there are no casualties of innocent bystanders."

The woman stopped, exhaling and breathing back in as she waited to face the music.

Ty was the first to speak. "Sounds good to me. What about the rest of you? I don't mean nitpicking the details yet. How do you feel about the plan in general?"

Everyone liked it. They had no better options, and if what Eleanor said was true, it could be hugely productive but without massive risk.

"All right," Ty grunted. "It's a deal, then. Hold on, though, Eleanor. One more thing." He abruptly turned and half-limped back to the truck, throwing open its back door and climbing in. Amahle wanted to help him, to ensure he didn't hurt himself, but she sensed that whatever he was doing, he wanted to do it alone.

After about fifteen seconds of shuffling around, he crawled back out with an extra armored uniform in hand. He tossed it to Eleanor. She caught it, but her knees buckled a bit at the unexpected weight.

"Welcome to the club," Ty said.

CHAPTER NINETEEN

Amahle poked around in the various things she and Gage had stuffed in different places around the truck. With a gnawing sensation of unease and frustration, she began to worry that the slip of paper with the Hellbreakers' secret radio frequency had got lost in the chaotic shuffle of the last couple of hours.

While her hands worked to clear away random items from the glove compartment, she looked up at the screen where the movie was wrapping up. A revolt had broken out among the villagers, and the evil Inquisitor was trying to flee the town while innocents burned at stakes or languished in dungeons. A carload of teenagers off to the left was laughing heartily at the whole spectacle in an effort to impress one another.

Gage climbed into the front cab from the other side. "Are you looking for that radio designation Gus gave us? I believe I put it in my pocket after you handed it to me." He slipped a hand into the side of his pants.

"Yes," Amahle mumbled. "That would've been helpful to know a moment ago." Then again, she'd started looking for it before she'd bothered to ask him.

Gage produced a crumpled scrap and handed it to her. "This is it. I'm sure of it."

Glancing at the paper, she nodded. "Yes. Thank you. Now, let us see if our new friends are still available. Wait, didn't they say something about only contacting them at dawn and dusk?"

"Yes," Gage frowned. "I forgot, too. We must call them in the morning, then. Let us hope they will be willing to ride into possible battle on short notice. I suspect they will not mind."

Amahle was inclined to agree. They didn't seem like the type to shy away from the chance to spill blood.

Looking through the windshield, she noted that Ty and Dante were explaining something to Eleanor, perhaps giving her a crash course in how the Executioners operated on the ground and what to do in emergencies. Daria was poking around with a map, probably plotting the route they would take to their destination tomorrow.

Amahle closed her eyes and rubbed them. "We should spend the evening preparing for what's to come. I think we need to let ourselves get enough sleep, too."

Gage agreed. "I might also have time to examine the bracelet. I will do so a safe distance from you; do not worry."

"Thank you." She climbed down from the truck and went over to Ty, intending to ask him if he had any spare guns or knew where they could procure some. If any serious, close-quarters battles lay ahead of them, she would need an automatic or semi-automatic weapon.

Gage relocated to the truck's rear compartment. He took out the bracelet, set it on a blanket, and poked it with a small wrench from the truck's toolkit while examining it in detail with a flashlight.

It was, like many Atlantican artifacts and Coven gadgets, mostly of a smooth silver-chrome color set with tiny blue dots that were probably Atlanticore crystals. Gage lacked the lab equipment to test anything with a proper degree of scientific certainty, but pure experience and firsthand knowledge told him that his impressions were likely correct.

If the bracelet had some kind of passive effect—if it was doing something right now—he couldn't tell. He suspected that like most machines, a switch or button activated it. In which case, there was little telling what might happen.

He had a pretty good idea. Singh's yoga expertise, impressive though it may have been, couldn't account totally for his unnatural ability to hold scalding metal in his hand for entire *minutes* without injury. Humans could traverse coal beds barefoot if they moved right and maintained good control over the unity of mind and body. To simply stand on hot coals for an extended time and remain unscathed was beyond the scope of natural reality as humans understood it.

Gage ran his fingers over the stones set within the metal, half-fearing electrocution or another unstable reaction. But nothing happened. Then he similarly felt along the inside of the metal loop. There were two indentations, barely perceptible, but when he placed his fingers inside them, that didn't result in any obvious effect, either.

"Hmm." He paused, staring at the bracelet. The image of Jori Singh rolling up the sleeve of his robe flashed again in his mind. Then Gage grabbed the device and squeezed it in different configurations.

Finally, when he put pressure on one of the blue stones on the outside *and* one of the indentations on the inside, he felt something happening. A cool tingling spread over his hand and forearm, and for an instant, he thought he detected a faint bluish shimmer in the air around it. The light was faint enough that under the bright sun on the pool patio, it might've been invisible. In the darker conditions at present, though...

Gage loosened his grip but kept the bracelet in his hand. He moved it around and noticed that it was bunching up the blanket and forcing it aside without directly touching it—there was about a half-centimeter gap between his knuckle and the fabric.

Next, he crawled through the truck until he found a box of wooden matches. Lighting one with his free hand, he held the flame up to the wrist of the hand holding the bracelet.

He felt no pain. There was no discoloration of the skin. And it looked like the fire was curling to the sides, once again about half a centimeter from contact.

"Incredible," he murmured. As he turned, intending to hop down from the truck and share his discovery with the others, he saw Amahle looking at him.

"Amahle. I have discovered what the bracelet does. It creates a field of invisible force that blocks or dissipates energy and matter. Look."

While she watched with interest in her tired eyes, he lit another match and demonstrated the effects once more.

Amahle shrugged. "That would explain the tea kettle. A pair of good gloves would work just as well. I don't understand why the Coven goes to such lengths to create things that other, simpler devices can already accomplish." Recalling how the defective Atlanticore pistol had exploded, she wondered if anyone in the Coven had heard of dynamite.

Gage clenched his jaw and pushed his glasses up the bridge of his nose with his unshielded hand. He looked frustrated. "Do you not see the potential of this technology? On so small a scale as this, yes, its usefulness is limited. It could expand to encompass a person's whole body. Or maybe even multiple people. It could provide something like an emergency shelter for those caught in hazardous conditions."

Amahle shrugged. "Yes, in that case, it would be easier and faster than carrying a tent and trying to set it up in a hurry."

"Well, I'm glad you can see some of the possible benefits."

She gave a vague nod. It was obvious that she wanted to pass out and sleep the whole night. Around them, the drive-in was beginning to clear out, but nobody came to ask them to leave. Tyler had probably secured permission to remain there overnight. Due to it being on a slight plateau, it would make a good secure location to make camp for the night.

"I will be back," Amahle stated. "Ty is taking me into town to buy a new gun. After that, I will be going to bed. You should do the same. If the last few days are anything to judge by, things will likely be as difficult tomorrow as they were today."

CHAPTER TWENTY

The static cleared as the Hellbreakers' secret channel came through. Outside, the last of the dawn birds chirped in the trees around the terrace.

"Hello," Gage said into the microphone. "This is your new friends. You told us to call you at dawn or dusk. Come in, please. Over."

It sounded like someone on the other end was adjusting their radio and getting ready to respond. Amahle looked down at the weapon in her hands, hefting it to get a feel for its overall weight and balance and mentally reviewing the manual of arms.

It was a Soviet SKS rifle, a popular weapon on Atlantica, though there were fewer of them in circulation recently than there had been the last couple of years. Partially thanks to the Executioners' crackdown on heavily armed gangs, most average citizens and petty criminals stuck with pistols and shotguns for personal protection. The most dangerous and well-funded groups would always have access to state-of-the-art rifles and submachine guns no matter what.

The SKS, while a slightly clunky-looking weapon—like most things manufactured behind the Iron Curtain—nonetheless had a pretty good reputation as a gun that provided a decent balance among several factors.

Accuracy was decent but not on par with a true marksman rifle, particularly since there was a significant drop at long distances. Its range was still superior to pistol-caliber weapons. It fired the fairly powerful 7.62 x 39mm round, which was sufficient for most targets and roughly on par with the cartridge used by her partners' AR-10's. It fired in semiauto and took ten-round stripper clips in its internal magazine, making it similar in basic operation to the American M1 Garand. Plus, it was known to be reliable.

On the downside, there was a danger of slam-firing when a shooter first loaded the clip and the bolt charged. While not really bigger than her Winchester Model 70, it was larger and heavier than most submachine guns. She would have to hope it would prove its worth as a good all-around weapon, able to handle any situation adequately, even if it was less than ideal for certain specialized operations. In any event, it was the best-seeming option available to them from the under-the-table arms dealers in town. The locals had access to more firepower than Amahle would've guessed, but nothing quite on par with what Executive Security could procure with a snap of the Board's fingers.

Her Winchester would remain in the truck in case she truly needed to make a long-distance shot. Her .32 revolver stayed at her side for emergencies. Everyone else in the crew was packing a similar amount of heat, except Eleanor. She had only her .380 pistol. Then again, her role was primarily to act as the "face" of the group in peace and to retreat to the rear or center of the formation in battle.

The radio noise fuzzed out, and a man's voice with a noticeable Australian accent came through. "Hello there. The two new friends we met yesterday, I'd wager?"

"Indeed," said Gage. "We're sorry for the short notice, but we have information on a target we intend to move against. This will, if our sources are credible, allow us to strike a major blow against the Coven. If you're interested, we request your aid and cooperation and would like you to be ready to move out in one hour."

There was a pause, then the man said, "That's great, mate. Let me tell the commander. Sit tight."

Amahle glanced out the window to the side. The others had loaded into their vehicle. Daria and Dante, seated up front, watched them for the go-ahead.

They'd decided earlier that the best way to approach the coastal water-processing facility was via a fairly direct route, yet one that still avoided most of the main roads. It would add about an extra half hour to the trip; nothing too serious. Fewer eyes would be upon them in the meantime.

The voice of Augustus Freeman came through the radio next. "We'll go where you lead. What's the place and how do we get there? Plan of attack?"

Gage frowned. "We intend to use no more violence than is necessary. There are fewer problems and risks that way. Of course, we might have to fight anyway." He described the place and the easiest route to reach it.

"Oh, we're closer to it than you are. We'll leave directly and meet you there. Over."

After meeting Amahle's sharp gaze, Gage spoke again. "Do not go all the way to the facility. Meet us in the farming village of, umm, Acacia Hollow, which is on the way. We'll rendezvous there and proceed together to the facility. Over."

It sounded like Gus conferred briefly with his men, then he said, "Agreed. We'll see you there shortly. Out."

"Out." Gage switched off the radio. Then he cursed. "I forgot to ask them how many men they have available. We still don't know exactly how strong their force is. It might be that they have others besides the ones we saw at Singh's house."

Amahle opened the door to give the go-ahead to the others, but first, over her shoulder, she pointed out, "Well, they had enough people last night to be sufficient for our purposes today, I should think. If they have still more, so much the better."

She called to Daria and gave them a thumbs-up. Daria and Dante nodded and returned the gesture.

Amahle shut the door. "Let's go."

Without further words, Gage started the engine, shifted gears, and took off behind the other truck. The pair of disguised Auto-cutioners rumbled down the slope and into Northvale, then took the west road, which led through the forested foothills and toward the western coast. The facility and adjacent town lay a significant distance north up the shoreline. It was an area none of them were overly familiar with.

The first hour of the drive passed without incident. Once again, things seemed almost uncannily peaceful, although the west road from Northvale didn't go through Atlantica Metro. Instead, it went toward a coastal fishing community where Ty had done some of his earliest work as an Executioner, then bore north-northeast into the hills since the coastline beyond the fishing town was mostly treacherous cliffs.

The village that Gage had mentioned, Acacia Hollow, was in a small valley near the northwestern edge of the highlands and perhaps a twenty or twenty-five-minute drive from the water purification facility. Amahle noted that after passing another intersecting street directly from the city, the road here was pavement. The Executives must have invested in getting the asphalt laid so supply trucks and their vehicles could more easily go back and forth between Metro and the water plant.

Ahead of them, Daria slowed as they descended the gentle slope into the village. It looked quiet. Around the town's periphery, no one was working in the fields.

Amahle noticed something right before the tree line rose to

block it off. "Wait. There are trucks here. The Hellbreakers must have already arrived."

Gage muttered, "Yes, I saw them. I still don't think we should be so quick to trust them and work with them. They might be of help, but they could as easily cause us problems that we don't need to deal with."

The South African said nothing in return.

They slowed as they drove into the village proper and its oddly deserted main street. Daria brought her vehicle to a stop, parking alongside the road next to an empty depot yard.

As Gage rolled up alongside them, Amahle rolled down her window and called, "We're going to check things out over there." She pointed. "We saw trucks that way. Our friends seem to be waiting for us. Let us go alone at first. Come for us if we don't return in ten minutes."

Daria replied, "So be it. Be careful."

Gage drove ahead, then turned left. The vehicles they'd glimpsed were mostly toward the northwest corner of the valley, in what looked like the common ground between two or three farming plots, and not far from a large barn.

Amahle noticed agricultural vehicles standing idle near some of the other fields. It all looked...wrong, somehow.

"Gage," she began. "Do you think the Coven might have known we were coming and set up a trap? It might be that they've killed or captured the Hellbreakers and are waiting for us, too."

Grimacing, the Nepali shot back, "Possibly, yes. Everything we do from here on carries tremendous risk. What choice do we have but to investigate? If there's a trap, better to spring it now than to be surrounded at the facility later when our guilt and intentions would be clearer. Here, we can at least flee and claim that it is all a misunderstanding."

He was right. Amahle checked her rifle. It was loaded and in good working order.

Beyond the edge of the town proper, they came to the cluster of vehicles—two pickup trucks with extended cabs and two large vans. Depending on whether anyone rode in the backs of the pickups, Amahle estimated a total force of anywhere from sixteen to twenty-four men, roughly two squads. A good-sized force if they were truly on the Executioners' side.

Past the trucks, they saw a cluster of figures standing before the barn. Amahle recognized their diabolical armor at once. One of the men, possibly Gus himself, held a flaming torch in one hand.

"What?" Gage gasped. "What the hell are they doing?"

Two of the men toward the back had noticed them approaching and turned to wait. The others quickly followed suit.

Gage stopped the Autocutioner about twenty-five yards from the group. Neither had to suggest aloud that they remain in the vehicle until they'd spoken to their new partners. The wisdom of doing so was obvious to them both.

Amahle leaned her head out the window. "Hello. What is going on here?"

The man with the torch handed it off to someone else and jogged forward a few paces. It was Gus. "Hi! We've got the villagers rounded up. So, they're taken care of. Are you guys ready to go?"

Gage likewise stuck his head partway out of the vehicle. "What do you mean, taken care of? We're coming out."

In unison, the pair jumped down from the truck and strode toward the Hellbreakers. Both carried their rifles on slings, positioned so they could be brought to bear in a second or less if necessary, but appearing non-threatening for the moment.

Amahle squinted past Gus and toward the windows of the barn. People milled around inside it, quite a few of them.

Gus chuckled. "They started getting antsy on us so we herded them in there and told them we'd set the building on fire if they gave us any more shit." He gestured behind him. His demeanor was one of a college kid who'd played a prank on someone.

Gage snapped, "You did *what?* Do you intend to go through with such a thing?"

Gus was close enough that he stopped while the pair trotted closer to the rest of the Hellbreakers, as well as the barn. "No," the young commander shot back. "Unless they forced us to."

Nic, the blond Australian guy who seemed to be Gus's right-hand man, stepped in. "Aye, they were causin' trouble, and we didn't have time to talk to them all nice-like. A few tried to resist. Some people aren't too smart, are they? We didn't kill anyone, though."

Amahle saw that some of the villagers within the barn sported bruises or abrasions on their faces and bodies, as though the Hellbreakers had beaten them with the butts of rifles or kicked them while on the ground.

"This was unwise," she stated. "These people will remember this and be mistrustful for years to come, even if you claim to mean nothing by it." She'd seen it happen before. Peaceful, rustic types never reacted well to bands of armed men bossing them around and hurting their neighbors.

Gage was trembling with anger as though on the verge of a screaming fit. Amahle had never seen him like this.

"You *fools,*" he rasped. "Let them out immediately and apologize. We'll be lucky if they don't help our enemies simply to spite us. To spite *you,* anyway. Once they're free, follow us to the facility and stop wasting time." He glared at the whole crowd of them and pointed. "Let me remind you all that we don't want any more casualties than necessary. This is to be a clean and efficient operation."

The young men all looked surly and irritated. Nonetheless, Gus gestured with his head, and a couple of them opened the barn and attempted to laugh the whole incident off. The farmers avoided looking at them out of fear or stared back at them with simmering rage.

Gage and Amahle lingered long enough to be confident that the Hellbreakers didn't intend to do anything stupid. Then they returned to their vehicle.

The Gurkha repeated, "Follow us." He started the engine and drove back to the main street, not bothering to wait for their new allies.

They found that Dante had dismounted and was holding his shotgun; they were probably preparing to come looking for the pair at any moment. "Hey," the physician shouted, "what happened?"

"Nothing," Amahle called back. "There was a misunderstanding with the locals. The situation is under control. Move out, and we'll follow. The Hellbreakers are behind us." The engines of their trucks were growing louder and closer.

Dante shrugged. "If you say so." He climbed back into the Autocutioner. Daria looked suspicious but said nothing. Ty and Eleanor were somewhere in the back, out of sight.

As the two in the white truck fell in behind the four in the blue faux van, Amahle remarked in a soft voice, "This should not have happened, but we can make amends for it later. Something similar happened right before I joined the order if you remember. Daria will be able to talk to these people, and Tyler will think of a way to set it right."

Gage didn't respond right away. He only looked ahead at the road leading up and out of the valley and toward the coast. "Let us get this over with."

CHAPTER TWENTY-ONE

The Executioners and the Hellbreakers had formed a motorcade. Or, really, more of a paramilitary caravan. There were too many vehicles to pretend it was much of anything else. Furthermore, some of the Hellbreakers were indeed riding under the open air in the backs of the pickups, openly dressed in their bizarre armor and toting their guns.

They would have to rely upon their fake IDs and Eleanor's cover story to get their proverbial foot far enough in the door to shove it open and rush the place. Actual stealth and subtlety wouldn't be an option.

As Amahle recalled, the plan was for Eleanor to pass them off as a security inspection crew. If they were lucky, it would get them through the front gate and maybe even the front door. It wouldn't pass muster once the higher-ups heard about it. No one was under any illusion that it was a perfect plan.

They would probably end up having to blast their way in. The Higher Powers willing, they would be able to achieve their objective of capturing or neutralizing their targets and blast their way *out*.

Daria's truck was out in front. Amahle guessed that Eleanor

was probably riding in the passenger's seat since she would be the one to do most of the talking and handle the identification nonsense. Gage was right behind her. Ideally, they would piggyback through the gate without being checked individually. There was no guarantee it would happen.

Behind Gage's vehicle were the two trucks and two vans of the Hellbreakers. As they got closer to their destination, Amahle saw in the side mirror that the men in the backs of the pickups had wised up and were now lying beneath a blanket. Still, while she welcomed their guns and their enthusiasm, she wasn't sure she trusted them to pull off any kind of maneuver involving tact and finesse.

If the shooting started, they'd have to hope that the Hellbreakers would be able to hold off Executive Security, doing the dirty work of covering the Executioners as they looked for the two Junior Board members who owned the facility.

Amahle pulled out a pair of photos Eleanor had provided to study. The Executives they sought were a man and a woman. The former was named Sergio Damiano. In Amahle's opinion, he looked a bit like Dante, only without the hard edges that someone like Dante inevitably acquired and ten or fifteen years older.

The woman was called Ida Tranh, apparently of mixed white and Asian descent, with a short bob haircut and glasses. Eleanor herself was most responsible for identifying them, but it didn't hurt for the rest of the team to have some idea who they were looking for, either.

After the valley where the village of Acacia Hollow lay, the land rose slightly to a couple more hills before flattening out as they neared the coast. Amahle kept a close eye on the number and density of civilian settlements. After the business with the barn, she didn't want the Hellbreakers getting too excited if there were bystanders around.

They drove through the empty, semi-jungle countryside for

fifteen minutes or so. The forest and brush thinned and developed land appeared ahead of them, right about the same time they spotted the blue strip of the Atlantic Ocean.

The town that had grown up around the water treatment plant was small, and it looked as though they'd set most of the houses and businesses back from the facility. It probably made noise or discharged unpleasant smells into the air, so ensuring a certain amount of buffer space from residential and commercial buildings was wise. Amahle breathed a low sigh of relief.

They drove through the village, making no effort to disguise their approach. Since they were posing as legitimate security personnel, it made sense to take a direct route and move with easy confidence. A few locals gawked or squinted at them as they passed, but no one accosted them or seemed alarmed.

Gage mumbled, "Once again everything seems almost too peaceful. Can you see any Executive Security vehicles waiting within the town? I cannot."

Amahle glanced around. "No, but if there are some, they would likely be hiding out of sight from the main road. I would have liked to scout for them in advance. I'm afraid we didn't have time for that."

The water purification facility loomed ahead, looking like an odd cross between a small military installation, a power plant, and a simple office. Fencing surrounded it on three sides. On the fourth was the sea. There were two smallish outbuildings off to the sides. Beyond the gate in the fence that faced east was a two-story office. It appeared to be attached to a larger and more industrial building that extended into the water and whose smokestacks gave off a steady trickle of silvery steam.

"Here we go," Amahle breathed. Her rifle lay out of sight unless one of the guards stuck his head through the window. She would be able to bring it up and into play in less than a second.

The gate wasn't as formidable as Amahle had feared. It was made of steel bars and had an electronic lock and a guard booth.

Secure enough to keep out trespassers on foot, and coils of razor wire topped the fence around it. However, an Autocutioner-sized vehicle moving at speed could probably knock it down. Thus, if Eleanor's plan failed, there were other options.

Daria's truck slowed and stopped right in front of the gate. Gage halted behind it, leaving about two trucks' length between them.

Amahle suggested, "Get closer if they open the gate so we can slip in right behind Daria. If they don't open up, we might have to ram it."

"That had occurred to me, but thank you." Gage's demeanor was frostier than usual. The weight of what they were about to do was bearing down on him, and he was probably still flustered by the ugly scene in Acacia Hollow.

A security guard, a tall, heavy man of about forty, emerged from the booth. He appeared to be wearing a soft armor vest under his shirt, and he wore a pistol at his side. His role was to deter low-level troublemakers and sound the alarm if necessary. The real heavy hitters were probably somewhere within the compound itself.

Amahle cracked her window and tried to listen to the conversation. Behind her, the Hellbreakers had parked a good hundred yards back. She wondered if they would try to rush the gate once it opened or if they meant to hang back and pretend to be part of a different group. It irked her that they hadn't planned their attack in more detail.

It was hard to hear everything said, but the guard kept nodding as Daria and Eleanor spoke. He asked basic questions, and they gave him comparable answers before handing over a set of badges and papers. The man flipped through, glancing at each for about two seconds before moving on to the next.

Gage said, "Eleanor has information for us as well. If they let her in, I will drive through and, if the man starts after us, we'll pretend that we didn't see him and simply don't know what's going on."

"Good idea," Amahle conceded. "If they start shooting, all of that can be discarded."

Gage's tone was grim. "I know."

The guard handed the ID stuff back to Daria, then went back to his booth. Five seconds later, there came a beeping and the gate rolled open with a rustling clank. Daria put the truck into drive at once and rolled forward.

"Go," Amahle urged.

Gage hit the gas. Not hard enough to make it too obvious what he was doing, but enough to propel them fast enough that the distance between the two vehicles closed rapidly. Right as he and Amahle crossed the threshold, the gate began to close again, and the guard ran behind them, waving one hand and shouting while his other hand fell to his hip by his gun.

Gage kept driving. They barely cleared the gate as it shut behind them, blocking off the guard, who stamped in irritation. He ran back to his booth and Amahle saw him speaking into a microphone or walkie-talkie while staring at them.

"Well, we're not in serious trouble *yet*," she quipped. "He seemingly cleared the fake IDs. So he's probably telling the people inside to double-check us. We will go with your idea to claim innocence as long as we can."

Her partner nodded. He steered the Autocutioner with his right hand, while with his left he grabbed the strap of his rifle and hoisted it up toward his lap.

So far, no small army of security goons was rushing out to greet them. Things were going nearly as well as they could have hoped for.

Daria stopped the truck on an open lot before the entrance to the main building, parking in such a way that she could loop around and drive off quickly without having to put the truck in reverse or navigate any obstacles. Gage followed her and parked about seven yards apart.

"Good," he muttered as he shifted into park and prepared to turn off the engine. Ahead of them, the others were stepping out of the vehicle.

Amahle wondered where the security cameras were. Ty in particular was hard to mistake for anyone other than Ty. As soon as someone who recognized his face caught sight of him entering the building, the game would be up. On a whim, she flicked on the radio, which was still on the Hellbreakers' frequency.

Gus answered almost immediately. "You're not supposed to be calling us at this time of day. So, when do we—"

"Wait," Amahle said. "Cover us. Move in only if there is trouble. So far—"

"Hey!" Another voice, probably Nic's, came over the speaker. "Black vans movin' in from the side streets. Guess there *is* trouble. Ha, ha!"

She hitched up her SKS on its strap, trying to ignore the sudden sinking feeling in her gut. A supply truck had pulled around from one of the outbuildings to the corner of the compound, and a pair of workers were loading boxes onto a dolly. "Let's go. Now. We need to get inside before anyone does anything stupid." The radio was still on, meaning that the Hellbreakers had probably heard her. She flicked it off and opened the Autocutioner's door.

Then an engine roared behind them as the lead pickup truck in Gus's caravan rocketed forward. It was going to ram the gate.

"Fuck!" Amahle exclaimed. She hopped down to the ground but immediately took cover behind the engine compartment. Daria, Eleanor, Ty, and Dante were at the entrance to the front office and had crossed the threshold.

The guard at the front booth appeared again, holding up a hand and drawing his pistol. He fired a single shot at the truck, which sparked uselessly off the frame.

Then the truck swerved around sidelong, and Amahle glimpsed something that set her jaw falling open. Commander Augustus Freeman, leading quite literally from the front, was leaning out the passenger's side window with a grenade launcher. He fired once, the weapon making a *thunking* sound as its payload careened right toward the space between the gate itself and the guard booth.

"*No!*" the guard screamed. The grenade went off. The blast sent a shockwave through the air that rattled the vehicle, and a blossom of orange flame and black smoke rose into the air. Amahle's ears rang. Metal *screeched* as the gate, the booth, and the guard were all blasted to pieces.

Then the Hellbreakers drove straight in. Behind and to the sides of them, four black vans—undeniably piloted by Executive Security teams—were closing in and squeezing off bursts of automatic gunfire.

Gage slapped his face. "For the sake of God," he groaned.

Amahle grabbed his shoulder. "Move! Let them handle the distraction. We need to get *in.*" Pulling him along, she sprinted toward the front doors. Ty, scowling at the sudden SNAFU, was holding the doors open for them while it sounded like there was shouting and commotion within.

Right before Amahle and Gage entered the building, the first two of the Hellbreakers' vehicles—the truck containing Gus and a van containing another group—veered in. Men in demonic armor jumped off or piled out, whooping and hollering and raising their guns.

The two workers by the supply truck had frozen next to the dollies they were loading. One of them started fumbling under his shirt for something. A trio of Hellbreakers noticed and opened fire.

The worker and his partner screamed as bullets riddled them, toppling over in misty clouds of blood. A few stray rounds also smashed into the boxes on the dolly, splintering them.

Tyler bellowed, "Goddammit! You fucking idiots. This isn't according to plan, and those men weren't a threat!"

Gus appeared from amid the chaos with an annoyed, vaguely contemptuous look on his youthful face. "One of them probably had a gun. We need to secure the gate, don't we? Besides, this place produces works of the beast. We don't want whatever they were loading to leave this facility."

The security vans were getting closer, and the shooting between them and the other half of the Hellbreakers' force was getting louder.

During a brief respite in the cracklings, Ty shouted, "Hold them off. We're going in." He ducked into the building, and Amahle and Gage followed.

Before the walls closed in around her and blocked off sight of what was going on outside, the last thing Amahle saw was the Hellbreakers, on foot, charging madly at the approaching security vans and blasting away with their rifles and submachine guns. When the thunderous reports of the firearms lulled, she heard them laughing and cheering as they flung themselves into battle with no particular regard for their safety.

"At least they do not lack courage," she grumbled under her breath.

Gage heard her. "It would be better if they didn't also lack *sense.*"

CHAPTER TWENTY-TWO

The front office area of the water purification plant was about what Amahle had expected. A spacious, genteel, but tasteful lobby with big comfy chairs and potted plants, along with a combination reception desk and second security checkpoint, including a metal detector.

Amahle snorted at that. They'd already blown their cover.

Dante, as the largest and youngest of the Executioners, was handling "crowd control," the polite term for intimidation of hostages.

"You! *Get down*," he snarled, aiming his shotgun at a pair of bureaucrat types huddled in the corner. They obeyed, dropping to their knees. "Eleanor, these aren't the two we're looking for, are they?"

Eleanor glanced at them. "No." Her face had a curdled look of distaste, perhaps at the thought of how what they were doing would look to the average person who didn't know what was going on behind the scenes.

Daria was aiming her Browning pistol at the throat of a security guard and bringing him around from behind the desk. Like the man in the booth outside, he wore a normal uniform and carried only a handgun.

Once he was out on the main lobby floor, Daria carefully circled behind him and took his gun, a .357 revolver, before slamming the butt of her pistol into the back of his head. He grunted and fell unconscious to the floor. She slipped the gun into her waistband, returned her Browning to its holster, and took up her Uzi in both hands. "Which way do we go?"

Ty glanced out the front doors. "So far those idiots are keeping the cavalry occupied. Move in and form two separate teams. We're not going to split up, but I want a point team and a rear team. Gage, Amahle—you're on point. Eleanor, go with them since we need you to ID the targets. Daria, Dante, and I will be in the rear. That's probably where the heaviest opposition is going to come from. Now, move."

There wasn't time for much in the way of emotions, but something within Amahle momentarily swelled with warmth and admiration. Despite his lingering wounds, Tyler refused to put himself anywhere other than at the forefront of the fighting. She didn't doubt that he would sacrifice his life for the sake of their mutual success if that was what it took.

She hoped he *didn't* have to die, though. Him, or any of the others.

She and Gage leapt out in front, striding through the metal detector and ignoring the alarm it set off. Eleanor moved in behind them. She said, "I believe the hallway to the right leads to the main facilities, and the left is mainly offices, the cafeteria, bathrooms, and so forth. I don't know where Damiano and Tranh would be."

"Left," Gage suggested. "If they're Executives, they would probably prefer to be in offices rather than in places where real work happens."

He trotted ahead, his AR-10 at the ready, with Amahle three paces behind him and Eleanor another two paces behind her. As they moved around the corner, they saw their three companions forming up to pass through the checkpoint and then secure the T-intersection of the hallway.

More disturbingly, Amahle had a brief glimpse through the entrance's glass doors of what was going on outside. The Hellbreakers were approaching the building. She couldn't tell if they were beating a defensive retreat or simply trying to help out after eliminating the opposition. Gunshots still rang out from the front lot area, though.

The three beat feet down the hall. It seemed longer than Amahle would've guessed by judging the building's size from outside. Doors lined each wall to the sides, and it opened to a large chamber at the end, without any bends or corners the whole way.

Gage said, "Let us check each room. I will take the left. Amahle, take the right. Eleanor, stay back a few paces and stay out of our way. If we see someone, we'll have you look at them when it's safe."

Amahle muttered, "I'm surprised at the lack of security inside the building. It makes me wonder if we have unpleasant surprises waiting for us."

Gage didn't respond. Instead, he took two steps forward and kicked down the nearest door to his left. Aiming his rifle and sweeping the space within, then peering through the gap between the door and the wall to which it was hinged, he declared, "It's empty."

Amahle moved up on the right and tried the knob of the first door. It swung open without resistance, and she shouldered her rifle.

Within lay a single desk and two chairs. A corpulent woman in plain business attire sat behind the desk, staring straight ahead at the muzzle of Amahle's SKS.

"Oh my God," she whispered. Then louder as she turned her

face aside, *"Oh my God!"* She pulled open a drawer and reached into it, her hand closing shakily around a pistol.

There was no time to convince her to surrender. Amahle shot her through the armpit, destroying both lungs and probably her heart as well. The woman groaned and slumped back in her chair, drooling blood. The pistol fell to the floor.

Amahle shook her head. "Clear," she said in a flat tone.

As they moved on down the hallway, they encountered virtually no one else save another office worker. This one, an old gray-haired man, gave himself up peacefully. Gage stuffed him into a closet, removed the pistol in his desk drawer, and left him be.

Furthermore, half of the rooms were bare of furniture. There was nothing to suggest anyone had ever used them at all.

Eleanor commented, "This building might be a façade more than anything else. Perhaps we should've taken the other hallway."

Everyone looked back over their shoulders. Ty and the others had taken position at the T-intersection at the back of the lobby and were moving slowly down the same hallway Amahle and Gage had charged down.

Noticing them, Ty called, "Our friends outside are moving in. I pointed the other way. We can let them soak up the heat in that direction while we finish up down here."

Then from somewhere beyond one of the open, seemingly empty offices, a man sprang out at startling speed with a roar and clamped his arms around Eleanor's shoulders.

Dante cried, "Eleanor!" He was too far away to do anything.

Amahle pivoted and aimed her rifle, cursing beneath her breath. Having to shoot over someone's shoulder was incredibly dangerous. The same instant she saw what was going on, the situation changed.

Eleanor's eyes were bulging with fear, but she acted quicker than Amahle would've expected. Much smaller than the man who'd tried to grab her, she slipped straight down out of his grasp before he could tighten his arms around her. Then she sprang up with her pistol drawn and fired it four times.

The man wore the same outfit as the regular security guards. The first two .380 rounds slammed into his chest and knocked him off-balance but failed to penetrate his concealed vest. Somewhere in the middle of her burst, Eleanor came to her senses and raised the gun, firing the last two into the man's throat and face at an angle so the bullets would hit the wall rather than flying down the hallway toward Ty, Daria, and Dante.

The guard gurgled on blood and fell over in a heap. Eleanor stood, frozen in shock at what she'd done.

"Christ," Dante muttered, his voice carrying down the hall despite how softly he'd said it.

Gage squeezed past Amahle to place a hand on Eleanor's shoulder. "It's all right. You did what you had to do. Well done. Now, come along, please."

Eleanor relaxed, mechanically turning back toward the far end of the hall, and walked slowly behind her friends as they proceeded to the end.

There was one more office to check. It too was empty, but Amahle looked it over more thoroughly than she had the last one. She had no idea how the guard who'd attacked Eleanor had escaped detection. She was still somewhat unused to fighting indoors in such tight quarters, and it bothered her that she'd made such a serious error.

On the plus side, Eleanor proved more capable in combat than anyone guessed.

The chamber at the end of the hall turned out to be the cafeteria. Someone had left a half-eaten meal on one of the tables, and a window hung open. Whoever had been there had made a hasty escape sometime after the shooting had started.

Eleanor, who was starting to come back to her senses again, looked at the repast. "I doubt Junior Board members would eat such cheap food," she mused. "I don't think the person who was in here was one of the Executives."

Ty kicked the wall. "Dammit. All right, back the other way."

No sooner had he given the order than a crowd of Hellbreakers appeared in the hallway from the lobby and jogged down the corridor in the other direction toward the processing facilities proper.

"Shit." Dante glanced at the others. "Those guys are trigger-happy. If there's security down that hall, good, but they might blow the Execs away too while they're at it."

Ty waved. "Follow them and do what you can. We're running out of time." He looked out the cafeteria windows, and half a second later, all of them spotted what he'd seen. Two more black vans pulled up outside, and full-armored men with rifles spilled out. "Go!"

This time, Dante took point as they ran back the way they'd come and crossed the juncture point to follow the Hellbreakers. Their impetuous allies had already vanished around a corner farther down, and gunfire was thundering again from somewhere deeper within the facility.

An instant after Dante crossed the T-intersection, some of the security goons outside opened fire.

"Down!" Ty barked.

They all dropped to their knees or bellies as bullets ripped through the walls, tearing holes in the wood and plaster. Dante alone was past the intersection. He leaned around the corner and fired a couple of blasts with his shotgun. Daria reached the juncture next and fired half a magazine of nine-millimeter bullets into the lobby before dashing across the opening. There came a brief halt in the goons' attacks as they took cover where they could find it.

Ty was up next. He sprang to his feet, held his rifle braced against his stomach with its muzzle pointing toward their foes, and charged straight ahead, firing sideways on full auto and screaming with bloodcurdling intensity as he moved. His lingering injuries probably assaulted him with pain, but he ignored it.

Amahle dragged Eleanor behind her, ducking low as she fired three rounds from her SKS around the corner to cover their movements further. Someone shot back, but the three-round burst went high by a hand's breadth, blowing chunks from the wall above her head.

It looked like at least eight men in the lobby, but two had fallen. One was dead. The other had been wounded and was writhing in pain on the floor. His comrades hadn't tried to retrieve him yet due to the repeated barrages of fire from the Executioners.

Before she passed into concealment in the other hallway, Amahle squeezed off a quick shot at the wounded goon. The 7.62 round blew a red hole in his abdomen and came out his shoulder. He stopped squirming at once.

Eleanor was once again half-stunned, but she seemed to be recovering her mental faculties faster and faster each time she encountered violence and death.

Gage was the only one left on the wrong side of the hallway. While the security team took blind potshots, he aimed his rifle and began firing short bursts of three or four rounds at a time. He advanced a few feet after each one and finally emptied the rest of his magazine as he jumped across the opening. Amahle gasped as an enemy slug struck him in the front torso area, knocking him into a spin. She caught him right past the edge of the wall and pulled him through.

Ty had reloaded and fired another half-magazine through the walls, covering them as they worked around the corner. In moments, the remaining men in the lobby would chase after them.

Amahle checked Gage. "Are you hurt?"

He gritted his teeth and patted himself down. "Ah, I do not

think so. It was a glancing blow." There was a long but shallow dent in the front plate of his armor. The impact of it had thrown him off-balance, knocked the wind from his lungs, and perhaps bruised his chest, but that was all.

"Good." Amahle sighed. "Let's go. Tell me if you cannot move fast enough."

Fortunately, he could. Despite being short and older than the rest of them, he kept pace as they moved down the next corridor. It ended not far from the corner at a double door that *had* stayed securely locked until the Hellbreakers blasted the hinges apart.

The Executioners advanced over the wreckage and into the industrial part of the main structure. This was the true heart of the compound that the Execs claimed was devoted to seawater desalination.

The area that opened before them looked more like a giant garage than anything. Aside from the fact that the various pipes they'd seen from outside ran through it. Some pipes funneled water underground to unknown functions. Others carried steam up and away from unseen sources. The metal cylinders turned the storage space into a colonnade of sorts.

They could tell that the pipes carried water, steam, or both since that was what flowed, shot, or spilled out from the ones ruptured by gunfire.

Bodies lay scattered across the floor. At a glance, Amahle counted eight or nine of them. One was a Hellbreaker, given the red-stained armor he wore with a black pentagram on the chest and the cross etched into the stock of his rifle. The rest were personnel from the facility. Some were security guards. Others were civilian workers who didn't appear to be armed.

Ty cupped a hand by his mouth. "Hey—*Hey!* What are you assholes doing?"

The mass of pipes blocked off most of their vision, but they saw the Hellbreakers driving a crowd of people before them, their guns continuing to thunder every second or two. More bodies *thudded* to the floor.

Amazingly, someone heard them. Nic the Australian jogged back. As he moved, he ejected a magazine from his rifle and slapped in a new one. "What's the problem, mates?"

Daria, whose eye was twitching in a rage that nearly equaled Ty's, shouted, "You're killing everyone! You aren't supposed to massacre the civilians, you fools. Did you even leave anyone outside to guard the entrance?"

Ignoring the first part of what she'd said, the man smirked. "Two of our best men. Excuse me." He sprinted away from them, weaving between the pipes to rejoin his comrades in their indiscriminate slaughter.

To Amahle's shock, Gage hissed, "We should take them out right now."

Eleanor stepped in front of the whole group, her face drawn with alarm. "We have to stop them. From here, if I remember right, the only way out is down a hatch that leads to the secret facility. It's underground. Everyone will be pressed in down there, and there will be a total massacre. We'll lose public support. We—"

Ty cut her off. "Move! Stop them." He waved and lurched forward, hobbling at a speed that was nearly a jog despite his obvious pain.

Eleanor fell in beside them as all five Executioners broke into a run. Though they had never been here before, they had fought together in enough different environments that it was unnecessary to issue detailed commands. They advanced in one section at a time, scouting and clearing it, leaving no avenues open for ambush, everyone covering for everyone else.

By the time they were close enough to the mass of people on the far side of the building to act, most of them were gone. The remaining staff and guards must have fled to the underground portion of the compound, and Amahle saw the Hellbreakers descending through a hatch in the floor as well.

She caught sight of Augustus as he launched himself into the opening, catching the ladder partway down. She had a clear shot. She could have fired.

"Gus!" she cried. "Wait. Stop this foolishness!" Her gut tightened, recalling the way he and his men had saved her at the mansion and his youthful charm...but also his apparent enthusiasm for unrestricted murder.

His head swiveled toward her. He flashed a big grin and climbed the rest of the way down, out of sight. The last two of his followers went next.

Footsteps pounded the floor somewhere behind them.

Ty yelled, "Gage!"

Among the group, Gage was still farthest back. He swung a hundred and eighty degrees, raised his rifle, and sidestepped around a pipe before opening fire on the entrance to the hallway they'd left behind—three bursts of six or seven rounds each, each a peal of brutal thunder.

Amahle ducked around another pipe in the opposite direction. She faintly saw more Exec Security goons spilling through the doorway to the garage area, some of them leaping to the sides to take cover or seek a better line of sight, while at least one toppled over in the agonies of death.

While Gage reloaded, Amahle raised her rifle and fired all the cartridges that remained in it. It was enough to give their adversaries pause, and during that interval, Dante, Ty, Daria, and Eleanor slipped into the hatch.

Ty shouted, "Come on!"

Gage blasted another four or five rounds from his AR-10 from the fresh mag, then retreated toward the opening. Amahle fell to the floor and crawled over behind him, willing herself to ignore the reports of bullets zipping past them, tearing up the floor, or punching new holes in the much-beleaguered pipes.

The hatch was circular and about a meter and a half wide. Amahle swung down onto the ladder, impressed by how fast Gage was moving immediately below her. She reached up and found the interior handle to swing the hatch shut. It *banged* into place.

She couldn't discern any mechanism to lock it. Still, at least the heavy steel would repel gunfire, and having to open it again would slow their pursuers, if only by two or three seconds.

Amahle dropped off the ladder once Gage was clear of it. Her feet struck the floor hard, but her legs and hips were supple enough to cushion some of the impact, and she rolled forward for good measure. When she came back up into a kneeling position, her jaw dropped again.

A short, featureless steel corridor opened into a vast, vault-like space. An irregularly pulsating and flashing blue-white glow illuminated it, accompanied by a weird humming. Catwalks made of bright metal spanned the perimeter of a cavernous depth that stretched deep into the earth.

People were shouting again. More gunfire erupted.

Amahle bounced to her feet. The others were already in position to move into the vault.

Ty glanced around at all of them. "Dante, Gage, Amahle, on point. Me, Eleanor, Daria, in back. Go." His voice was oddly soft, but his lips had pulled back, exposing clenched teeth.

Amahle dashed ahead between the three who would guard the rear of their formation. She was two or three paces behind Dante and Gage as they went through the opening at the end of the short corridor and fanned out onto the catwalk. Behind and above, she heard the second security team opening the hatch.

Unless there was a secret exit down here, they were trapped. More enemies and profoundly unreliable allies lay ahead, and enemies blocked off their avenue of entry from behind. Even if they found the two Execs they sought, there would be no way to escape except by killing a numerically superior force in tight quarters.

As Amahle dashed out onto the catwalk, her brain had trouble processing what her eyes saw. Instead, it focused on the sounds behind her. A single gunshot, followed by a loud *hissing* noise, and the tramping of three pairs of feet.

Daria explained, "I shot a steam pipe near the hatch. That ought to slow down our friends. As for how *we* will get back through it later, who knows?"

Ty replied, "Yeah, we'll deal with that when we—oh, my God."

Amahle's eyes focused, and at last, the scene before her became coherent.

More bodies littered the grated surface or slumped against the railings. The Hellbreakers had lost three more of their own, but the death toll among the facility's workers and guards was twice as great.

It was also clear that the cavern below them was more grotto than anything. It ended in the sea itself. There wasn't enough light to see the water, but Amahle heard and sensed its presence.

The most striking thing was what lay beyond the initial section of the catwalk, near the far end of the hollowed space before them, about a hundred meters away.

The device was enormous. Its base was a solid cylinder rising from the water below. It occupied an area the size of a small house, surrounded by a ring of catwalk that skirted its upper edges. A glowing blue core was the source of the unsteady light; it reminded Amahle of an electrical storm. Surrounding it were several rings that revolved in a centrifugal pattern, spinning in opposite directions. Each held Atlanticore crystals that likely powered the whole contraption.

Gouts of water channeled into the grotto from the adjacent ocean poured over the lower reaches to keep the thing cool. Steam rose continuously around it, mostly caught by fans that funneled it into the exhaust pipes they'd seen above.

Then something else occurred to Amahle. The rings around the core were like massively larger replicas of the bracelet Gage had taken from Singh. What the device's purpose was, she had no idea.

Nearer the machine, the Hellbreakers had been bottlenecked at a narrow catwalk section before it divided into the two paths that stretched to either side of the giant centrifuge. Fireteams of Executive Security, fully decked out in paramilitary gear, occupied each of the two branches and had pinned the attackers down in a crossfire.

The Coven must have had reinforcements underground, guarding the machine, which presumably was the real reason the entire facility existed. The few remaining civilians had retreated somewhere behind the device. As Amahle watched in stupefied horror, another of the Hellbreakers staggered back, half his head blown off, and pitched over the railing into the waters below.

The young men with the unholy armor and sanctified weapons had whipped themselves into a frenzy. Despite being at a disadvantage, they screamed and howled as they frantically reloaded and fired, refusing to retreat, obsessively trying to outgun their opponents through sheer rage.

It was the contraption, Amahle realized. The sight of it had driven them mad.

Amahle shouted, "Gus! Fall back. You're going to get everyone killed! We can still—"

Another peal of rifle fire cut her off. Gus looked back at her over his shoulder for half a second. Then he turned once more to stare at the glowing centrifuge. In an eerily shrill and hoarse voice, he shrieked, "The beast! The works of the beast..."

CHAPTER TWENTY-THREE

Dante shook his head. "They've lost it," he opined. "Mental health isn't my specialty, but I'd be referring them all to a psychiatrist if they came into my—"

A barrage of shooting drowned out the rest, but they all got the gist of it.

Behind them, someone stumbled out onto the catwalk, thrashing around and wailing. It was one of the security goons who'd been behind them. He must have tried to run through the steam jet and gotten scalded.

Ty turned and shot him twice, ending his pain and blasting him back against the far railing. Then he fired two more shots into the corridor to discourage the rest of them. He looked back at his comrades. "We need to pull those idiots back and have them handle rearguard, so we can break through and look for the Execs."

Amahle and Gage were already running up behind them, keeping their heads low, knowing full well how much danger they were in. Amahle struggled to ram in the next ten-round stripper clip. The rifle's mechanisms were rather stiff. But she managed.

Gage shouted, "Fall back, Hellbreakers. Fall back! We can win this if we—"

"No!" Gus retorted. "It ends now. We're bringing all of this filth to its end. They can't do stuff like this. It's against God and nature!" He raised his rifle and fired a long burst, at least ten rounds on full auto at the centrifugal device. The bullets sparked off the metal, but the dents they left were big enough that further gunfire might do real damage.

Amahle noticed that the security forces beyond the choke-point had seen them approaching, and two of the men were aiming at her. Her SKS came up automatically, and she squeezed the trigger three times. Both guards fell, one straight back with a hole through his eye. The other twirled sidelong, leaking blood, and collapsed atop the nearest rail.

She threw her voice toward the Hellbreakers. "Stop being ridiculous. We can take down their operation later. Now is the time for cool heads."

Nic's face was suddenly visible amid the group, and he pointed his gun at Gage. "Back off, you two. You're startin' to annoy the piss out of us."

The sight of him threatening Gage set off an explosion of rage that Amahle hadn't anticipated. She often tamped down on her emotions and was sometimes surprised by their intensity when the unexpected occurred. "Don't you dare!" she snarled, aiming her rifle.

Then Gus turned again, and without any further words or warning, shot her in the chest.

Amahle let out a sound that was halfway between a groan and a sharp, sudden "oof." The bullet slammed into her. It flattened against her armor but still knocked her off her feet, and searing pain shot through her torso and down her left arm. She almost dropped her rifle as her back *thudded* against the catwalk's steel grating, and a vacuum might as well have emptied her lungs.

"Hey!" Dante raged. "That's it. Fuck you, assholes!" He raised his shotgun and fired, not at the security goons but the Hell-breakers.

Then, as Amahle's vision swirled and swam and her chest burned with the struggle to breathe, everything became total pandemonium.

Twenty guns fired at once, drowning out all other noises as bullets flew in every conceivable direction. Everyone was a target. Everyone now fought against everyone else.

Amahle started to sit up, trying not to pass out. She knew the bullet hadn't penetrated her armor. Still, it could've broken ribs, cracked her sternum, or possibly ruptured muscles and organs from the impact's sheer force. Gus had shot her dead-center at a perfect ninety-degree angle.

For the first time in a long time, she wanted to cry. The physical pain and the less obvious kind that accompanied betrayal were unbearable.

Suddenly Daria was kneeling beside her, feeling around her torso and trying to drag her away from the main line of fire. Tyler stood over her while shooting. Eleanor was off to the side, her pistol in hand, frantically looking back and forth between the main battle ahead of them and the growing shadows of the other security team behind. The men there seemed to have found a narrow gap around the steam jet and were slowly crawling through it.

Amahle's vision cleared, and she could breathe again. "I'm all right," she gasped. "Mostly. Help me stand."

Daria was about to protest. Then a bullet whizzed past her head. She broke into a sharp string of Polish, raised her Uzi, and fired it one-handed in the general direction of both groups of their enemies. She braced her hip against the railing while Amahle struggled to her feet.

She would be okay, more or less. The next week, or the next month, would hurt. She felt confident that she hadn't taken a mortal or disabling injury.

Daria barked, "Dante!" There was enough time between barrages of fire for the tall physician to hear her. He emptied a final shell from his Ithaca, blowing one of the Hellbreakers over the edge of the catwalk, then glanced back and forth. He blinked. At last, he ducked back to check on Amahle.

"Sorry," he said. "I was pissed. Where'd you get hit?"

Amahle put a hand on the approximate spot.

Dante frowned. He loaded extra shells into his shotgun while he spoke. "Oof. Probably got a rib or two popped loose, maybe a bruised diaphragm. You'll live as long as you don't have serious internal bleeding, okay? If you start getting dizzy, tell me right away."

Two bullets rang off the steel about a foot to the side of him.

Amahle raised her rifle. "I will try to remember that. Other things are going on." Then, before she knew what she was doing, she plunged straight ahead into the fray.

She *was* dizzy, but it was impossible to say if it was from internal blood loss, as Dante seemed to fear, or simply from the general trauma of the blow she'd taken. Everything around her became a mechanical haze, a roistering melee of chaos that somehow seemed to exist within a cycle of order, not unlike the unstable core of the Coven device within the rings that protected and empowered it.

Amahle was aware of motion and her hands firing the rifle and loading another stripper clip. She had only the vaguest idea of what was happening. Then her vision cleared, her consciousness sharpened, and she saw what was around her once again.

She, Gage, and Eleanor had—somehow—ended up far along the catwalk that bent around the giant contraption to the right. They'd passed the chokepoint. Glancing around, she saw bodies everywhere. At a huge cost to their numbers, the Hellbreakers must have broken through, and the last of the security team had retreated elsewhere.

Augustus Freeman and his men, who numbered perhaps ten

at most after the slaughter they'd been through, mindlessly blazed away at the centrifugal rings and the glowing core. Cracks appeared in the shining metal. The *hissing* of steam around the device grew louder and angrier.

Closer to the corridor they'd come through after the hatch, Tyler, Daria, and Dante battling it out with the second security team to cover the rest of them. They outnumbered the Executioners, but the Coven's minions were the ones who currently had to contend with a chokepoint.

Eleanor shouted, "Come on! This way. Please, we still might have time."

Amahle stumbled toward her, aware of Gage by her side.

Two scientists or workers in white coats had appeared from somewhere deeper within the facility and were approaching the Hellbreakers. The latter were distracted by their single-minded objective of destroying the bizarre machine.

The egghead out in front, a small older man with huge spectacles, waved his arms. "Stop! You're going to destabilize it. It will destroy the whole—"

His voice turned into a squawk as Gus' hand shot out and clamped around his throat. Lifting him straight up, the Hellbreakers' commander hurled the man over the railing toward the device. His body struck one of the rings and blasted back in a shower of blue sparks before it hurtled to the water below.

The other scientist, younger and larger than the first, nonetheless got the message. "Shit!" He turned and ran.

As Eleanor led Amahle and Gage around to the far side of the machine, they saw the two catwalks converging again. The fleeing scientist was ahead of them. He ducked into a doorway on a small structure that Amahle hadn't seen before since the centrifuge device blocked it.

It looked like a glorified shed built into an outcropping of rock in the grotto's wall. Within were rows of complex machinery and a narrow passage leading somewhere deeper into the compound's hidden depths.

Gage reached out and grabbed Eleanor's arm, pulling her aside while he took point. She fell in step with Amahle.

As they reached the doorway to the control chamber, the second of the two scientists was pulling a lever and pressing a button. He looked up at them with bulging eyes and the expression of a teenage shop employee caught stealing from the register.

"I have to flood the chamber," he protested although they hadn't accused him of anything yet. "It's the only way to stop a total meltdown! The core will overheat. Those fools ruptured it."

Gage said, "How much time do we have?"

The man's mouth made strange shapes before he blurted, "I don't know. A few minutes."

Eleanor stepped up. "Where are Sergio Damiano and Ida Tranh?"

The scientist glanced aside at something on the floor. "Um. Ms. Tranh is right here. I don't know where Mr. Damiano is, okay?"

Gage pushed the scientist aside and sprang into the room. Lying below the line of sight from the control shed's windows was a small Asian woman in a dress suit. She'd taken a bullet through the shoulder and was half-conscious as her hand vainly clamped over the wound, trying to stop the bleeding.

Outside, there was a metallic *creaking* sound followed by a powerful rush as water from the sea spilled in through a gate near the strange machine. It surrounded the device's base and rose, creating plumes of white steam that filled nearly half the cavern.

Eleanor stared at Tranh. "I don't think she's going to make it. This might have all been in vain."

From the dark passage at the other side of the shed, a

disturbingly familiar voice chimed in. "I can help her. If you will let me."

Out of the shadows stepped Jori Singh.

Amahle stared directly at him for what seemed like ten seconds without grasping what she was looking at. It was undeniably the same man she'd seen gunned down at the pool. Yet he was alive and showed no particular ill effects from having had his torso ventilated half a dozen times, followed by sinking underwater for several minutes.

Gage sighed. "Oh, dear. This isn't right at all."

Singh was wearing slacks and a button-down shirt. He strolled casually out to the middle of the shed's floor. "We do not have much time. I can heal Ms. Tranh if you permit me a minute or two of peace. Keep those people outside away from me."

The scientist had flattened himself against the window. The glass shattered behind him and a gout of blood erupted from his neck. He clutched madly at the wound but collapsed after only a second or two, dead.

Amahle came to her senses. "Do whatever you must." She stepped over the unfortunate scientist's body and aimed her rifle out the window. One of the Hellbreakers was shooting at them, and it also looked like one or two of the fresh security men had got past Tyler and the others. She took potshots at all of them, half-emptying her rifle and sending them diving for cover.

Gage had moved protectively over Singh as the man crouched next to Tranh. He placed his hand over the woman's and in turn over the wound.

A barrage of gunfire echoed through the grotto as slugs peppered the shed, cracking more glass, punching through weak points in the walls, and damaging the equipment, some of which began to smoke or spew flames.

Amahle dropped prone. She could blind-fire out the doorway from where she was at, but there was a chance she might hit one of her friends. Instead, she crawled forward. Her ears were taking serious abuse from all the noise of firearms going off indoors, so she didn't hear the pounding of boots until the figure appeared in the doorway.

"No!" Gus shrieked, again in the ragged, high-pitched tone he'd used when glimpsing the machine. "We killed you! You're in league with the fucking Devil, aren't you?"

He meant Singh. The tall Indian looked up at him with calm eyes.

Gage pounced at the young commander, moving quickly, but he was still the slower of the two men. Gus caught his rifle by the barrel and ripped it from the Gurkha's grasp, flinging it aside. It *clattered* onto the catwalk and pitched over toward the water—which had now risen at least three meters. The rushing of the sea grew louder.

Gus and Gage crashed into each other, snarling like animals. Amahle rose to a crouch and tried to get a bead on Freeman, but the pair were moving around too fast for her to hit him without putting a hole through Gage while she was at it.

Eleanor had backed into the corner, frozen in fear and wonder.

The struggling men bumped into Singh, knocking him forward so that his elbow unwittingly jammed into Ida Tranh's stomach. She moaned horribly and spat up blood.

Singh snapped, "You must not interrupt me, or it will not work. She will die without consistent care from—"

Amahle had enough. She ducked back into the shed, seized Singh by the arm, and hauled him to his feet before throwing him out the door. "There is no time left for her. We're taking you instead." She aimed her rifle at him to make sure he got the point.

He blinked, showing a twinge of fear and confusion. Even now, with everything going on, it was *less* fear than an average human would have.

Amahle shouted past the man's shoulder. "Gage! Eleanor! Get out of there. We have to go. The water is still rising."

The struggle between the two men had stopped. Gus, bigger and younger, had pinned Gage beneath him, with the older man's back braced against the edge of a machine. Slowly, Gus bore down on him, bending him backward. In another moment, his spine would break.

Amahle still had no good shot. She stepped sideways, hoping to at least get a bead on Gus's arm, anything to stop him from paralyzing and killing her friend.

Eleanor's hand suddenly shot up into sight, and the pistol *cracked.*

Gus let out a strangled cry. "Dammit! What did you..." His hand went to the back of his neck, and he fell over sideways, releasing Gage, who slumped to the floor.

Amahle sprinted into the shed. As much as she would've liked to finish off Commander Freeman—since Eleanor didn't seem to have scored a mortal hit—saving her friends was more important. She shouldered her rifle on its sling and grabbed Gage by the shoulders, shoving him out the door. Then she took Eleanor's hand and pulled her out as well.

Below them, the water was only about ten meters below their feet. It had risen more than half the distance between its original level and the catwalk.

"Come on," Amahle insisted, growing dizzy again as her chest pained her once more. The adrenaline that had got her this far was wearing off.

The four of them stumbled forward, taking the long way around the increasingly unstable device to avoid the remaining Hellbreakers. The young men had run out of ammo for their rifles and submachine guns and now shot the machine with their sidearms. The cracks in the metal leaked angry blue light, and the electronic hum had become a grating rumble.

Abruptly, they bumped into Dante. "Hey!" he exclaimed, taking in the sight of them all but focusing on Singh. "Who the hell is that? Whatever, follow me. We dealt with the assholes behind us. But this place is flooding, and it looks like that *thing* is going to turn this whole place into a patch of overheated carbon particles."

"Yes," Gage croaked, rubbing his throat and back. "We know."

Jogging toward the short corridor that led out of the grotto, they found Ty and Daria waiting for them. Corpses lay strewn against the railings. The first two Executioners gave Singh a weird look but didn't waste time asking questions. Instead, Daria sprinted ahead of the rest of them.

She picked up a dead man and tossed him in front of the steam jet she'd created earlier. "There. He's past caring, so he might as well block the worst of it. Still rather hot, so step quickly past this part." She hopped over the corpse and past the weaker eddies of steam that curled around his torso.

The rest of the group followed suit, with those unscathed helping the wounded clear the jet and ascend the ladder. Amahle waited toward the back of the formation. As she mounted the ladder, struggling to ignore the swelling agony in her chest, she heard the hysterical voices of the Hellbreakers behind her.

Gus had emerged from the shed and rallied the others. It sounded like he was trying to convince them to escape, too— they'd done enough damage to the "work of the beast" to claim success in destroying it, so there was no sense in becoming martyrs.

Amahle wondered if the fanatics would trail them. She didn't feel like fighting another battle today.

She emerged through the hatch and into the garage area. The ground was rumbling slightly, and the colonnade of pipes all rattled. Some of the ones that had escaped the earlier bullet barrage had ruptured from excessive pressure in the last minute or two.

"Run to the best of your ability," Ty instructed them.

Only Dante, Daria, and Eleanor were in any condition to

sprint at top speed. They stopped halfway across the floor and waited for the others.

Time slowed to a torturous crawl as the group struggled down the hallway and through the lobby. In addition to the low-level earthquake, a curious tingling and a general sense of peril and doom filled the air.

The machine was going to blow at any moment.

Dante, out in front, flung open the rear door of the faux van and grabbed Singh. "Be our guest." He pushed the man into the back compartment before slamming the door shut. Then he helped Amahle and Gage back to their vehicle, hopping in to ride with them while Tyler, Daria, and Eleanor piled into the first.

Amahle was on the verge of relaxing when an awful thought occurred to her. "The people in the town. What if the explosion destroys the whole place?"

Gage started the engine. "We will do what we can to warn them. Between all the gunshots and the trembling ground, I should hope that most of them would be wise enough to realize that something is terribly wrong."

He had a point, Amahle decided.

As they drove out through the wreckage where the gate had been, Amahle rolled down her window and shouted into the streets, "The plant is going to explode. Get everyone clear. You must evacuate. The plant is going to explode..."

There was hardly anyone out that she could see, but a young couple gawking as they rolled past nodded and ran. A few other people moved away from the facility as the two trucks rumbled by, whether on foot or in their cars.

Amahle, Gage, and Dante were perhaps half a mile from the so-called water treatment plant when the core melted down.

At first, there was no noise, but silence, as though the explosion had forced everything else around it to be quiet and pay attention. Then in a flash of blue-white light, the outlines of the facility and the outer reaches of the villages collapsed inward, like something had sucked them beneath the earth.

Then came the true blast, a sonic boom that thundered across the landscape, rattling the teeth of gophers a mile away and sending millions of pieces of debris scattering into the atmosphere.

"God," Dante moaned. "Have *any* of us seen anything like that? It wasn't a nuclear blast, was it? Gage, talk to me. You're our technology guy."

Gage sighed. "I have no fucking idea, Dante. It has been a most trying day."

Ahead of them, the other Autocutioner slowed to a halt. Gage parked alongside them.

Leaning out the driver's side, Daria called, "Is everyone okay? We seem to be fine. Let us hope the people of the village were so fortunate."

Amahle declared that they weren't hurt. At least, not by the explosion. She stared at the smoldering wreckage. "I also wonder if..."

Vehicles were approaching. The blast had been so bright that it was difficult to see any details near the site, but gradually things took on shape and color again. A red van and a blue pickup truck were coming straight toward them.

"So," Amahle muttered. "We weren't the only ones who escaped." She checked to ensure that she'd loaded her rifle. She had.

The two vehicles stopped about a hundred yards away. Gage watched them with a dour expression. When no one else spoke, Amahle cleared her throat and projected her voice as loudly as she could.

"Gus?"

There was total silence for about five seconds. Then someone shot at her.

She jumped in place. The bullet *dinged* off the doorframe

about two feet to her right. Someone needed to practice his longer-range shooting. Then again, since the Hellbreakers had used up their other ammo, he might have fired at her with a pistol.

Amahle's eyes bulged while her lips curled into a vicious snarl. "You motherf—"

"Enough," Gage interjected and hit the gas. The truck rolled forward around the other Autocutioner and back onto the road. Daria followed them. In the rearview mirror, the two vehicles of the Hellbreakers—who had lost more than half of their number, if Amahle wasn't mistaken—drove off to the side and down a back road that led to God knew where.

Dante shook his head, sensing his friends' wounded sense of trust, their anger, and disappointment. "I guess the alliance didn't work out, then."

CHAPTER TWENTY-FOUR

Once they were a safe distance from the coast, Gage contacted Daria via the emergency radio frequency. They agreed to take an unnecessarily long and circuitous route back to the city, crossing the entire breadth of the island's hinterlands before looping back down the southeast coast toward Daria's old home near the city docks.

It was currently late morning. They ended up driving the entire rest of the day, not arriving at Atlantica Metro's eastern outskirts until an hour past dark.

They talked little and paused only once to relieve themselves and pick up food and drinks from a corner store. Their stopping place was one of the small towns increasingly springing up throughout the valleys in the hilly, forested interior. After they'd purchased their provisions, Gage pulled Daria aside.

"Has he talked? Has he said anything?" His eyes were eager, verging on needy.

Daria frowned. "Your friend, Mr. Singh? He told us that's who he is, but I'm puzzled by it since you said he was shot to death, drowned, or both. Otherwise, he's told us nothing. He doesn't seem to be in a very good mood and only stared into space when

Eleanor tried making conversation. Ty threatening him didn't accomplish much, either."

Gage frowned. "I see. When we return...home...I will speak to him."

"You are welcome to try." Daria's tone had a slightly sarcastic edge. "Speaking of home, I don't believe I've been there in two months, so I must apologize in advance if the place smells musty and lacks much in the way of a fully stocked pantry."

Over a year ago, Gage's first case as an Executioner had brought him and Dante into hostile contact with a group of Slavic ruffians who ran an all-purpose crime emporium behind the façade of an auto body shop. They hadn't been the Executioners' actual target, but the business had been ugly enough that hard feelings had persisted.

So, about a month later, they or their associates had managed to discover where Daria lived, probably through mutual contacts in the world of smuggling. Someone had driven a bulldozer through Daria's living room and tossed a Molotov cocktail into her bedroom for good measure. She'd been out on a case at the time. Nonetheless, she was none too happy when she returned—particularly since she hadn't participated in haranguing the Romanians to begin with. They'd retaliated against her simply for being friends with Gage and Dante.

So, Gage and Dante had skimmed off the top of their paychecks from the Executives to help pay for the repairs. It took a couple of months, but the house was finally back to its old self right in time for Daria to effectively move out of it and spend the bulk of her time at HQ like the rest of them.

Still, it was nice to know that the house was *there* if they needed it.

The area seemed peaceful as the two vehicles rolled down the street. The neighborhood adjacent to the docks was a blue-collar one that was crowded and often rowdy, but the locals were either tired tonight or engaged elsewhere.

It only made the Executioners that much more alert. The Coven was still gunning for them, or so they had to assume. Executive Security might have cleared out the civilians in preparation for a major ambush.

No such strike came. After their initial recon sweep, the five parked on opposite sides of the small house, dismounted, and let Eleanor and Singh step down. Ty and Dante took their involuntary guest to the garage, presumably to secure him, while Daria led the others into her mildly dusty living room.

"Sit and relax," she instructed them. "I don't have much food, but I do have vodka. We're in too much danger to get smashed, but a single drink for the rest of you will calm our nerves, I think. Which equates to two drinks for me."

Moments later, she'd distributed glasses of the clear, fiery liquor, and everyone except Singh sat around in a rough circle. They still had their weapons with them. Daria had turned on her outdoor floodlights. At the same time, they lit only a small, dim lamp within to minimize reflections on the windows and see any uninvited guests who might show up.

Ty led the discussion. "Daria. Thanks. We all needed this." He downed his vodka in a single gulp.

The rest did likewise, draining their drinks quickly and setting the glasses down on the tray. Amahle noted with approval that Eleanor seemed to handle the liquor as well as the rest of them.

"Okay," Ty continued after wiping his mouth. "We need to take stock of where we're at. A bad place if we're honest with ourselves."

Daria sighed. "Yes, yes, I didn't have time to clean, and I can't bring myself to hire a maid."

"Har, har," Ty shot back. "You know what I mean. We've had a shitty week. Life hasn't given us any breaks. That sort of thing. We finally found allies and lost them in the space of one day because they turned out to be goddamn psychos.

"We've found out that the Coven isn't playing around anymore. They're not only tinkering with half-baked small arms that make house-sized craters when they don't work so well. They have government-quality facilities where they're working with Atlanticore shit on a level that can wipe out a town."

Gage nodded. "Yes, that's an accurate assessment."

"Unfortunately," Amahle added.

Eleanor raised a hand and glanced at them. "I'm sorry that the information I provided wasn't of more help. Things didn't go well. At least we've learned what they're capable of. That facility was very remote. Some of the people who escaped from the village might talk, but otherwise, the Executives can bury the fact that it happened. I suspect they have other such facilities. A similar incident at one in the middle of the city..."

Dante traced the rim of his empty glass. "Yeah. Let's *not* do that again."

The discussion continued for another five minutes. They all agreed that come morning, there would be hard decisions to make and deep planning to conduct, but no one felt like plunging into it yet. So far, they were safe. They would sleep in shifts.

As the conversation trailed off, Gage stood. "Excuse me." He nodded at his friends and went out into the garage.

Jori Singh sat in a chair. Ty and Dante had done an excellent job of securing him, having tied him up in every way they could think of before they ran out of rope and paracord. They'd secured the whole mass to an iron beam buried five feet in the ground under the floor's concrete slab.

Gage pulled up a chair and sat facing the other man, so their feet were about a meter apart.

"Mr. Singh, I would like to speak to you."

The man rolled his shoulders to the best of his ability. "Then speak. No one is stopping you from letting noises spill out of your mouth."

Gage blinked. Given how gracious and borderline unctuous

Singh had been at the mansion a day and a half ago, his sullen, snappy demeanor seemed to come from nowhere.

Still, it made sense after all that had happened. Ida Tranh and some of the scientists and security guards at the coastal compound might have been friends of his. Plus, he'd probably invested much in the strange centrifugal device.

Gage grunted. "But first." He reached out and unbuttoned the front of Singh's shirt. The ropes binding him made it impossible to take it completely off, but he could part enough of it to inspect the man's chest.

There were patches of rippled skin, puckered scars where the Hellbreakers' bullets had struck him before his apparent death. They appeared to be months or years old. Gus and his compatriots had gunned Singh down mere *hours* ago.

"This is most interesting. So I must ask—what is the Coven doing, and how are the Executives supporting it? You gave me the long and rambling but rather vague version before. Now, I want the shorter and more specific version."

At first, Singh said nothing. He only stared at a point beyond the wall as though he intended to ignore his host. After a minute, he mumbled, "We do not always get what we want, Dr. Gurung."

Gage exhaled slowly. It was going to be a long evening.

After half an hour of fruitless questioning, Singh finally said something of partial value. "I could have helped Ida Tranh. If only you and your friends had protected me from interruption, as I requested, and been a little more patient. One more minute might have been enough."

He didn't move his head, but his eyes moved instead, focusing on Gage's face for the first time. "That you prevented me from healing her is a thing that I'm not sure I can forgive."

Part of the man's aloof façade crumbled. Moisture glimmered around the bottom of his eyes, and his lower lip trembled.

For an instant, pity and compassion struck Gage. Arrogant though he was, and despite his associations with the Coven,

Singh seemed like more of a scholar and healer than anything else. Tranh must have been dear to him.

Then the wave of emotion vanished from Singh's face. He was still morose but back in control of himself. He added, "So far, both the Executives and the Coven have tried to play nice with you people. We hoped you would see the value in what we're attempting to do and join us in full. Now, I'm afraid we're past that point."

Gage leaned back in his chair. Singh's demeanor wasn't threatening. If anything, he was sinking deeper into depression. Yet there was a cold and deadly undertone to his words. He was making a statement of absolute, set-in-stone fact.

"The situation with you and your friends is a tragedy born of hubris. Such is the story of the Executioners. The little saga involving Augustus Freeman and his merry band is much the same. People are oblivious to the chasm that yawns before them. They plunge ahead when they should stop."

Gage tried to process what the man meant. He noted that Singh knew Gus' name without having to be told.

A footstep sounded behind the Gurkha. He turned and saw Amahle stepping out of the shadows by the door that led into the house. She looked past him, staring instead at their captive.

"That is just as well, Mr. Singh." Her voice, too, carried an icy tone of certainty. "Because the Executioners are not going to stop. Soon, we will cut out the heart of this monster you have created."

The story continues with book Six, *Scorched Earth*, available now at Amazon.

Claim your copy today!

AUTHOR NOTES MICHAEL ANDERLE

JANUARY 29, 2022

Thank you for not only reading this book but these author notes as well!

Justice Begins…

Many of you know about Kurtherian Gambit and that the main character, Bethany Anne, has a bit of an attitude about Justice? In this universe, *ATLANTICA*, I continued that same premise, but I decided to play with the concept.

Basically, what happens when "anything goes" inside someone's house? What happens when you take chances inside your house, but a shot exited the walls?

Would home-building be different? Would your guests' sole purpose be to shout, "Keep bullets IN the house!" Would we have some funny commercials, kinda like those in *ROBO-COP*, where the punchline was "I'll buy THAT one for a dollar!"

Since I was raised in Texas, I grew up with a heightened sense of "your home is your fort." What happens on your property is sacrosanct. That includes justice, so if someone comes onto my property and tries to get into my house (breaking and entering), when they get hurt, that is on them.

For example, if there were razor blades set up so if a person tried to break into the house via a window and sliced themselves up, that's on them. Mind you, that was how I grew up thinking, and (surprise to me) when I was told by my wife that in California, the robber would be able to sue me.

And win!

"Whatever for?" I asked, shocked. "They are on MY property, doing ILLEGAL stuff, and what happens to THEIR responsibility for doing this shit?"

The discussion went downhill from there.

For those who are interested, the reasoning is that the welfare of your fellow man is worth more than whatever is inside the house. I'm of the opinion that they should consider this before they try to steal something. She and I had to agree to disagree on this one. I could sort of see the intention, yet that argument takes nothing into account about the mental well-being of those who feel scared and can't implement whatever they want in THEIR HOUSE due to this law.

Anyway, I went off on a tangent above, but I wanted to give you some insight into this series and this unique aspect of ATLANTICA's legal background.

I hope you have a fantastic week or weekend. Talk to you in the next book!

Ad Aeternitatem,
Michael Anderle

OTHER ATLANTICA BOOKS

John Chambers Books

Her Mother's Pendant (Book 1)

The Mystery Deepens (Book 2)

One Last Choice (Book 3)

Valentina Winters

The Red Countess (Book 1)

One Night to Kill (Book 2)

One Death Too Few (Book 3)

Terra Kris

She is the Law (Book 1)

Law or Justice (Book 2)

Justice Served (Book 3)

Santana Sokolov

Law of the Jungle (Book 1)

Inner City Jungle (Book 2)

Rumble in the Jungle (Book 3)

BOOKS BY MICHAEL ANDERLE

Sign up for the LMBPN email list to be notified of new releases and special deals!

http://lmbpn.com/email

For a complete list of books by Michael Anderle, please visit:

www.lmbpn.com/ma-books/

CONNECT WITH THE AUTHOR

Connect with Michael Anderle

Website: http://lmbpn.com

Email List: http://lmbpn.com/email/

https://www.facebook.com/LMBPNPublishing

https://twitter.com/MichaelAnderle

https://www.instagram.com/lmbpn_publishing/

https://www.bookbub.com/authors/michael-anderle

www.ingramcontent.com/pod-product-compliance
Lightning Source LLC
Chambersburg PA
CBHW022125310726
48972CB00007B/2206